IN A CLASS BY HERSELF

IN A CLASS
BY HERSELF

A NOVEL BY

Linda Crawford

Charles Scribner's Sons, New York

Library of Congress Cataloging in Publication Data

Crawford, Linda.
In a class by herself.
I. Title.
PZ4.C89916In   [PS3553.R286]   813'.5'4   76-16561
ISBN 0-684-14759-9

This book published simultaneously in the
United States of America and in Canada—
Copyright under the Berne Convention

Printed in the United States of America

For Edie Soderberg, who helped with one beginning
And Sandra Scoppettone, who helped with another

IN A CLASS BY HERSELF

SPRING

One

"We always thought Evie would do something with writing," her mother was saying. "She has a real flair for it."

Evelyn, passing by, wondered who was on the other end.

"They've asked her to do a follow-up on the article I sent you," Mrs. Girard went on. "So she'll be leaving here tomorrow on assignment."

Evelyn noted how her mother relished the phrase "on assignment." It had a professional flavor and she was proud to have picked it up, thrilled to be able to say it. And say it she would, whenever possible: "Evie has to go on assignment, so her visit's cut a bit short." . . . "Leave one quart of milk and half a dozen eggs. Just Mr. Girard and I will be here since Evelyn is going on assignment." . . . "I could probably make it Thursday now, Madge. Evelyn's gone on assignment." . . . "Ever since Evie went on assignment, the house has seemed a little empty."

"Well, it is. It's real nice . . . the opportunity . . . and I think she's using it very well which is most important."

Mrs. Girard, watching Evelyn pour a large glass of milk, motioned toward a pot of coffee on the stove.

"I will, Nell. I certainly will . . . well, real nice . . . yes, I will . . . real nice . . . 'bye."

"There's juice in the fridge, honey, and I think this coffee should be hot. I turned it on when I heard you upstairs. There's bacon, eggs, bread for toast, or English muffins. Oh, and there's some of Marguerite's coffeecake left, I think. That's real good warmed up. Or cereal up in the cupboard . . . fresh strawberries you might like for that. And a piece of melon or half a grapefruit. I think they're all cut and fixed. There's some Wisconsin cheese Bert sent that tastes real good with eggs if you . . ."

Evelyn wanted to scream but held up her hand instead.

"I'll just have this glass of milk now. Thanks, Mom. Is the paper around?"

"Right at your place. Right here."

All Evelyn wanted was fifteen minutes alone with her glass of milk, the paper, and silence. She needed those things to steady her hands and clear her mind. God, why those last three or four drinks the night before? The taste in her mouth was putrid.

"That was Nell on the phone." Her mother settled in across the table from her. "She thought you looked beautiful yesterday."

"Mmmmnnn . . . nice of her to say."

"Bob Fraser came up to me at the reception and said, 'Lily, Evelyn has grown into a very stunning young woman.' And Maureen thought you looked like a model. She asked if you'd ever thought of modeling."

"Really? They should see me this morning."

"That shade is particularly becoming on you. It might make a real pretty street-length dress if you wanted to have it shortened. The lines are simple and classic. You might get a lot of good out of it, Evie."

"Mom, you've said that about every bridesmaid dress I've ever had and not one have I ever worn again and I don't suppose this one will be any different."

Miss Girard's clarity is stunning.

"Well, it's such a pretty shade on you . . ."

"Mom," Evelyn cut in, more edge in her voice than she'd intended, "I'll think about it . . . okay?"

Mrs. Girard murmured something inaudible and made a show of busying herself as Evelyn glanced down at the paper.

Evelyn had come to town for the wedding of one of her brothers and she had been under her parents' roof for almost a week. The strain was beginning to show. Every so often she suffered peculiar, and terribly childish, seizures. She put her fingers in her ears and waggled them, contorted her face into grotesque masks, stuck out her tongue, and crossed her eyes. All this, of course, she presented to her parents' backs. Her mother didn't drink and was made nervous by those who did; her father was an unacknowledged drunk. Evelyn found herself wanting to say things like, "No, no milk thanks. I'll have a bottle of Scotch." And a lot of the time she felt unspeakably rude, nearly strangling with the effort of making pleasantries. A week was much too long at her age, twenty-seven.

She had come from New York for the wedding and received the star treatment from her family and their friends. She was, after all, a writer. They bestowed this title on her because she worked for a newspaper and because she didn't correct them. She never called herself that, of course, but then she didn't have to. When asked what she did, she would reply in a most understated and offhand manner, "I'm a reporter." And, nine times out of ten, she could count on the response, "Oh, you're a writer."

This label was not new, however. People had been assuming she was a writer, calling her one, introducing her as one, treating her as one, for years. She had been calling herself one internally, and intermittently, since she was six and passed winter Saturdays in the attic, surrounded by a poet's props: notebooks, pens, a large bottle of soda (to be drunk directly, no glass), some pieces of bread, and hunks of cheese. The pose occasionally even included writing a verse or two in her cramped child's hand. Such activity could have been taken as a sign of promise but not the poems themselves. Her subjects included her baby brother, spring housecleaning, and elevators. Her style was unremarkable, although it in-

dicated an awareness that both rhyme and meter were desir-
able, if possible.

Several years later she won a first prize and an honorable
mention in two categories of a city-wide essay contest. The
first prize went to a rhapsodic paean to sailboats, the honorable mention to a stirring explication of the symbolic meaning of a local charity drive.

In college she complained that the dreary required papers
kept her from "really writing." She wrote excellent dreary
required papers and completed a few short stories, one of
which a professor urged her to consider publishing. After two
refusals she withdrew it from the market. She devoted her
master's thesis to demonstrating the intricate link between
Henry James's life and his work, only two pieces of which
she'd read, the first novel and the last, and both of which
she'd loathed. When this was highly praised and, again, publication was suggested, she felt so fraudulent that she fled to
New York, leaving her doctoral plans behind.

Her newspaper work consisted, for the most part, of inter-
viewing people during long lunches at posh restaurants. Anticipation of these appointments made her sick with terror.
She often vomited before and got rather drunk during, never
noticeably, of course. Her subjects were performers, occasionally from the worlds of music, dance, or the theater but,
most often, from television. She felt her stories about them
were usually stilted and empty, the merest cut above gossip-
column copy, and she worried that they would ruin her for
finer things, none of which she found time to attempt.

But other people—her family, her friends, even some co-
workers—marveled at her position, achieved so young, so
replete with glamour, so endlessly fascinating ("You mean
you met Karen Valentine? You had lunch with her?"). Occasionally, however, she received a newsworthy assignment,
like tomorrow's to examine a job-training program for disadvantaged young women.

She wanted only one thing of this day: to get through it with maximum quiet. The odds rose sharply as her father pulled into the driveway. From the time that elapsed between his car door slamming and the house door opening, she knew he'd had a few ("a couple of belts" was the way he'd put it, if he put it at all). When he drank he slowed down immediately and radically. His conversational pauses became gaping chasms. Sometimes they opened up between sentences, sometimes between the words of sentences. But no matter where they yawned, it was understood in the Girard household that nothing was to intrude on the silence, most especially words from anyone else. When that understanding was breached, and a sound occurred, Mr. Girard exploded in an exhalation of disgust—his answer to so many things—and often feigned an exit from the room, as if to say, "Oh, for God's sake! How can anyone speak under these conditions!" But he would always stop before he reached the door, return to where he'd been sitting, and start over again, even more slowly. He also walked with a slight list that he usually managed to keep just this side of a stagger.

"Hello there, dear," he said with forced heartiness, executing one half of a wobbly Charleston step. "Is your dance program filled?"

If she had a nickel for every time she'd heard him ask that —just a nickel!

Evelyn had risen and begun walking toward the stove as he entered, putting herself on the floor, as it were. He slid an arm around her waist, took one of her hands in his free one, and swayed in place, making breathy little rhythmic sounds.

"I'm sittin' this one out, honey." She tried to keep her tone light and her body from wrenching as she pulled away from him.

"Is your program filled?" he asked Mrs. Girard, who was passing through on her way outdoors.

"All filled . . . every dance."

He reached out to pat her behind, barely brushing it as she moved rapidly past him. Pouring coffee, Evelyn heard him, in the laundry room next door, lift a bottle down from the shelf, swallow, twist on the top, and replace it. If he didn't drink openly—and he almost never did anymore—he felt it didn't count.

"Evie . . . just one question." He came back into the kitchen and sat down at the opposite end of the table from Evelyn. He took a cigarette from the pack in his shirt pocket, lit it, and pushed it around the ashtray, rearranging the old ashes. He pulled a hand across his eyes, reached for a handkerchief in his back pocket, and blew his nose loudly.

"Forgive me, dear." He put the handkerchief away, picked up his cigarette, and looked at Evelyn, his eyes still full, his mouth moving. It was hard to tell if this movement presaged speech or inundation by emotion. Those two things looked very alike on him, an added difficulty when one was trying to determine whether or not to enter one of his pauses.

"Un question." He held up his index finger and deliberately gave the words an atrocious French pronunciation.

"Je suis prête," said Evelyn, straining for banter and getting nowhere near it.

"Dear, please! Watch your language! Your mother might hear." His mock horror gave way to a little chuckle. He was pleased with his snappy patter.

"Do you not think . . ." He snuffled and made a great display of pulling himself back from the edge of total immersion in tears. "Do you not think . . . that Mom is the most beautiful woman in the world?"

Oh, Jesus, thought Evelyn, the old you-have-a-saint-for-a-mother-but-a-schnook-for-a-father routine.

"She's certainly right up there," Evelyn said. "Of course, I'm breathing down her neck in that department."

He chuckled with appreciation and took what seemed to

Evelyn an inordinately long time to pull out of the laugh.

"Evie," he said finally, his face and tone very grave now, "did you ever go into a restaurant . . . and they bring you a plate of food . . ." He made a small strangling noise and looked from side to side as though seeking a target for what was coming.

"Yes, that has happened to me," said Evelyn.

"Oh, God!" He was impatient with her interruption. "And they bring you a plate of food and it just makes you sick." He hissed this out with great venom.

"No," she replied, unwilling to concede every time, "I can't say it has."

He looked incredulous. Obviously, he had not gotten his point across.

"I mean, you can't even see the plate! Every last bit of it is covered!"

"You don't have to eat it all, Dad."

The purity of her language is dazzling.

"I have told the waitress," his voice tightened as she refused to acquiesce, "that I do not want salad, I do not want a potato, I do not want vegetables, I do not want crabapples and parsley, I just want the entree."

He held his hands up in a cupped circle indicating that the entree he wanted was something small and round.

"And here comes this plate so full of stuff . . ." The strangling sound echoed in the back of his throat again. "Well, it just makes you sick!"

He got up, unable to sit still with his outrage, and disappeared into the laundry room. Mrs. Girard came in while he was out of the room and began taking small covered dishes and foil-wrapped packages out of the refrigerator and setting them on the counter.

"Here's some of that Jello salad you liked so much Thursday night, honey," she said as he reentered.

"Never touch the stuff till after sundown, dear." He turned to Evelyn, feigning exasperation. "I have told the old girl that time and time again."

"I can heat up this Shrimp Dijon you liked last night," Mrs. Girard said.

"No thank you, dear. I saw it made." He gave Evelyn a conspiratorial wink, trying to align her with him against Mrs. Girard and her efforts to get him to eat.

"Would you like jelly and onion on raisin bread?" Mrs. Girard inquired, undeterred.

"Oh, for God's sake . . ." This squirted out through his clenched teeth. She had, as usual, pushed a little too far. "I will get what I want when I want it." He enunciated each word fully, spitting them at her.

"What about you, Evie?" Mrs. Girard looked slightly hurt but resilient. "There's some real nice sliced beef here or Gertrude's black cherry Jello salad . . ."

"I'll fix something a little later, Mom. Why don't you just sit down and have your lunch? Don't worry about those of us who can't make up our minds."

Evelyn congratulated herself on the last line. She was so good at placating them both, lining up with them simultaneously.

The silence that followed was interrupted only by Mrs. Girard's chewing and Mr. Girard's preparations for speech. Evelyn kept her eyes on the paper, reading the same sentence over and over.

"Evelyn." When he called her that it meant he would ask something he felt was probing. "Have you ever thought of being a stewardess?"

"Only when you ask me that question," she replied.

He laughed, letting her know that he knew he was sometimes tiresome but that this time was different.

"No, seriously, honey . . . did you ever *really* consider it?"

"Dad," her voice rose slightly, "I'm terrified of flying. I hate, loathe, and despise every moment I have ever spent in an airplane and I would never spend another one if I didn't have to, so somehow being a stewardess has never presented itself to me as a strong vocational possibility. Anyway, I do something else."

"I'm sorry. I'm sorry already." He gave it a heavy Yiddish inflection. "There's harm in asking?"

"There's no harm in asking, Dad. Is there any point in asking?"

"There should always be a point? Geez, what a grouch!" Pretending to be hurt, he gratefully seized the excuse to exit. Soon his ball game would be on and he would belt and snort (his only two words for drinking) his way through the afternoon, hollering, cursing, arm-waving, fist-shaking, venting, all at the perfectly acceptable target of the TV screen.

Evelyn was a great taker of notes. She took them for different reasons at different times: to remember events and feelings . . . to compile data for eventual transformation into literature . . . to sort out what was happening to her . . . to document her existence . . . and, sometimes, to verify it. She labeled the bodies of notes according to their purpose: journals, diaries, notebooks, jottings.

She was at present in a journal period, documenting and sorting, trying to do so with some degree of honesty. She had been noting for days the specific rigors of being locked with her parents but this afternoon she saw it with a burst of generalized clarity.

"I think I see the origin of the horror," she wrote, "at least partially. It's the repression, the silence—the terribly soft tread to the laundry, the whisper of untwisting the cap from the bottle, the almost noiseless swallow, the muffled refastening of the bottle top, the murmuring slide back onto the shelf, the hushed retracing of the path back to the chair. Nothing must ever appear on the surface. As long as it's not visible, it doesn't exist. And all of life becomes pussyfooting, treading gently, speaking softly. Do everything carefully and quietly. Always be cautious. Never take risks. I've never seen it so clearly. Each little piece of life is handled so gingerly— and handled is the correct word, not lived. All so silent."

"Evie." Her mother's voice floated up the stairs. "Dinner's almost ready."

Evelyn's insight had sent her into a deep sleep and kept her there all afternoon. Her hangover seemed dimmer now but, of course, she wouldn't have time for a drink before dinner. Ever since her father had stopped taking his drinks out of a glass, dinner occurred promptly at six. She wasn't sure why. He certainly didn't demand it and, most often, ate very little of it anyway. Once he had probably asked, whining, plaintive, "Why can't we, for God's sake, have dinner at six o'clock?" And Mrs. Girard had cast the die.

Since he had eaten nothing but Oreo cookies for the past two days, Mrs. Girard, in desperation, had made something surefire: browned ground beef spooned into the center of a mound of mashed potatoes. Feeling guilty for imposing it on Evelyn, she talked it up brightly while she was serving, defining its purpose, asking forgiveness, and seeking justification, all at once.

"This is one of Dad's favorites," she said, preparing his plate. "He always seems to enjoy it."

While he made disparaging sounds, Evelyn watched her mother place a scant spoonful of mashed potatoes in the middle of a regulation-size dinner plate and sink a modicum of ground beef into the potatoes' center.

Evelyn couldn't help herself. "I'm glad to see he doesn't overdo, even when it's his favorite."

"And somehow it always tastes even better on a cool night, I think," Mrs. Girard went on. "I don't know why that should be but it always just hits the spot somehow."

"Mmmnnn . . ." It was all Evelyn could manage.

"The Benedicts thought they'd stop by tonight. They're real anxious to see you before you leave."

"Oh? What time will they come?" Evelyn walked to the refrigerator and got a can of beer, ignoring her mother's attempt to ignore her.

"They'll be along after dinner. Does it taste good to you, honey?"

"Very good, dear," he murmured, ashamed somehow of this special food.

"Well, Dad," Evelyn said, after a very large gulp of beer, "where will Mich end up next season?"

"Dear . . . are you kidding? In Pasadena on New Year's Day."

"I'll contact my bookie the minute I get back to New York."

"Dear . . . would you remember the 'forty-eight Ohio State game?"

"No, I really wouldn't," said Evelyn.

He looked surprised and disappointed. "Ohio ten—Mich twenty-eight? My God, that last quarter! Bennie had them trying everything . . . quick over the middle, the long one, short punches off tackle, end around for ten, twelve, fifteen. Oh, my God." His eyes misted over as he remembered.

"Well," he continued, anger restoring his grip, "this monkey they have now . . . I mean, Evie, if I can call every play from the stands . . . it's two or three straight ahead, a couple off tackle, a few more straight ahead again. Oh, for God's sake, you just have to wonder . . ."

He pushed his plate aside, half the mound still sitting in the middle. "It's second and ten, Purdue's forty, five bloody minutes to go. Mich trails by ten and you think, What's he got to lose . . . he's gotta put it in the air."

He paused, marshaling his energies. "Three off tackle on

second, two up the middle on third, fourth," his voice was rising now, "he kicks!"

He flung his arms in the air, then brought his hands down to his head where he combed his fingers furiously through his hair, as though trying to erase the memory. The movement spun him out of his chair and, finding himself up, he just kept walking, toward the laundry. He was still shaking his head when he returned.

"We've got some nice fresh pineapple for dessert," said Mrs. Girard.

"None for me, dear," he said, making it sound as though he'd actually considered but decided against.

"I'll have some later, Mom," Evelyn said, clearing away the dishes and bringing her mother a dish of fruit.

"It gives me pimples," said Mr. Girard.

"I always think fresh pineapple is especially nice," said Mrs. Girard. "Oh, Evie, they had an unusual salad at the City Club the other day. It might be something you would like. It was sort of a modified Waldorf with fresh pineapple and small papaya cubes and a sesame dressing that was real good."

"I tend to eat green salads these days," said Evelyn gently.

"It was real nice and light and didn't leave you feeling all heavy afterwards," Mrs. Girard continued. "I hate that heavy feeling after lunch. It just makes you sluggish the rest of the day."

"Now I never have that problem, dear," Mr. Girard put in, attempting a joke at his own expense.

"Oreos just don't give you that heavy feeling, do they?" said Evelyn.

He laughed loudly and much too long.

"Evie," he said, when he'd recovered, "do you ever take a slice of raisin bread, nice and thick . . . spread it with jelly, and slip on a generous slice of sweet Bermuda onion?"

"No, Dad," she answered, "I never do."

"Well, that is quite a sandwich."

"I'd agree, without even tasting one."

Evelyn was beginning to hear the strain in her voice.

"Guess I'd better freshen up a bit," she said, rising.

She has caught the sound of the middle class unerringly.

"Girls," said Mr. Girard, "we will meet back here in one half-hour in sun helmets, panties, and bras. The games chairman has spoken."

Evelyn remembered the first time she'd heard him say that, one long-ago, sober summer morning at the beach. Hard as it was to believe now, it had been quite funny.

"The games chairman should keep his mitts to himself," Evelyn said, twisting away from his outstretched hand which was poised to pinch.

"Miss, is your program filled?" He rose, unwilling to let her go quite yet.

"I don't dance, buster." She walked quickly to the refrigerator for another beer and vanished upstairs before he could make his way around the table and take her for a partner.

"Pegeen . . . you're looking lovelier than ever. And Ben, my boy, let me have that coat. You should hang onto this . . . they'll come back."

The sound of greetings drifted up to Evelyn, who was standing in front of the bathroom mirror, hesitant. She was at that point where she knew she looked passable but, if she could stand to do more, she could look much better. She often felt this way with a hangover.

Evelyn was tall, thin, dark, even-featured, and, she thought, quite ordinary. Actually, she was heading toward something quite exceptional but she couldn't see it, especially now. Every time she looked in a mirror in this house it gave her back an old reflection: acne traces on the skin, hair lank, uncertain about the eyes.

"Evie . . . so good to see you." Peg Benedict kissed the air beside Evelyn's cheek. "We thought you looked so lovely last night."

"Thank you. So nice you could stop by."

"Hi, Ev." Mr. Benedict grabbed her hand and drew her toward him. "Good to see you."

"Would any of youse like a touch of refreshment?" asked Mr. Girard.

He had a sister who made him apoplectic with her inability to say a straight English sentence. As he said, she always had to "ham it up." Evelyn was fascinated to find him doing the same thing, exactly as though the trait were genetic. God, she hoped it never turned up in her!

"Scotch and water for me, Dad," she said.

"Make it two, Al," said Ben.

"Do you have a Coke, Alfred?" Peg asked.

"Have we got Coke? Margaret, my dear, have we got Coke?"

Mercifully, he didn't stay to answer his own question but listed off in the direction of the laundry. How he loved the chance to go there on legitimate business.

"It was such a lovely wedding, Lily," said Peg.

"Well, it was, wasn't it? We certainly thought so. The church looked so pretty, didn't it?"

"Lovely."

"Well, Evie," said Ben, "maybe next time you're home it'll be for your wedding."

"Never can tell, Ben." Evelyn twinkled back at him, thinking it seemed pointless to tell him she had just fallen madly in love with a woman.

"Do you still see Boris, honey?" her mother asked. "We see his by-line in the paper here every so often."

"Mmmnnn," said Evelyn. "He's been writing a lot of stuff for the news service wire."

"Gee, we had such a good time that evening we spent with him in New York," Mrs. Girard went on. "He took us to Chinatown to a real authentic little spot and then afterwards we walked all around. It's so interesting to see their markets, all the different vegetables and all."

Mr. Girard returned carrying two glasses.

"Margaret, my love, un Coke." He gave a deep bow. "Evie . . ." He handed Evelyn a tall glass full of rather light liquid. She'd told him several times just a splash of water would do but each time he looked hurt and poured roughly half and half. Then he left the room again, was gone a few minutes, and came back with Ben's drink and a beer for himself. Beer wasn't alcohol, as far as he was concerned, so he drank it quite comfortably in public.

"So how's the father of the groom?" Ben asked.

"Just fine, Benny boy . . ." Mr. Girard paused and they all froze, waiting. He took a deep swallow of beer, placed the can carefully and soundlessly on the table near his elbow, and leaned forward with his arms dangling between his legs, his head lowered. Then, with great effort, he pulled up his head and focused his brimming eyes on Peg and Ben.

"Did you ever . . ." He started to go under but fought back with one enormous, trumpeting inhalation through the nose. "Did you ever see . . ."

The Benedicts were as used to this as anyone outside the family but even they were shifting about a bit.

"Oh, God . . . did you ever see a more beautiful bride than Joycie?" He blurted it as though it hurt passing through his mouth, as though having been held back so long, it had to be ripped out.

"She was just lovely," Peg said to Mrs. Girard, unable to continue looking at him.

"Peau de soie gives such a nice soft effect, doesn't it?" said Mrs. Girard.

"Dear, please! Watch your language," Mr. Girard chided, laughing noiselessly at his joke.

"Lily," said Ben, "does Joyce remind you a little bit of Jane Fonda?"

"Are you out of your mind?" Mr. Girard exploded.

"Gee," said Mrs. Girard, "I hadn't really thought of it but I can see how you might think there was some resemblance."

"Are you out of your mind?" Mr. Girard rasped. "Why, she doesn't look a thing like her."

The force of his disagreement propelled him out of his chair. "My God, Ben," he muttered, leaving the room.

These exits of his, which were frequent, had a common denominator. He always sought to leave the impression that he was stepping out until one or all of the room's occupants returned to their senses and made reasonable conversation possible once again.

"Just sometimes from the side, she looks a little like her," said Ben. "Do you know what I mean, Peg?"

"Yes, dear, I know what you mean," said Peg, eager to close the subject. "Tell us about your job, Evie."

"Oh, I'm still doing the same sort of thing."

"Have you ever interviewed Jane Fonda?" Ben asked.

"Ben," said Peg sharply. "Your mother said you had lunch with Paul Lynde the day before you came home."

"Yes."

"He's not always in real good taste, is he?" said Mrs. Girard. "You just never know when he might slip into something."

"Did you ever meet Sally Struthers, Evie?" Mr. Benedict asked.

"Yes, I did."

"What about Rob Reiner? Did you ever meet him?"

"No . . . no, I didn't." Evelyn desperately wanted another drink and another place to be. She was trying to figure out how she might get at least one of these, gracefully, when her father pitched forward into the room and lay in its center, flat on his face.

For an instant of absolute stillness, they all regarded him with the same sort of warmth and concern one would lavish on the centerpiece of a banquet table. It was a stunning moment.

"Al." Mrs. Girard broke away from her chair and knelt down. "Are you all right?"

"My God," said Ben. "Shall I call Maury?"

"Dad." Evelyn rolled him over and sat him up. "Lean on me and get up."

"Maybe he should lie down, Lily," Peg whispered. "We'd better call Maury."

"Come on, Dad. Mom, give him a hand on the other side."

Mrs. Girard helped to hoist him off the floor and, between them, they walked him toward a bedroom.

"Shall I give Maury a call or have you got a doctor closer?" Ben called after them.

"Not now, Ben," said Evelyn. "Just a minute. I'll be right back."

Mr. Girard was completely silent. When they got him to the edge of the bed, he rolled onto it, turning away from them. Evelyn quickly returned to the Benedicts.

"Freddie Samson had a real bad fall recently," Ben said. "He spent about a week at University Hospital for tests and . . . what was it they found, Peg?"

"Inner ear, I think. I know how stubborn your father is, Evie, but maybe you could pressure him before you go. When's the last time he had a checkup?"

"I don't know. Ages ago, I'm sure."

"Well, he seems to be resting quietly," Mrs. Girard murmured, coming halfway into the room and stopping suddenly.

Resting quietly! My God, thought Evelyn, in less than five minutes they've created their own myth and bought it.

"I'll have to get in touch with Maury," said Mrs. Girard.

"Maybe we'd better be on our way, Lily," said Peg.

"Well . . . perhaps . . ." Mrs. Girard stood, unmoving, while Evelyn got their coats.

"We were saying to Evie," Ben said, "that Al really ought to have a whole battery of tests. Freddie Samson had a real bad fall not long ago and he was in University Hospital for a week of tests."

"Inner ear, I think," said Peg.

"Well, I'm sure that's what Maury would recommend," said Mrs. Girard. "It's always good to have everything checked."

"Let us know, Lily. So good to see you, Ev."

"Take care, Evie. Don't stay away so long next time."

Mrs. Girard was dialing before the door closed behind them.

"Well, he had a fall," she was saying. "No, he's lying down now. He doesn't seem to be in any discomfort."

As Evelyn poured herself a Scotch, no water, she could hear her mother through the wall.

"Yes, he'd eaten dinner. We had ground beef and mashed potatoes which he likes, so he'd eaten a little something. Peg and Ben were here and Evie hasn't left on assignment yet so she was here and we'd been sitting and talking . . . he just seemed to fall straight forward . . . yes, into the middle of the room . . . I will, Maury . . . yes, I will. And thanks so much."

She hung up the phone and turned to Evelyn, who was leaning in the doorway. "Maury wants Dad to get in touch with him tomorrow to set up an appointment for a whole battery of tests."

"Mother," said Evelyn, "he was dead drunk!"

"So they should be able to get him in by the end of the month. It's always good to have everything checked."

"Person to person to Miss Regina Ross," Evelyn said to the operator. "The number is OR seven three eight hundred, room seven fourteen."

"Hello." Regina's voice was breathless, as usual.

"I didn't expect you to be there," said Evelyn.

"Oh, my God, darling. Is it you? Hang on a minute."

Evelyn could hear ice against glass and was glad she'd made herself one before calling.

"I just this instant walked in the door." Evelyn heard Regina swallow. "Had dinner with Daddy Warbucks at Lutece."

"Sounds like today was Father's Day everywhere," said Evelyn.

"How's yours? God, I miss you."

"Hideous. He fell in a drunken heap in the middle of the living room tonight and my mother's booking him into a hospital for tests, hoping it's inner ear. I miss you too . . . terribly."

"I had dinner last night at Armando's and it was perfectly awful without you, unbearably lonely. I met Stephen and Rob at eight and we didn't eat until midnight. That might give you some idea of the sort of evening it was. I notice today there are some linguine flakes on my sweater and several whole strands in my purse, indicating that the actual eating of the meal may have been somewhat less than tidy."

"I didn't feel absolutely perfect this morning myself," Evelyn said. "I sat up with my father last night through four or five extra Scotches. Of course, the conversation was worth it. We discussed Nita Naldi, Roosevelt, and Bobby Jones. I wouldn't have missed it."

"My recall of last night is not total," Regina said, "but I do recollect faintly a conversation with a dwarf who was seated at the bar, until I insisted he join us. I told him about my passion for what I chose to call miniaturism, defining it, I believe, as a love of all things tiny, and he was absolutely fascinated. Said he'd never run across that before. Stephen reminded me this morning that I'd asked him up tonight for a tiny drink so if you hear a knock . . ."

"Do you intend . . ."

"I have no intention of even going to the door," Regina shrieked. "But Peter is supposed to be coming by before we go to dinner so it may be a little tricky."

"I have to go to Maine tomorrow," said Evelyn.

"What? My God, darling, what for?"

"A story on a women's job-training program."

"Jesus . . . for how long?"

"Shouldn't be more than two days and at least it'll be more interesting than my scheduled interview with Rose Marie."

"God knows," said Regina. "Will you be back by Wednesday night? Clarice is giving Teddy a birthday party."

"I ought to be. I can't believe I won't see you tomorrow."

"God, has it only been a week? It seems forever."

"I know. I hate it."

"It is the most hateful, the most loathsome . . . oh, Christ, I think there's someone at the door. If those fuckers had put in a peephole when I asked them! Of course, the dwarf would be below eye level, I guess, but at least I'd know it wasn't Peter. Fuck! I'd better get off and see."

"I'll call you tomorrow from Portland. I love you."

"I love you, darling. Safe journey and back soon. Night-night."

"Night." Evelyn put down the phone and sat very still. Those qualities that had drawn her to Regina—her flamboyance, her constant motion, her hyperbole—were the same ones that now made her feel particularly lonely. The absence of her extravagance was so noticeable.

Miss Girard is a superb stylist, a first-rate craftsman.

"Miss Girard is also a terrific drinker and ought to have another right now."

As she spoke into the empty room, she raised her glass in a little salute. Both speaking and saluting were certain indications of impending drunkenness and she recognized the signs. Knowing it would be a late night—she had to do a laundry, pack, and, she feared, have yet one more conversation with her parents—she took a Dexamyl with the last swallow of Scotch. Feeling better immediately, and knowing she'd be growing sharper by the minute, she went downstairs briskly and headed for the laundry.

He was just lowering the bottle from his mouth as she came in and their eyes locked in an embarrassed stare.

"Funny you should mention it," said Evelyn, attempting lightness. "I was just going to have one myself."

"Saves on glasses this way, ya know." He delivered his line in an elongated country drawl, the sort of voice that would go with pullin' di-rect on the jug, she supposed.

"Why, I never thought 'a that." She grabbed a bottle of brandy by the neck and took a slug. "By golly, you're absolutely, one hunnert percent right."

She hated herself for going along with him, especially when he laughed in appreciation of their bond.

"Now let me fix ya one up good and proper," he said, not quite sure yet where he stood.

"No, I'll do it myself." Her voice rebuffed him and she felt him slink off as she turned her back to pour.

He was such a depressing drunk! So slow and so corny. She resented him for impeding her rising spirits and tried to pull them up again with two massive swallows of his not very good brandy. By the time she filled the washer with clothes and splashed some soda in her glass, she had her edge back. The soda was for her mother's benefit. She became truly alarmed if she saw anyone drinking anything dark. Several glasses of light-colored liquid didn't bother her nearly as much as a single dark one.

Her parents were waiting for her in the living room, wrapped in silence.

"You two should keep it down a little," said Evelyn. "Do you want the neighbors calling the police?"

She knew it was weak but it got a strained smile from Mrs. Girard and a gurgling sound from her father.

"I want it understood," she continued, "that if we are going to sit here and talk, I must be allowed to get a word in edgewise. I cannot be fighting this ceaseless chatter every moment."

"We'll try and hold back, dear," said Mrs. Girard, striving for irony and achieving pathos.

"Watch it, noisy," Mr. Girard barked at her. "Dear," he said to Evelyn, "if only I could get Mother to cut down on the gab. Honestly! I don't know what we're going to do with her."

Mrs. Girard smiled slightly at his mock exasperation.

"And another thing I wouldn't mind a bit," said Evelyn, "is being able to see you."

Her father's penchant for dimly lit rooms was at some kind of grotesque zenith tonight; the only light in the living room was a dull streak from a hall two rooms away. Mr. Girard winced as Evelyn turned on a small table lamp across the room from him.

"You're probably wondering why I've called you here tonight," said Evelyn, desperately staving off the silence.

"Peg looks good, doesn't she?" said Mrs. Girard, trying to help.

"I have never seen her looking lovelier," Mr. Girard answered, moved to tears by the recollection and his statement about it.

"Ben looks good, too," said Mrs. Girard.

Evelyn didn't know how long she'd be able to stick with this.

"Why, the schnook," her father snorted. "Jane Fonda . . . can you imagine . . ."

Evelyn tore into the pause, knowing suddenly that she'd reached her limit.

"What time should we leave to make the nine o'clock plane, Mom?"

"About eight, I guess."

"I'd better get my things together."

"Yes, you probably should."

"What time will you have breakfast on the table, Dad?"

Leave 'em laughing, she thought.

"Yes, dear," he muttered, completely lost in his pause.

"I'll leave my order in the kitchen."

"Okay, dear," said Mrs. Girard vaguely. "That'll be fine." His haze had enveloped her, too.

"See you in the morning." Evelyn turned away, unable to dispense any ritual kisses. Before going upstairs she poured herself a very dark drink and tucked the bottle under her arm.

Two

"Illusion and silence—silence and illusion. This house is so full of both. Will I ever extricate myself from them? If the silence were stillness and the illusion fancy, all would be well. But the silence is clamped on roiling innards and the illusion is a hard necessity."

Not bad, thought Evelyn, leaning her head over the edge of the bed to read from the journal on the floor. "Roiling innards" was a bit excessive, but other than that it wasn't bad, particularly for something composed on the brink of a less than sober sleep. She could tell she'd been slipping into sleep by the journal's contorted position on the floor, less than sober by the handwriting and the fact that she didn't remember writing a word of it.

Miss Girard's statement has both precision and eloquence.

Evelyn turned onto her back and felt for the first time the damage her head had sustained in the night. It was swollen and shot through with pains running in two directions, front to back and side to side. Her tongue was so enlarged she had difficulty moving it around in her mouth and it ached. Her eyes felt grainy and hollow.

Hearing her mother below in the back part of the house, she flew downstairs to the kitchen, grabbed a beer, and flew back up, all without a whisper of sound. With the first swallow she took four aspirin and two Dexamyl tablets, sufficient propulsion to get her dressed and to the breakfast table.

The pills began to work while she was showering. By the time she emerged she could focus on her image in the mirror. It was a bit blotchier than she'd have wished but it could have been worse. It so often had been. She felt grateful as she smoothed on pale makeup, taking the red down a bit. Her hands still were not steady enough to do any work around the eyes so she left her liner and mascara sitting on the basin as a reminder.

The head pains were now less specific, the best she could hope for. They never went away entirely but concentration on other things could hold them at bay. She took a Dexedrine capsule to ensure that and, by the time she was clothed, she felt the day would be possible.

Compared to the day before, the drive to the airport was a model of pleasant relaxation. The fact that it signaled the end of her visit, the fact that she always tried harder at the end, and, of course, the pills all combined to make it so.

Evelyn's preferred airport drinking pattern was two martinis, straight up, in rapid succession, before even finding out her departure gate; two more as soon as she had; and two more as soon as possible after passing through it. But today, because of the early hour, the brandy she was carrying in her purse would have to do.

"It was just such a treat to have you here, Evie." Mrs. Girard looked absolutely stricken, as though she had just said, "I can't believe you're going away forever."

"So nice, dear," murmured Mr. Girard.

"I'm so glad I came," Evelyn lied, kissing each of them. "Hope it won't be so long until next time. And now, I can no longer contain my eagerness to place myself in that airplane. I suppose it's the one out there with people hovering around the engine. Oh, God . . . lamb to slaughter. Well . . . take care."

She gave each a quick pat on the cheek and walked away. The lame chatter was meant to extricate her, which it did, and ease the process, which it did not. The thing rising inside her now took her breath away. She knew the pills had given her sufficient insulation and distance so that it wouldn't last long, but, in that moment of turning away, it tore through her body and threatened to escape. Had it gotten out, it would have been something between a sob and a shriek, a sound without a name but as mournful as any. As it was, her passage to the plane was silent.

She went directly to the back (a navy flier boy friend once told her it was safest in a crash) and into a seat by the window. To be able to drink with the least possible visibility was more important, at this point, than her terror of flying. She'd figure some way to keep from looking out. The brandy went down smoothly and by the time it hit her stomach she was completely severed from the farewell scene.

"Is this seat taken?" She looked up into a completely round face, slightly flushed from the effort of moving down the aisle with what looked like four briefcases.

"No, it's not." She spoke pleasantly enough but turned back immediately to the magazine in her lap.

" 'Tis now." He grinned. As he lifted one of his bags to the overhead shelf, she could see a patch of stomach where his shirt separated slightly just above the belt. It was white and hairless and she instantly pictured his entire body the same way.

"All the way through to Portland, too?" Hearing the rhyme, he chuckled and repeated it, snapping his fingers in accompaniment to his syncopated phrasing.

"Yes." She kept her head down, hoping he'd pick up the signal.

"It's a dandy little town. I get there every so often. Always enjoy myself." He was shifting about, settling in. "The last time I was there . . . let's see . . . must have been about a year ago . . . I noticed there was a fair amount of building going on but it hadn't changed much. Ever been?"

"No, I haven't."

"Dandy little town." He squirmed in his seat, trying to reach into his back pocket, emitting little grunting noises as he did whenever he moved. He pulled out a small notebook and checked something in it against a piece of paper he'd taken from his jacket.

"Customer list," he said, as though she'd asked. "Sample cases." He pointed to the shelf above.

Evelyn nodded and smiled weakly.

"Have ya heard the one about the traveling salesman?" he asked, letting her know he knew he was a joke.

"I suppose you get that all the time," she said.

"Oh, doesn't bother me," he assured her. "I'm the type of guy can take a joke, even if it's on me. The wife says I'm so easygoing if I went any easier I'd be asleep."

"Mmmnnn," said Evelyn.

"In my line of work, you can't afford to be touchy," he went on. "Your thin-skinned fella, or one who's sensitive, just doesn't belong in sales."

"No, I suppose not," Evelyn murmured, raising up her magazine before her with unmistakable meaning.

"I enjoy meeting people. That's the real key. Not just customers but people on the way, such as yourself. I'm Arnold Pratt, please call me Arnie."

"Evelyn Girard," she said, taking his outstretched hand. "Don't call me Evie."

"Ladies' choice." He chuckled. "Evelyn it is."

He leaned back in his seat, pleased with himself. "That'll be easy for me, ya know. I have a sister Evelyn that also hates to be called Evie."

"I don't hate . . ." Evelyn began, then caught herself. "Frankly, Arnie," she said, after a moment, "I don't really give a damn."

That convulsed him. He threw his head back in a laugh that kept the folds on his neck vibrating against his collar so rapidly the motion blurred as she stared at it.

"I didn't know . . ." he gasped, "I didn't know I had a card on my hands."

"You don't, Arnie. Believe me, you don't."

The plane began to move slowly toward the runway. During takeoff Evelyn always clung to her seat mate. It was nice if they were acquainted but, if not, a stranger served. She knew she must not lay a finger on Arnold Pratt, if she could possibly help it. He would be difficult enough without any encouragement. So she dug her nails into the armrests and leaned back, closing her eyes.

"Clutches you a little, does it?" he asked.

"It's not one of my favorite things, Arnold."

"You're welcome to hang on here."

She raised one eyelid slightly and saw his beefy hand extended, palm up. "That's terribly sweet of you but I'm . . ."

Suddenly the plane was climbing and her hand slapped into Arnold's. She hung on ferociously, her nails biting into his flesh. When he put his other hand over hers, she flipped her hand over and clawed it too. No use missing the chance, she thought.

"Up we go, nice and smooth," said Arnold. "It's a beauty of a lift-off. You oughta watch."

"I can't," she hissed.

"A beeeeauty," he repeated.

Broken little prayerlike fragments ran through her head: Please, God . . . let me . . . oh, Jesus . . . I'll never . . . Christ, please . . . oh, God. Takeoff seemed to be unusually long.

"Lift-off accomplished," he announced as Evelyn felt the plane level off.

"I hope I didn't hurt you," she said, staring at the deep red tracks in his flesh.

"Don't be silly," he said, rubbing his hand nevertheless. "Glad to be of assistance."

She pulled the brandy bottle from her purse and took a

deep swallow before holding it out to Arnold.

"Never touch the stuff." He paused. "Before noon. But you go right ahead."

"I have, Arnold."

"So you have . . . so you have." He was somewhat shocked but trying hard to cover. "I am a firm believer in a touch of spirits for medicinal purposes."

"Medicine has nothing to do with it, Arnold, my boy." She gave it a Mae West twist that absolutely dissolved him.

She has a scrupulous ear, absolutely faithful to life.

"Well, my chickadee . . ." He attempted Fields but lost him in a wave of laughter. Evelyn raised the bottle, winked at him, and poured a snifter's worth down her throat. That, for some mysterious reason, served to keep the wave rolling. When she held up a pill she'd fished out of her jacket pocket, winked again, and popped it in her mouth, he went to pieces. Just as she began to fear he might slip over some invisible edge, a stewardess loomed over them and he regained enough control to order coffee.

"Is it good for you to laugh like that, Arnold?" Evelyn asked.

"Laughter never hurt anyone. That's what I always tell the wife. She goes, 'Arnold, you certainly have a hearty laugh,' and I go, 'Marcia, my dear, laughter never hurt anyone.'"

"Hearty, eh? Marcia would appear to have a way with words."

"Oh, Marcia is real smart," he said. "I always said she was twice as smart as me and three times prettier. And to prove it . . ."

He squirmed around, lifting one enormous thigh off the seat so he could reach into his back pocket. The plastic covering the pictures was cloudy and cracked.

"Here." He pulled them out of their cases. "You can see better this way."

He handed her one. "Marcia," he said. "Joey, he's seventeen . . . Susie, she'll be fifteen next month . . . and Patricia, she's eight. That's the tribe."

"Fine-looking," said Evelyn.

"Take after their mother." He gave her a poke with his elbow and winked.

"Mmmnnn . . ." She felt she'd paid enough now for the privilege of disfiguring his hand during takeoff and picked up her magazine.

"Not only a card but an intellectual, too?" He'd seen she was reading the *Atlantic.*

"This hardly qualifies me," she said, gesturing with the magazine.

"It would where I come from."

"Where *do* you come from, Arnold?"

"Downstate Indiana, little town called Boonville, to be exact."

"Uh-huh . . . well, I'd better finish up this article. Research for my assignment in Portland." She knew as soon as she told the lie that it was a bad one but he was quiet and she hoped he'd missed the opening.

"What exactly is your line of work?" he asked.

"I'm a newspaper reporter."

"Well, what do you know."

"Very little most of the time, Arnold, if you want the truth."

Her mind is incisive.

"I do, I do . . . surprising as that may seem for someone in *my* line of work. It's funny . . . people think sales is so much double-talk but, to coin a phrase, honesty is the best policy there just like anyplace else. 'Course you have to have a good product. I'm in dinnerware."

He looked at her expectantly and she stared back, unable to imagine any appropriate response.

"I'm in trouble," she said finally, hoisting the bottle as he began to chuckle.

"It's a plastic-coated stoneware, can't chip, doesn't wear, lasts forever."

"Nothing lasts forever, Arnold."

"Guaranteed lifetime of at least thirty years."

The stewardess appeared and he was silent as she slipped down their folding shelves and slid trays onto them.

"Light, two lumps, hold the bumps." He grinned up at the stewardess.

"Cream and sugar are on your tray, sir." She gave him a smile of dazzling emptiness. "I'll see what we can do about the bumps."

"They always get a kick out of that," he confided to Evelyn.

"You're the card, Arnold. There's absolutely no contest."

She splashed some brandy into her coffee cup and was replacing the cork when she felt Arnold leaning toward her.

"Hey, Brenda Starr," he whispered. "Stop the presses. How about a dash for Arnie?"

"Arnold, I'm stunned," she said. "Sun not yet over the yardarm and all that. Am I corrupting you?"

"Corrupt away," he said as she poured. "Today's a special occasion . . . not every day at nine in the morning that I meet a beautiful girl such as yourself. Cheers."

"Cheers, Arnold." She felt things getting a little frayed around the edges and floated more brandy on her coffee.

"Plastic coating prevents scratching and chipping," he said, "both things that you'll get with your plain stoneware."

"Aaah," she said, waiting for the brandy to hit.

"It also gives a little sheen that brightens up your colors. Regular stoneware can look a little washed out, at least to my eye."

He was truly unstoppable and she resigned herself.

"How did you get into dinnerware, Arnold?" she asked.

"Funny you should ask," he said. "I was thinking only last night . . ."

As he told her of his progress toward and entrance into

dinnerware, she stared at a sweet-roll crumb on his lip. Despite the continuous motion of his mouth, it would not be dislodged. It clung even as he rose and reached overhead for a sample case.

"You can see for yourself," he was saying, "which is always best anyway. The eye can't lie, I always say."

He sat down heavily, pulling the case onto his lap.

"This isn't the full line, of course, but you get an idea of the style and your color choice is in the accompanying brochure."

His breathing was somewhat labored but still the crumb remained. He undid the clasps of his case with a flourish and flung open the lid.

"Ta-daaa," he trumpeted, holding the last syllable.

A flash of harsh aqua, a color she loathed, assaulted her.

"The color is sea blue, the pattern Thistledown."

"How many patterns are there?" Evelyn asked.

"An even dozen to choose from, delivery within a week."

"And how many colors?"

"Your color choice varies with the pattern but within each pattern there's a minimum color availability of four shades."

"Minimum of four," she repeated. "Well . . ."

"Run your hand over this," he said, placing a plate under her fingers.

"Mmmnnn . . . very smooth."

"Can't chip, doesn't wear, lasts forever."

"Ah, yes, your thirty years of forever."

"If you'd be interested . . ."

"Arnold," she cut in, "before you say another word, let me tell you there is no possibility of my buying any dinnerware now, absolutely no possibility. So you can relax and not feel you have to . . . you can just relax, enjoy your brandy, and ponder the meaning of something that lasts forever, guaranteed for thirty years."

She splashed some brandy into his cup, refilled hers, and listened to her own voice. It held just a trace of drunken inflection, not enough for anyone else to pick up.

When they were about fifteen minutes from Portland, she selected from her vial a German air force pill, reputedly given to Nazi pilots to keep them awake and flying for days. She intended to do some groundwork when she arrived and the German bomb should give her several good hours.

"Where will you be staying?" Arnold asked.

"Holiday Inn," she said, immediately regretting it. "But, Arnold, we must not go on meeting in public. People will talk."

"Please, madam," he huffed, attempting to pick up her cue but landing somehow in the nineteenth century, "do not be so bold."

She put her head down, embarrassed, not knowing how to tidy up the loose ends here.

"Arnold," she said finally, raising her head, "give me your card and when my stoneware chips and wears I'll get in touch with you. I'm always in the market for something that lasts forever."

"With pleasure." He whipped one out of his jacket pocket. "And your address? I'll send you a complete set of brochures."

Evelyn recited her address, wondering why she wasn't giving him a false one.

"And," he held out his hand, "for the landing."

"Oh, I'm much better at landings," she said, hating herself for lying, hating him for looking hurt.

"To your solo landing." He raised his cup. "May it be a great success."

"Tell it to the pilot, Arnold," she said, feeling her stomach plunge as the plane slid downward. She pushed down as hard as she could with her feet and clenched her upper teeth against her lower until her ears rang. But her hands remained nonchalant.

"Well done, little lady," said Arnold as the plane bumped against the ground.

"Nothin' to it, Arnold." She took a swallow of brandy before packing it away.

"It certainly has been a more pleasant trip this time . . ."

"Oh, Arnold," she interrupted him, "I bet you say that to all the girls."

He seemed suddenly at a loss for words and had a look on his face she'd seen before. God, if there was one thing she couldn't stand it was the idea of brightening someone's gray little day. She couldn't bear the sadness that produced in her.

"Gotta tear, Arnold." She got past him into the aisle just as the plane finally stopped. "Knock 'em dead. I wish you record sales . . . and thanks for the hand."

She walked quickly up the aisle until she was stopped by the wall of fellow passengers spilling out of their seats. When she turned and looked back at Arnold Pratt, he was staring out the window, his limp hands resting on the sample case in his lap. On the bottom edge of his lower lip, undisturbed, was the crumb.

Approaching the Holiday Inn in a taxi, Evelyn felt superb. She asked the driver what she thought were probing yet delicate questions about the area, charming him out of his regional coolness. She absorbed the passing scene greedily.

Put quite simply, if Miss Girard were any better a writer I would be frightened for her.

She took possession of her room quickly and thoroughly, setting up a work area near the telephone—typewriter and paper, research file, notebooks, thermos of coffee—and, across the room, a small relaxation center—Scotch and brandy, ice bucket and glasses, magazines and books, journal.

At about one o'clock she entered her work area. She read

through the research, did several telephone interviews and typed up the notes, set up appointments for face-to-face interviews the next day, and jotted down impressions to be used for color. When she finished it was two-fifteen. She wondered if the Nazi pilots' actual flying time had been speeded up.

Moving into the relaxation area, but carrying her coffee with her, she looked through a dozen magazines and finished a book. That brought her to three o'clock.

She tried Regina but there was no answer. She showered, washed her hair, manicured, and dressed very carefully. It was three-thirty when she poured yet another cup of coffee and sat down with her journal.

"How very strange it is to find myself in this place," she wrote, hearing immediately a strain of affectation but powerless to stop it. "Work is done but there is time left in the day and, how well I know, it will be a time suffused with longings. Perhaps they are always there, awaiting time and space, needing those to exist full-blown. And when they see a clearing, they rush in to fill me. Unfulfilled, they cause a sadness that pierces some distant place in me. Fulfilled, they make me know for an instant that infinity is possible. Just for an instant, I can loosen my bonds and slip beyond the limits . . ."

Evelyn felt herself plunging into something downright Shelleyesque and she wasn't really in the mood. Scotch, she had found, could take away airs as quickly as anything. She poured one on the rocks and dialed Regina again. Still no answer.

"What is it that causes one to pose even for oneself?" she continued, her objectivity sharpened by the Scotch. "To present fabrications internally when, during the presentation, one knows very well they are fabrications? Who's kidding who? What's the point?"

That seemed to Evelyn a good place to leave off. Since she

planned to make it a very early evening, she felt it would be appropriate to be at the bar by five. That left her an hour. The ringing of Regina's phone annoyed her and she put down the receiver noisily.

"My darling," she wrote, "how impatient I am when I cannot talk to you. How impatient I am with everything in this world that isn't you! Everything else seems so flawed, so boring. I am so full of wanting you that all other things are intrusions. Thank God for pills and booze this last week. I've abused them both but they've gotten me through."

Reminded, Evelyn went to her pill bottle and took a Daprisal. When the phone rang she jumped, spilling Scotch on the dresser.

"Yes?" she said, still shaking from the sound.

"Evelyn? It's Arnie . . . Arnie Pratt."

"Oh, Arnie. I couldn't imagine . . ."

"Just wanted to make sure you got settled all right."

"That's terribly sweet of you. Yes, I got settled."

"I finished up a little early, just down the street from you. Thought I could buy you a drink."

"Well, I'm still tied up here . . . I don't know . . ."

"Tell you what," he broke in. "I'll be in the bar there in half an hour. Stop in if you can."

"Okay, Arnie, maybe I'll see you there. Thanks for calling."

Evelyn really did not want to spend the evening with Arnold Pratt. No part of her wanted that. Yet, as she hung up the phone, she felt absolutely certain that she would.

"It needn't be," she repeated over and over, dialing Regina for the fourth time without any hope that she would answer. When she didn't, Evelyn slammed the receiver onto the floor. Then, easing her way through another Scotch, she redid her makeup and changed her clothes.

By five o'clock her chemical mix was working nicely. So what if Arnold Pratt was at the bar?

And he was, dead center and looking expectant.

"Evelyn." He called out and waved as though he were trying to get her attention from the opposite end of an amphitheater. She hated him and her embarrassment as the bartender's head snapped up.

"You know, Arnold," she said, sliding onto a stool, "I spotted you right away, picked you right out of the crowd."

She hoped the bartender's smile indicated appreciation of her irony. The other man at the bar apparently didn't hear.

"What'll it be, miss?"

"Scotch on the rocks for the lady," said Arnold, gleeful at her look of surprise. "Am I right?"

"You've never been righter," said Evelyn. "Want to tell me your secret?"

"Well," Arnold began with relish, "when you took the brandy out of your bag on the plane I saw a bottle of Scotch and, according to the way you drank the brandy, I figured you'd drink Scotch on the rocks."

"You're a regular old detective, you are," she said, with a thick English accent.

"Elementary, elementary. It's just the facts, ma'am," said Arnold, mixing Sherlock Holmes with Dragnet. She must remember that leads of that sort were dangerous with him.

"Scotch on the rocks," the bartender announced. As she placed her hand around the glass, Evelyn tried to give him a look that encompassed the story of her day, at least that part of it which included Arnold Pratt: I-met-him-on-a-plane-and-he-found-out-where-I-was-staying-and-called-and-said-he'd-be-in-the-bar-and-I-would-have-been-here-anyway-so-you-could-not-exactly-say-I'm-with-him sort of look. From the look the bartender gave her, Evelyn felt she'd fallen somewhat short.

"Here's lookin' at you, kid," she said to Arnold, really looking at him, noticing his fresh shave, clean shirt, changed tie.

"You too, kid." He winked, raised his glass, and made her feel, she guessed, just about as far away from Ingrid Bergman as it was possible to be.

"Well, Arnold, what kind of a day was it for dinnerware?"

"Fair to middlin' . . . but you know what they say."

"Wrong, Arnold. I don't know what they say."

"Fair's better'n flat, flat's better'n foul."

"Oh, come on, Arnold. This time you've gone too far. Who says that?"

He chuckled, pleased that she was teasing him.

"Just about everybody in Boonville, sooner or later, I guess," he said.

"To Boonville." She saluted him and swallowed deeply.

"I always enjoy a good sense of humor and you sure have one," he said, shaking his head to indicate enjoyment.

"Well, you know what they say, Arnold."

"No, I can't say as I do. What do they say?"

"Humor is as humor does."

"Aaah, they do, do they?" Arnold had lost her and, to cover his confusion, he signaled the bartender.

"Another round here, please."

"Make mine a double," she said, still trying to communicate with the bartender, this time saying, Look, I'm a drinker. You can understand *that*, can't you?

"Two doubles," Arnold said quickly.

"You mustn't try to keep up with me, Arnold," she chided. "The brandy's probably what made your day just a fair one."

"Oh, I know my limit," he said, rather hurt. "Don't you worry about old Arnie."

He took a very large gulp, throwing it back as though it were a shot. She thought she felt him shudder as it went down.

"Why won't you call me Arnie?"

She twisted toward him abruptly, startled by the plaintive note in his voice.

"Why? Why, I don't know . . . I . . . I just don't know. Do you really prefer it so much?"

"I think it gives things a friendlier touch."

"A friendlier touch?"

"Arnold is so formal. Course business associates call me that and so does the wife but for a little drink between friends . . . make it Arnie, huh?"

He placed his hand on her upper arm, as though to pull her into some confidential circle. It rested there for a moment before he squeezed.

"Whatever you say, Arn. Oooops, looky there! Now you've got me shortening it too much."

She realized she was beginning to sound like him and fell immediately silent.

"They make a real fine drink here," said Arnold, feeling her quiet and needing to break it. "Real fine. There's a place down the street though that can't be beat . . . called the King's Coach, I believe. Fella there pours singles like doubles."

"Sounds like my kind of place, Arnie."

She could count on a big laugh with any remark about her drinking and this one was made even bigger than usual by his uneasiness with her silence. He prolonged his laugh to fill up space.

"It would be my pleasure to buy you a drink there later," he said, as his laughter faded.

"Oh, I don't think so, Arnie . . . but it's a sweet offer. Big day tomorrow, you know."

He was crestfallen but tried valiantly to remain casual.

"Never say never. I learned that years ago and it's stood me in good stead ever since."

"I'll remember that, Arnie. I never, by the way, say never to another drink. It's just that . . ."

"Bartender." He interrupted her, snapping his fingers and

pointing at her glass. "Then do me the honor of dining with me."

Christ, she wished he wouldn't talk that way!

"Arnold . . ." she began.

"Arnie," he prompted, "and remember, never say never."

"Arnie . . ." she started again.

"Nothing ventured, nothing gained," he said. "What have you got to lose? A few drinks, some good food, good talk. They serve a fine meal here."

"Arnie, I wish I could explain . . ."

"Not necessary . . . absolutely no explanations needed. You don't have to answer to old Arnie. Just say yes."

If Arnold Pratt had a line, she had a feeling she'd just heard it. What she couldn't believe was that it worked.

"Okay, Arnie old boy, you win." As she heard herself saying it, she felt in the pocket of her suit jacket for the pill she'd placed there earlier. Arnie noticed the gesture.

"And this is the one I take to make me eat dinner." She held it up between her thumb and forefinger before popping it into her mouth.

She is in a class by herself.

Arnold loved that, giving her arm a light punch with his fist and chuckling. She suspected it wouldn't be long before that same fist was making little sweeps of understanding beneath her chin.

"Well," he said, "now that we have some time, enough of the small talk, eh?"

"Absolutely, Arnie. Say something large."

"Bartender," he motioned with his hand, "two more doubles."

She had to admit it wasn't bad but Arnold's own appreciation of it kept her from responding. She simply stared at him while he struggled with the tears of his laughter.

"Marcia is dead right, Arnie. That is a hearty laugh."

"It's exercise for me, the way I do it . . . like being on a vibrating machine."

"That's an interesting slant: laughter as exercise."

"To bigger things," said Arnold, raising his glass, "in talk and drinks."

"A splendid toast, Arnie. I'll drink to that."

She was just trying to imagine what large conversational topic they might tackle when Arnold offered his.

"What do you sleep in?" he asked.

"Nothing, Arnie. Why do you ask?"

He stared at her, rather glassy around the eyes. His mouth was open slightly and unusually red. He looked as though he could go either into a coma or a leer.

"Hey, I thought you'd know the gag," he said, pulling himself back from wherever he'd been.

"What gag?"

"What do you sleep in? A bed."

"Arnie, that settles it. Now I'm absolutely sure you missed your calling. Do you write your own stuff?"

"Oh, that's a real oldie," he said, perfectly straight. "I'm just surprised it's new to you."

"I'm full of surprises. Just stick around."

"I intend to."

Evelyn heard something different in his voice, unnameable but distressing.

"And, in line with that," he continued, "what is your room number? I'll order a bottle and some ice from this guy now and it'll be in the room after dinner."

"Arnold," her tone was sharp, "no room number and no drinks after dinner. I work tomorrow . . . early."

"Lost my head, lost my head," he muttered, again trying Fields but no better at it than he had been that morning.

"And for my next surprise . . ." Evelyn waited until he raised his head. "I'm hungry."

"Aaah, the little lady wishes to be fed." He couldn't let go of Fields. "She wishes to put some vittles into her tummy."

"That's exactly what she wishes. What do you say?"

"Your wish is my you-know-what," said Arnold, sliding off his stool and attempting a bow.

"Don't get fancy, Arnold." She took hold of his arm, afraid he might bow right into the floor.

"Arnie," he snarled, pulling away from her, then trying to cover the wrench with an elaborate flourish of his arm.

"Arnie," she kept her tone light, "are you by any chance a mean drunk?"

"Me?" He looked hurt and incredulous at once. "Evelyn, you gotta be kidding. This is old Arnie."

"I know it's old Arnie," she said. "It's also old bourbon."

"Evelyn, let me tell you something." He took hold of her shoulders and stood looking at her earnestly. "The only problem I have with too much booze is keeping a straight face. Marcia, the wife, always says, 'Arnold drinkin' is Arnold foolin'.' I just get silly. So don't you worry."

"I'm hardly worried," she protested. "Just curious."

As they walked toward the dining room, he cupped his hand under her elbow, squeezing it once or twice along the way. By the time they arrived, he obviously felt very much in charge, snapping his fingers to attract the headwaiter, pointing out the table he wanted, ordering "a Chivas for the young lady" before they were even seated.

"You needn't have done that," she said, touched by his bravado.

"Of course, I needn't," said Arnold. "Evelyn, think what it would be like if people never did things they needn't do."

"I'm very bad at double negatives," she said. "They confuse me thoroughly."

"Let's just say this is a special occasion."

"I have trouble with that, too."

"Look," he leaned toward her across the table, "you can't know what a treat it is for me . . ."

"I don't want to know, Arnie."

That brought him to a screeching halt, staring at her from mid-table.

"Okay, Evie . . ."

"Evelyn."

"Evelyn. No ties, no commitments, no promises."

"No ties? No promises? For God's sake, Arnie, we're just having dinner together!"

"That we are." He signaled for menus.

They were very large. Each entree was given a thumbnail sketch in the lushest of language, something that always made Evelyn suspicious. Arnold recommended a beef dish described as "succulent medallions of the finest beef, cooked gently to perfection and served in a delicate sauce *au jus* with aromatic herbs—none better than!" Evelyn said that was fine with her.

"And a little vino to go with? Something red?" He twinkled at her.

"That would be lovely, Arnie," she murmured. He at least seemed eager to support her habit. That made her, at this moment, feel kindly toward him.

"Curiosity must be a great asset in your line of work," he said, dismissing the waitress rather grandly.

"It helps."

"Doesn't hurt any in mine either. If you're curious about what makes people tick, you're ahead of the game."

"What makes you tick, Arnie?"

She asks the right questions and never settles for easy answers.

"Boy, you're sharp." He shook his head in wonderment. "You don't miss a thing."

She failed to see what she'd zeroed in on, what he found so astonishing.

"What does?" she asked. "Money? Sex? Image? Power?"

"Whoa there! Hold on. That's pretty powerful stuff for the dinner table."

"You said you wanted big talk, Arnie."

"Fair enough, fair enough. But first . . ." He gestured toward the arriving wine.

He made a big show of sampling both bouquet and taste, holding the glass beneath his nose a full five seconds, the wine in his mouth about the same.

"They get a kick out of that, you know," he confided, as the waitress moved away. "Disappoints 'em when you don't do it."

"Is that right?"

"I sometimes even ask for presentation of the cork."

"They must really love that."

"They sure do. Makes 'em feel they're dealing with somebody important, I guess. Actually," he leaned across the table, dropping his voice, "I don't even know what I'm smelling or tasting for, if you want the truth."

"Coulda fooled me, Arn."

He chuckled at the big one he'd put over, raising his glass to Evelyn.

"Skoal," he said.

"Same to you," said Evelyn.

"Now as to what makes me tick . . ." He sat back and pulled at his mouth, already slightly purple from two large swallows of wine. The silence, for Arnold, was unusually long. He finished his glass of wine during it.

"Let's see." He poured another. "All the usual things, I suppose. Contrary to what you might think, I'm just an average guy."

He slid down a bit in his chair, appearing to sink deeper into thought.

"I can tell you what's making me tick right this minute."

Evelyn felt him try to clasp one of her legs between his under the table, but he missed and she decided to ignore it.

"I don't think you have to, Arnie."

"No? Then you tell me."

"Medallions of beef," said the waitress, appearing at Evelyn's elbow.

"Succulent, aromatic, right over there," said Arnold.

"Very hot plates," the waitress announced, putting one in front of Evelyn. "Very hot plates," she repeated, setting down Arnold's.

"Very hot, very hot," Arnold muttered. He looked odd but Evelyn decided to ignore that, too.

"Looks wonderful, Arnie. Do you always eat here when you're in town?"

"Sometimes I do, sometimes not." He didn't want to have this conversation. She didn't want any other.

"Are there many other choices?"

"Not many."

"I noticed a place out by the airport that didn't look bad."

"It's all right. Nothing to write home about."

"Tastes as good as it looks," she lied, taking a bite.

Beneath the table she could feel his thighs flapping together like a giant jaw, opening and closing, trying to secure some part of her. The motion created a breeze that blew against her legs, no matter where she moved them. But still, the activity went unacknowledged by both of them.

"All the usual things, eh?" she asked.

"That's right." His face was flushed, his breathing shallow.

"Just an average guy?"

"I'd like to take my average prick and shove it in your usual pussy."

"Nice talk for the dinner table, Arnold."

"And it's not so average either."

"I'm sure it isn't."

"I could suck you up good, right under this table." His eyes were now protruding rather alarmingly and he had his hands balled up into fists. She wasn't sure she could keep her veneer intact much longer.

"Arnold, you say the sweetest things."

"Say, 'Suck me, Arnold, right under this table.' Say it."

It was becoming harder and harder to pretend they were discussing dinnerware but Evelyn was uncertain what tack to take. Quite obviously, Arnold was running out of control at this moment. Desperately, she took one last stab.

"And you call me a card! Arnie, my boy, you got it all wrong."

"You like my sense of humor?" he asked.

"It's wild, Arnie . . . a little offbeat perhaps but who cares? Right?"

"I had you fooled?"

"Oh, you fooled me all right. You're a regular old fooler, Arnold Pratt. That's what you are."

He took a sip of wine and went on with his dinner. Evelyn tried not to stare. When she realized her mouth was slightly ajar, she wrapped it around her glass and gazed at him over the rim. He just looked like good old Arnold Pratt. No grizzled tufts sprang from his ears; no lengthy tooth hung down over his lip; nothing dribbled from the corner of his mouth. She was absolutely baffled.

"Do the medallions hit the spot?" he asked. "Everything I said they were?"

"Perfect, Arnie. Just perfect."

"They also serve a fine cheesecake here so save some room for that."

"Uh-huh . . . okay."

"The wife is a nut for cheesecake. She probably feels about cheesecake the way you do about brandy." The comparison pleased him enormously. "Well, there's a Holiday Inn in

Pittsburgh she says has the best ever and I always bring her a piece home when I go there. The one here's almost as good."

"I'll be on the edge of my chair, Arnie."

"The better to grab you, my dear." He flapped his thighs together, making a whooshing sound.

Evelyn was dumbfounded. Did he know he was doing that or not? Did he have seizures or just a supply of very bad jokes? Was he a maniac or a fool with a low tolerance for wine? What, in God's name, was going on here?

"Arnie," she said, "let me ask you something."

"Fire away. Bang, bang, bang." His grin was enigmatic.

"Do you ever have blackouts when you drink?"

"Blackouts?"

"Loss of memory . . . can't remember the next day what you did the night before."

"Marcia, the wife, always claims I forget to do things after I've had a couple beers but I guess that's not the same thing."

"No. I mean just what the word says: parts of the time when you're drinking are blacked out."

"I could take out my cock and stick it in your big, black cunt."

"That's not exactly what I mean either, Arnold."

"I'll take out my cock and you suck, suck, suck."

"Arnold drinkin' is Arnold foolin' all right. Marcia sure has your number."

"Pull it out . . . pull it out."

"Arnie, if I can pull this one out, so to speak . . ."

"Stick it in . . . stick it in."

"Arnold, stop that," she hissed at him. "Just cut it out and eat your dinner."

"Eat you," he muttered, bending over his plate. She had scolded him like a child and he responded as one, putting his head down, toying with his food. At least he was silent.

She ate the little bit she could manage to chew and swallow and had the waitress wrap up the rest for later when the pills wore off. Somewhat less than sober herself, she was fascinated by Arnold's behavior as well as repelled. It reminded her of everything she'd ever heard about speaking in tongues, the only difference being that she could understand every single word he said.

"Hey," she nudged his arm, "where's the old Arnold Pratt we all know and love?"

"He awaits you, madam." His attempt at courtly gesture swept his glass from table to floor and she could feel the wine splash on her leg.

"Waitress," he called out commandingly. "Another glass here . . . and more wine."

"Arnie, do you think . . ."

"Please." He held up his hand, anticipating her. "How often do I get a chance like this?"

"A good question, Arnie. You tell me."

"Not very often, Evelyn. Not often at all."

"What do you mean, 'a chance like this'?" The phrase rang ominously in her head.

"A chance to sit with a lovely girl such as yourself, have a fine meal, sip wine . . ."

"Sip, Arnie? Did you say sip?"

He seemed confused by her interruption.

"Ah, how nice," she murmured as the waitress arrived, "yet another bottle for sipping. Please, allow me." She filled their glasses to the top and raised hers to eye level.

"Here's sippin' with you, kid." She winked at him.

"To you." He raised his glass solemnly, his eyes bright and damp.

God, she thought, I'd rather have him obscene than maudlin.

"Arnie, let me talk business a moment. What is your professional opinion of these dishes? I mean, speaking as an expert, how long do you give 'em?"

"Nowhere near thirty years, that's for sure." He lifted the saucer out from under his coffee cup and turned it in his hands. He wasn't kidding.

"You can see some fine lines around the edge here." He pointed them out. "Those'll turn into chips before long and this probably isn't even a year old yet. If only people would listen when you explain . . ."

He trailed off, gazing intently at the saucer.

"What this country needs is a good set of dinnerware," said Evelyn. "Right?"

He looked up, staring at her exactly as he had at the saucer.

"You got a good set. I don't care about big ones."

"Hold on there, Arnie. I have a feeling you're making a transition."

"I'd like you to put your tit right on this saucer, just put it right there."

"What an amusing idea." She thought she'd try going along and see what effect that had. "But tricky."

"I could show you some tricks. I bet I know tricks you never even thought of."

"I bet you do."

He reached under the table, putting his hand behind her knee and pulling, jamming her knee into his groin and her stomach into the edge of the table.

"Oh, that's a good one, Arn," she said, rather breathless. "And brand new. Haven't come across that before. Any more where that came from?"

"Plenty . . . plenty more." His face got redder as he worked himself against the abutment of her knee.

"I can hardly wait."

"You won't have to for very long. Waitress." He signaled for the check.

"Wait a minute, Arn. Do you think for one minute I'd leave this table without my after-dinner brandy?"

"You can have it in the bar." He was breathing quite heavily now and looking very determined. Evelyn wondered if going along was the answer. It didn't seem to be bringing him out of it.

"I'll go in, lay my cock on the bar, and tell 'em to give you anything you want."

"Ah, now that one I know . . . the old cock-on-the-bar gag."

"I'll gag you with it. Stick it in your mouth, so big you'll gag . . ."

"You're dead right there, Arnie. How'd you know that about me?"

"What's that supposed to mean?"

"I hate sucking cocks, Arnie. That's what it means. Sucking cocks is an activity I loathe."

Head-on confrontation is an integral part of her métier.

She wished she hadn't said that. She wished, having said it, that she'd kept the hostile edge out of her voice. She could see she'd merely whetted his incentive, a most unnecessary addition.

He paid the check quickly, grasping her leg between his knees while he counted out the money. He freed her leg only when he rose and came over to take her firmly by the arm.

"Arnie, surely you don't think I'd run off without my brandy."

"You'll have a lot more than brandy."

"Promises, promises. That's all I ever get from you, Arnold Pratt."

She realized that her attempt at casual levity was wearing very thin.

"I promise to fuck you within an inch of your life," said Arnold, propelling her from the dining room.

"There you go again."

"I'm goin' nowhere but into your pants."

"Arnold, you're an incurable romantic. You really are."

He steered her into a booth in the corner of the bar, not at all the spot she would have picked. Instinct told her, however, that this was not the time to resist.

"Make it a brandy stinger for me," she said, hoping he'd have the same and go under with it.

He ordered two stingers and sat quietly until they arrived.

"To you, Arnie," she said. "May the stinger not sting you."

"Don't worry about me."

"I'm trying not to, Arnie. Should I?"

"I didn't say that."

He was almost sullen now, resisting all her efforts to steer him into another mood.

"Surely we haven't run out of things to say so soon," said Evelyn. "What's your stand on the economy?"

He grabbed her hand and pressed it tightly into his crotch.

"That's no kind of answer, Arnie," she said, pulling back. "I fail to see the connection."

He reached again for her hand. "Tell me you like it . . . tell me."

"Ah, Arnie, there's the rub, you should pardon the expression. You see, I don't like it."

"Up and down," he murmured, "up and down."

"Over and out, Arnie. Over and out." She began to slide from the booth and got almost to the edge before he hauled her back.

"You're not going anywhere." His grip stung her wrist. "Relax and enjoy your drink."

"Arnie, it's hard to relax when you've got me . . ."

"Please," he hissed, "just be quiet and drink your drink." He signaled for two more.

She couldn't understand why she wasn't out of this by now. It had gone on quite long enough. If he restrained her, she could simply scream. What could he do? Was she titillated? Was she afraid? Both? Was she drunker than she thought? She studied him while he paid for the new round. He was slightly flushed, a bit too moist around the mouth, rather exaggerated in his movements but, basically, he just looked like good old Arnold Pratt—good old Arnold Pratt with a couple of extra drinks in him.

Beneath the table good old Arnold Pratt unzipped his pants and placed her hand inside.

"If you move your hand I'll turn over the table so everyone can see what you're doing to me."

"What I'm . . . Arnold, there's some confusion here."

"Keep your hand there. Do what I say."

"Arnie, how could you? You know that's my drinking hand."

"No more jokes. Just do what I say."

She didn't want to believe what she heard in his voice.

"Arnie, I've worked hard on this routine and now you come along and tell me no more jokes. You've got to be kidding."

"Shut up." He twisted his hand on her wrist, pulling the skin painfully.

"That smarts a bit, Arnie. Could you please not do that again?"

"Now just move your hand up and down . . . slowly . . . up and down."

He leaned his head back, closing his eyes for a moment. Then he pulled himself up very straight, his free hand resting casually on the table.

"That's it," he said, "up and down. Now tell me you like it."

"Why I haven't had so much fun since . . ."

"I said no jokes." His voice rasped and he tightened his grip again. "Tell me."

"I like it," she said, unable to get her voice above a whisper.

"Faster now . . . faster." She stared in disbelief as he finished his drink and held up his glass, signaling for more. "Say, 'Arnie, I love your cock.'"

She raised her own glass and upended it down her throat.

"It's terrific, Arnie. Absolutely terrific."

This time he dug his heel into her foot as he turned his hand on her wrist.

"I love your cock." She was close to gasping.

"Much faster when the waitress comes. Now . . . now."

He gave the waitress a big smile and flipped a bill onto her tray.

"Keep the change," he said.

"Thank you," she smiled, surprised by his generosity. "Thank you, sir."

As the waitress thanked him the second time, Evelyn felt Arnold spurt up against the under side of the table. Wet trickles streamed down her leg. His grip on her loosened somewhat and he slumped down slowly out of his rigid position. He sighed deeply and turned toward Evelyn, grinning.

"I'll drink to that," he said.

"You betcha," she muttered.

"Was it fun for you?" he asked.

"Fun isn't *exactly* the word I would have chosen."

"Exciting?"

"You're getting warm."

"Nope, now I'm cooling off."

"Ah, I see that jokes are allowed once again."

"Well, Evelyn, you know me . . ."

"Arnold drinkin' is Arnold foolin'?"

"You know something? You've got a fabulous memory."

"Well, I'll certainly remember tonight, Arnie. That I can promise you."

"No blackouts?" He winked and jabbed her gently with his elbow.

"No, siree. Not one second lost . . . not one."

"Me, too," he said. "That's just how I feel."

With that he seemed to slip into a reverie, as though he were already looking back, fondly recalling their evening. Evelyn simply drank, staring straight ahead.

"One for the road?" he asked, after a long silence.

"One what?" said Evelyn.

He was puzzled for a moment. Then he grinned and the grin turned into a laugh.

"Oh, I getcha. No, no . . . I'm afraid that's about all I can manage for tonight. Sorry."

"Perfectly all right, Arn. Believe me. Perfectly okay."

"One more stinger?" he asked.

"Sure," said Evelyn. "Why not?"

Three

The first thing she saw was her stockings, draped over an armchair near the bed. They looked diseased, like an old leper skin. She grabbed the toe of one and pulled it toward her. Close up she could identify the streaks: wine and sperm. At those points where the two mingled the color was dusty rose, one of her favorites.

As she turned to see the clock, she felt the bruise on her instep and looked immediately at her wrist, expecting the red mark she found there. Good old Arnold Pratt—good old drinkin', foolin' Arnie Pratt.

She had overslept by almost an hour. The realization made her feet hit the floor with an impact that sent shock waves up and down her body, but she was halfway across the room before the pain registered completely. When it did, she expressed it in alternating moans and whimpers. Emitting sounds relieved slightly the pressure in her head.

The cool bathroom tile felt good beneath her feet. She pressed down hard, wanting the cold to spread upward and take away her swelling. Eyelids, fingers, ankles, lips—everything felt puffy. She looked in the mirror. Everything was.

She let the water run until it was icy and carried a large glass of it with her to the telephone. She first rescheduled her morning appointments, then dialed Regina.

"Yes." It was the voice Regina used when she felt guilty for still being in bed. With it, she tried to disguise all traces of sleep and project brisk efficiency. It actually sounded rather like a scream.

"It's me," said Evelyn.

"Oh, thank God." Regina sighed and Evelyn could feel her sinking back into the pillows.

"Try and stay awake for just a bit," said Evelyn. "Please. I need to talk."

"Wide awake, darling," Regina murmured. "I want to be up."

"I can hear your eagerness. I tried to get you all yesterday, all last night . . ."

"You did."

"What?"

"We talked about three o'clock this morning."

"And I've been congratulating myself for remembering the evening. What did I say?"

"You spoke of your delightful dinner partner . . . Mr. Pratt, I believe."

"That's right . . . good old Mr. Pratt."

"My God, what a nightmare!"

"It is as nothing compared to the promise of today."

"What is it? What's wrong?" Regina was somewhat awake now and sounded alarmed.

"How can I put it?" Evelyn took a large gulp of water and heard Regina lighting a cigarette. "I look like I've been attacked by bees."

"Tiny bit swollen?"

"I could barely squeeze my finger into the dial holes."

"Oh, my poor angel. Can you get on a plane and come home?"

"Hardly. I didn't come here for dinner with Arnold Pratt, if you'll recall. God . . . I don't know how I'll do it."

"Jesus, baby. I wish I could help."

"You do. Your voice helps . . . as much as anything can. How long did we talk?"

"Long time . . . probably about an hour."

"Not a shred of it . . . not one. Christ!"

"If it's any consolation, I see here on my bedside table a huge glass with at least two dozen twists of lemon in it that I do not recognize. That is, I recognize neither the lemons nor the glass. Nor do I have any recollection of how they came to be on my bedside table."

"It's no consolation at all . . . but a dandy little mystery. Could you be free tonight?"

"God, when is tonight?"

"After today."

"I didn't think you'd be back."

"Neither did I but I think I have to be. Try and be free. We could have a late supper."

"I'll try."

"It would get me through the day."

"Come here when you get in. I long for you."

"As soon as I can. Please be there."

"I hope today gets better."

"It's the only possibility . . . for you, too." Evelyn made a kissing sound into the phone and was immediately embarrassed. It was one of those things that seemed so natural when someone else did it, so false coming from her. She had a long list of them.

"Bye-bye," she and Regina whispered simultaneously.

When Evelyn's hangover was especially vivid, dressing was difficult. Her clothes were either too loose or too tight; her stockings invariably ran as she pulled them on; the heels on her shoes seemed to be different heights. When she looked in the mirror it was as though she were reflected through a fish-eye lens. Her face was elongated and widened at once; her eyes bulged; her mouth writhed. Everything, all day, would look this way to her. The world would be caricatured. She had never discovered why alcohol played this particular trick on her perception, but it had done so for some time.

After stoking up with several pills and some coffee, she took a cab into the countryside, just in time for her interview with the program director, Colonel Evans. He was a distinct type, a mixture of bureaucrat and military man, retired for years but still using his title, a no-nonsense approach to things, aggressively genial.

"Glad you changed the appointment," he said, leading her down a hallway. "Gave me a chance to clear my desk."

He opened the door to his office and indicated a chair for her as he circled the desk and sat behind it.

"You certainly have cleared it," said Evelyn, gazing at the polished surface, completely blank except for a fountain pen stand and an empty wire basket.

He chuckled. "Manner of speaking . . . clear the desk. Helps though to have things neat. Keeps the head the same way."

He chuckled again and pointed toward a pot of coffee sitting on a hot plate in the corner, raising his eyebrows in a question.

"Please," said Evelyn. "Black."

She wondered if his aversion to pronouns was something left over from military service.

"Don't mind saying . . . awfully surprised to see you getting out of that cab," he said, handing her a plastic cup of pitch-black instant.

"Oh, why was that?" asked Evelyn, knowing why.

"Expected someone older. Unusual for a gal your age to be doing this sort of work. No older than some of our recruits."

"Actually," said Evelyn, "I'm a very young-looking forty."

"Fooled me . . . and I'm usually a pretty good judge." Satisfied with that exchange as an icebreaker, he leaned back in his chair, making a steeple of his fingers beneath his chin. He was ready for her to fire away.

Evelyn took a swallow of coffee and fought to keep it traveling downward.

"That is a ferocious cup of coffee, Colonel."

"Black it is." He laughed.

"Are you always so literal?" Evelyn was stalling. Her mind was empty. She could barely remember why she was here.

"Learn that in the army," he said. "Mean what you say, say what you mean."

"Do you mean to say . . ." It was an old trick of Evelyn's. When she found herself blank, she would repeat in question form what the interviewee had just said. It usually made sense and bought her a little time. Now it did neither.

"Pardon?" The colonel looked puzzled.

"No, no. Colonel . . ." There was a note of reprimand in her voice, designed to make him feel he hadn't quite been paying attention, another old trick. "Tell me why you are here."

"What?" Now he looked truly confused and Evelyn realized her phrasing wasn't all it might have been.

"Why was this chosen as the site?" Her tone again reprimanded him but he didn't seem to notice.

"Can't help these girls by putting them in the same old environment. No good sticking them in some inner-city hotel. Looked at a lot of these but just couldn't see the facilities as viable motivating factors."

Evelyn had focused on his continued omission of pronouns rather than on what he was saying and was startled when he stopped.

"Viable motivating factors," she murmured, hoping that she appeared to be mulling them over.

"Environment here can become one of those factors," he said.

"Yes, of course."

"Give new horizons." He flung his arm outward in the direction of a window. "Look around. Literally, a new horizon."

"Very true," said Evelyn.

Colonel Evans began to talk about money, mentioning

items in his budget, including a lease on the property and renovation of its existing buildings.

"Gonna ask if that's a lot of money?" he asked, not giving her time to say it never occurred to her. "Not looked at this way . . ."

She heard his voice and watched her hand writing and assumed it was transcribing what he was saying. But it was only an assumption. She was so distant she could not have testified to anything happening in the room. The pills were fighting to cut through the thickness in her head but they hadn't yet. She was afraid they wouldn't.

"Colonel," she interrupted him, passing a hand lightly across her forehead to indicate some nameless vapor. "Forgive me. I've had a slight bug that comes and goes and it leaves me a little woozy. If I could just . . ."

"Ladies' room?" His voice was heavy with understanding, causing her to play it even more fully.

"Just some cold water . . . it passes." She wobbled getting up and clutched at the back of her chair. Afraid she might have overdone it, she glanced quickly to see his reaction. It was deep concern.

"So sorry," she said, dropping her pronoun and leaning against him as he took her arm and escorted her to the hall.

"Straight ahead, on the left."

"Thank you, Colonel. Right back . . . so terribly sorry."

"Please, please. No rush."

She gave him a weak but brave smile and set off, hesitating slightly every few paces, reaching out once to steady herself against the wall. She felt him start toward her on that one and quickly straightened up, making clear, however, that the effort was great.

Inside the ladies' room she ran the cold water while searching in her purse for the pills. She took them with water slurped out of her cupped hands, thankful the room was empty. As she splashed water onto her face, she felt the ominous rumblings of diarrhea in her lower stomach. Much as she hated it, it was better than vomiting. Vomiting carried the pills away. Vomiting also made her cry.

She continued putting water on her face, then dried it as she monitored the progress of the inner rush. Her timing was perfect and she felt better when it was over. She felt—she always felt—that some of the poison had been expelled.

As she tried, with powder and a stick of Erace, to deemphasize the blotches on her face, she thought of questions she might ask. Only two things suggested themselves. She reduced them to minimum form—purpose of program, local reaction—so that she could repeat them over and over until she got back in the room and could write them down. If she didn't say them constantly between now and then, she felt sure they would escape.

Colonel Evans rose as she entered. "Get you anything?" he asked.

"Would you have any tea?"

"Certainly would."

As he crossed to the hot plate, she quickly wrote the two phrases in her notebook.

"I'm so terribly sorry," Evelyn said. "I thought I'd shaken the darn thing."

It was easy for her now to feign annoyance at the interruption. The pills were beginning to work and she had at least two questions to ask.

"Know how you feel." He handed her the tea. "Had a low-grade virus that hung on all last winter. Hard to throw those things off."

"It's such a bore." She was now the complete professional, carrying on no matter what, and she could see he was impressed.

"Colonel," she shifted in her chair to a position of keen

alertness, "tell me how you see the purpose of the program, your definition of its focus, its goal, if you will."

She knew that an unnecessarily long question didn't always make the interviewer seem on top of things but sometimes it did. She congratulated herself that this time it had.

"Development of the complete individual," he answered quickly.

"No easy matter . . . no small task," she murmured knowingly.

"Not just vocational instruction and never said it would be easy," he pointed out. "But program can do it, if anything can."

While he listed the components of the program, Evelyn watched him intently. There was a certain look, she'd found, that kept people talking for as long as she wanted to keep looking. The look assured them that what they were saying was absolutely riveting. She kept it fastened on the colonel for several long minutes. The interview must seem to last a decent amount of time and she had just one question left.

"And doesn't mean playing drop the handkerchief," he was saying.

"Certainly not," Evelyn put in, wanting him to know she understood. Judging from his tone, there were those who didn't.

"Means showing these girls how to improve looks and actions," he said. "Begin to take some pride in themselves, going to be more motivated to get a job and have a better chance of getting it."

He paused here, obviously in prelude to something important.

"Can't get a job in tight pink nylon pants and makeup from ear to ear." He spoke the words like a credo and watched eagerly for Evelyn's reaction to it.

"No question there, Colonel." She nodded her head firmly.

"And absolutely not true that they'll get skiing and golfing lessons." He brought his fist down on the desk for emphasis and Evelyn realized she wouldn't even have to ask her other question. "Not true that we're running a country club out here. Can ski and golf and swim in their spare time, of course, and use any recreational facilities indigenous to the area. But not here for that and any implication in that direction is completely false."

He seemed suddenly to hear his shrillness and stopped abruptly.

"So," said Evelyn, "there won't be any lessons . . ."

"Absolutely not. Strange ideas that get started . . ." He trailed off, not wanting to go any further in that direction.

"Well, Colonel, I wish you well." She closed her notebook and capped her pen. His embarrassment made it easy for her to wind up.

"No easy matter, as you said. But challenging." He was trying to regain the offensive before she left. "And worthwhile, no matter how great the effort."

Evelyn began to feel sorry for him as she watched him try to talk himself into belief in his project.

"Don't get a chance every day to tackle something like this," he said. "Don't often get a crack at this sort of thing."

It sounded like a litany, well worn through repetition, necessary to his existence.

"Well, as I said, Colonel, good luck." She put out her hand, eager to signal the end, needing fresh air badly.

"Walk you out." He took her by the arm as though she were still feeling faint.

"Once-in-a-lifetime deal, opportunity like this . . ." He couldn't seem to stop and she didn't interrupt him. "Doesn't come along very often."

"Thank you for your time." She extended her hand again. "I enjoyed it."

"Not at all, not at all."

Evelyn wanted terribly to ask him about the pronouns but she didn't.

Evelyn was obsessed with getting back to New York. She kept two other appointments, made a few more phone calls, canceled everything else, and was at the Portland airport by three o'clock. The plane she got on brought her into New York at the height of the rush hour. The ride from the airport to the city lasted two hours and fifteen minutes.

During that time, Evelyn systematically put aside the past week and concentrated fully on Regina. Until a few months ago, one of her life's imperatives had been to avoid thinking about women. She had even tried to avoid thinking during the week about a female lover she saw every weekend.

Monday through Thursday Evelyn spent her evenings with men, either on dates or in chance encounters, the latter usually occasioned by advanced drunkenness.

Friday night she took the train to the country. Jane met her and they went to Jane's house and there Evelyn remained until Sunday night or very early Monday morning. They had a lot of sex, not too much to drink, very little talk, and a great deal to eat. They played tennis, took drives, saw an occasional movie, and shopped in the local markets, two of which had highly masculine female checkers whom they made cracks about. They both suffered waves of guilt and horror at their secret shame but never discussed it even with each other. Despite their sexual activity, they were deeply repressed.

Jane was firmly, and proudly, middle-class, a characteristic Evelyn felt was mirrored in Jane's mania for appliances. She had them for every occasion: for grilling bacon, for toasting English muffins, for roasting chickens, for sharpening knives, opening cans, carving meat, for perking coffee, for grinding it, for chopping nuts, making shakes, grilling cheese, for broiling hamburgers, for frying them, shaping them, for cooking omelets, mulling wine, squeezing juice. She had a separate machine for every kitchen activity and she loved every last one of them.

Jane also had phobic doubts about her intelligence. She feared she was not as bright as Evelyn and dealt with her fear by attempting to know everything. She became a collector of facts. She sought them in the pages of news magazines, on television talk shows, in the question-and-answer sections of Sunday's newspaper magazines, and in miscellaneous reading. Evelyn always felt that the sole reason Jane read was to increase her fact supply. She had not, however, developed that faculty which could judge the relative importance of the facts she collected. It meant as much to her that she knew Jeanne Crain was married to Paul Brinkman as it did that she was familiar with the origins of the Vietnam war.

Her fear of the lesbian taint was, if possible, even greater than Evelyn's. She gave the very word a wide berth, describing anyone of questionable femininity as "a bowling alley type." When Evelyn once called her "honey" within earshot of a waitress, Jane's kick beneath the table drew blood. They took holidays together, usually to a foreign country, but when Jane found herself free of the strictures of her regular life, she became even guiltier. She expressed her guilt by withdrawal and sulking, a fact that made their holidays less than wholly successful.

They had met years before in high school, the first time a crush of Evelyn's came to fruition. They'd seen enough of each other then to cause Evelyn's parents to ask Evelyn's boy friend to speak to Evelyn about the amount of time she spent with Jane. They were worried, he said. He did not say about what. That was the closest Evelyn's parents ever came to confronting the matter. They hoped, she supposed, that it would go away. She certainly did. And thought perhaps it had when she tired of Jane and they went their separate ways.

However, after a series of not terribly serious romances with young men and one broken engagement, it cropped up again. During Evelyn's junior year in college, she fell madly in love with a female campus leader. They did a lot of double-dating, going directly from front porch good-night kisses with the boys into some dark corner of the dormitory where they ravished each other.

In her senior and graduate school years, she was enamored of another young woman and, at the same time, trying to secure the attentions of a young man reputed to be unreachable. He proved to be reachable after all but as soon as Evelyn reached him, he graduated and went into the navy. That left her with only her lesbian passion which flourished until she moved to New York.

At that time, Evelyn tried to excise her penchant for women. She gave herself over entirely to the world of men: she worked with them, flirted with them, played games with them, conducted affairs with them, had one-night stands with them, became pregnant by them, and, of course, drank with them, without which most of the rest would have been impossible. In the interest of tidiness, tying up loose ends, she mentioned to her psychiatrist at the time her previous "homosexual experiences" and their attendant fear and guilt. After she had spoken, he went on to other things and the subject never came up again. Since he ignored it, Evelyn tried to also.

When Jane reentered her life, she changed nothing but her weekends. Those she used as retreats where she replenished and restored herself sufficiently to last through the coming week. There was nothing restorative about the guilt, however. It was as though each weekend she checked into a sanitarium for forty-eight hours but stole the money to pay for it. Everything in her life seemed hopelessly dual and the discipline required to sustain the dichotomies was wearing. By the time Evelyn met Regina, she was extremely tired.

They had a friend in common and met at one of his dinner parties. Regina was late, coming in just as they were beginning to eat. Evelyn's first memory of her was watching across the table as she drew out of a very large satchel six packages of cigarettes, all different brands, and a jar of hot mustard. Feeling Evelyn watching her, she looked up and said, "Daniel never has anything but French's which is unspeakable, true swill." She didn't mention the cigarettes.

Regina was dressed completely in black—boots, stockings, sweater, skirt, and dog. He appeared to be welded to her ankle, seldom straying more than a few inches from it. Her hair was a color rarely seen on an adult, almost towhead white. It surrounded her face, an area of intense animation, like a golden circle. Evelyn found her enchanting.

When she'd lived in Nevada, Regina said—getting the first of several divorces—F.B., the dog, had been able to walk the length of a bar without ever touching a single glass. He'd also been able to circle a room without ever touching the floor, soaring from one piece of furniture to another.

"Regina," said Daniel, "you are always making the most extravagant claims for that creature. I'd be satisfied if he'd just stop staring at me while I eat. I can't swallow when he's looking at me."

When she'd lived in the Canary Islands, she'd traveled around on a motorcycle without brakes. When she wanted to stop, she just rammed it into the nearest obstacle. The small scar beneath her chin was due to that.

When she'd tried to commit suicide at the age of nineteen, she sat beneath a bathroom sink, facing out, and banged her head against the basin's underside many times. Her hope was to be discovered with her long blond hair spread luxuriantly on a field of red.

On the night of her wedding to a sixty-five-year-old muskrat hunter, she was found running through the Nevada desert, completely naked, unable to say how she'd arrived there.

The last time she'd visited London, she'd vomited on Sir Laurence Olivier.

Evelyn had these facts in hand before dinner was over. During a shared cab ride afterwards, she learned Regina was the assistant director of a play in rehearsal, couldn't eat anything white, was in constant fear of contracting leprosy, and lived in a midtown hotel so that she could get to the theater on time.

Two weeks later they ran into each other at the theater, decided to have a drink, found the place they'd picked was closed, and went to Regina's hotel. They drank and talked and, when Evelyn's memory picked up again, it was in the midst of a scene of total sexual abandon. She had, however, no recollection of where she was, who she was with, or how she had gotten there. The first two items came back to her quite quickly. She never retrieved the third. But, from the moment Evelyn realized she was in Regina's bed, it never occurred to her to leave.

Her sexual craving for Regina was so acute, her attraction so powerful, euphemism would have been laughable. This was, without question, lesbianism, a certainty which caused every old guilt, and some new ones, to rise to the surface. Evelyn watched as the carefully constructed fictions of her life simply crumbled. She scattered into countless pieces. By way of taking herself in hand, she drank more than usual and renewed her acquaintance with pills. When that treatment gave every indication of proving insufficient, she supplemented it with a new therapist.

She remembered now that she would see him tomorrow. Thank God she'd come back! She leaned her head against the cab's window, absorbing its coolness.

"Where are we?" she asked the driver after what seemed a very long time.

"I'm doin' everything I can, lady. Whadda ya expect when ya come in this time 'a day?"

"Nothing, really . . ." she murmured.

"Well, that's what ya get. Ya wanna fast ride, come in some other time."

"I'll remember that."

His hostility gagged Evelyn and they rode the rest of the way without a word.

Four

Regina's rooms were empty and there was no sign of where she might be or when she'd return. Evelyn was glad to have time for a shower and drink but knew she'd be enraged if Regina's absence lasted a moment longer than they did. She took two pills with the first swallow of Scotch and set the glass on the tub, within reach. Standing under the shower, she heard the phone ring but couldn't get to it in time. She should have taken it off the hook while she bathed. Regina might call.

She could feel rigidities in her body being loosened and swept away by the hot water pounding on her skin. She liked the sensation of Scotch running down her throat while the water washed over her body. She felt as though she had stiffened when she left here and remained that way for more than a week. Now everything was becoming fluid and soft again.

Miss Girard exhibits an absolute mastery of stylistic nuance.

She rubbed some color into her dead-white skin with the rough bath towel. She never understood why, at the moment her cheeks were blushing with chemical roses, her body was draining of any color whatsoever. She felt much healthier when she was slightly pink all over and she achieved that now with the abrasive towel. She dressed slowly, postponing the feeling she knew would seize her when she was ready and Regina still wasn't there. It was eight o'clock when she finished.

Evelyn promised herself that if Regina did not appear by

eight-thirty, she would leave. She glanced over the training program material, realized it was skimpy, but didn't feel up to creating padding at the moment. Finally, she just sat, drinking a fresh drink, watching the clock.

When the phone rang it sounded very distant and she didn't even move toward it until the third ring.

"God, I thought you still weren't there," said Regina. "I was starting to get worried."

"I was in the shower when you called before. I've been here for hours."

"Darling, you couldn't have been. I didn't leave there until just before seven."

"I must have just missed you. Where are you?"

"I'm at Eric's. He left some things at the theater and I had to bring them down here."

"Christ! Does that mean you're embroiled for the night?"

"No, I'm about to leave. Why don't you meet me at El Casa in half an hour."

"Perfect. I love you."

"Me too. See you soon."

El Casa was a Mexican restaurant with two outstanding virtues: the kitchen was open until one in the morning and the margaritas weren't watered. Evelyn ordered one as she walked in the door. By the time she reached a table in back, José was carrying it toward her—another virtue.

"And the other? She will come?"

"In a little while, José. I'm early."

Evelyn sat facing the doorway, excited at the prospect of seeing Regina again, trying to appear casual. Attempting to strike a pose of languorous relaxation, she tilted back in her chair but misjudged the angle and felt the legs start to go. Just in time, she threw her weight forward and crashed down, her elbows ramming into the tabletop. José turned at the sound but didn't know what it had been. He wasn't close enough to see the flush spread over her face. Realizing she was staring at him, she summoned him to the table as though that were the intention of her stare.

"Guacamole, *por favor.*"

"Yes, of course. Right away."

When Evelyn glanced back at the door, Regina was coming through it. Evelyn's entire body still registered a jolt of shock each time she saw Regina. When it passed, she rose and they greeted each other with brushed kisses on the cheek and white-knuckled grips on the arms.

"My God, I'm glad to see you," Evelyn said as they sat down.

"Jesus, darling, you look wonderful. I expected a ruin."

"Tequila has erased every trace of the horror."

"I could use a little magic myself."

Her hand in the air sent José speeding toward the bar. He was back with drinks and guacamole before Regina had even taken cigarettes and hot sauce from her purse.

"The first sip of tequila," said Regina, after a swallow, "always takes me back to the Acapulco bar where I sat for days drinking margaritas while the lovely Miss Haliburton pursued Inez . . ."

"Inez?"

"A Paraguayan whore she fancied in an effort to drive me totally berserk. She was the lover of Olga Mendoza, the fat, hairy daughter of the Mexican chief of police. Charming couple, Olga and Inez. Olga looked exactly like Charles Laughton but with a lot of stringy black hair."

"What about Inez?"

"Inez could barely be seen through the pancake and rouge. Cleaned up a bit she might not have been bad. She always wore shoes the color of her lipstick and enormous silk shawls."

"How did Olga feel about Haliburton?"

"First, she threatened to kill her. Then she said she'd have her father arrest her, although I don't think her father had had anything to do with her for years."

"Olga was the family embarrassment?"

"I think he stuffed her away someplace the instant her sexual preference became known. Hardly a political asset, our Olga."

"So what happened?"

"She finally did try to kill Haliburton . . . with one of Inez's shoes."

"Unlikely weapon."

"She found them in bed together and tried to drive the spike heel into Allie's head, but all she succeeded in doing was leaving one little red heel mark on her cheek, which was actually rather sweet . . . in a bizarre sort of way. Then they all became great friends and Allie moved in with them when I was shipped home to the madhouse."

"Ah, the good old days," said Evelyn. "Shall we have another drink to them?"

"Absolutely."

"I'm so glad to be here with you," said Evelyn. "The past week seemed forever."

"It was," said Regina. "An eternity."

"I want you."

"Oh, my darling, I want you too."

They sat quietly for a moment, made rather breathless by this outburst of longing. Then, simultaneously, they raised their glasses and drank, never taking their eyes off one another.

"Where is F.B.?" Evelyn asked, unable to stand the intensity.

"I left him at Eric's where he has fallen deliriously and fiendishly in love with Celeste, a gigantic red cat and the only other creature on earth I've ever seen him acknowledge. He won't even let Eric come near her."

"How does he manage that?"

"So far he's using his paralyzing gaze although he's capable of much fiercer ploys if necessary. I had a truly gruesome period a while ago, dragging things home from the bars every night, and he was particularly savage with them. He had a special growl that sent them fleeing into the night, usually without their underwear. Haven't you ever noticed the undie pile in the far left-hand corner of my closet?"

"I thought it was dirty laundry," said Evelyn.

"Oh, no. Those are F.B.'s trophies."

"Why just underwear?"

"The way I piece it together is this: I would tear the outer garments from these vile creatures as we were coming through the front door, leaving the garments piled somewhere near the entrance, taking the vile creatures into my bed clad only in their pretty underthings. When these were ripped off, they remained somewhere in the bed area, out of reach once the creatures went to the john and became F.B.'s prisoners. He never let them get back in bed but they could pass from bathroom to living room where they clothed themselves before leaving. You can't imagine the massive relief when I'd wake up with their underwear and not them."

"But I can. Men don't tend to leave their underwear but I certainly know the relief of waking up alone. It's almost unbearable to have to look at evidence first thing in the morning."

"Even drunk you never brought home women?"

"If I'd stumbled across any lady taxi drivers I might have . . . my passion for cabbies was boundless. But no, I didn't. Even drunk I was rigorously heterosexual . . . especially drunk."

Regina signaled José for two more drinks. "Tell me about the Holiday Inn. Is the food indescribably horrid?"

"No," said Evelyn. "Just boring. Are you hungry?"

"I suppose we could look." Regina took the menus from José when he returned with the drinks and handed one to

Evelyn, fixing her at the same time with a gaze of sexual intent.

"I'm not sure I can read if you look at me like that," said Evelyn. "But please don't stop."

Their eyes remained locked across the table until José cleared his throat discreetly.

"You wish to order now?"

"Very soon, José." Regina turned her dazzling smile toward him. "Just give us a few minutes and two more margaritas."

"I had dinner last week with Frances Jameson," Regina said, "and she served what she had chosen to call a Mexican casserole."

"Oh, God . . . one of her ninety-eight-cent specials."

"Couldn't have been a penny over forty-nine. My darling, it was so vile I had to feign a recurrence of my ulcer after the first bite, the first recurrence in fifteen years."

"Could I stand to hear the ingredients?"

"Could I stand to name them? Oh, but first the cocktails, the drinks before dinner. There were only two apiece and they came out of those tiny airline bottles. I couldn't believe it. It's like the time she gave half-pints as Christmas presents. Anyway, the casserole had lima beans, some disgusting nuts, a few plugs of bone-dry macaroni, bits of pineapple, some highly pungent tinned fish, and crumbled potato chips on top."

"What's Mexican about that?"

"She put in chili powder, lots of it, although not enough to kill the taste of anything else. Each ingredient was completely and perfectly itself."

"Why would she make something so repellent?"

"Because she is so unbelievably tight—darling, she used to give dinner parties with the proceeds from returning Coke bottles."

"I don't believe it."

Regina held up two fingers where José could see them.

"I've seen her do it. I once went with her while she traveled to some distant corner of Brooklyn by subway because they gave you back an extra cent on each bottle, shopped for tuna, noodles, and mushroom soup with the return money, and served it to eight people that night."

"What about booze?"

"It was understood that everyone would bring their own."

"She's hardly destitute, is she?"

"Hardly. She has money from her family and money from her operatic efforts."

"Is she any good?"

"An awful lot better than she was as a dancer, which is what she was when I first knew her and we were having whatever it was we had. I was acting then and we were in a show together. She was really dreadful . . . embarrassing."

"I wish I'd had the nerve to try acting," said Evelyn.

"Did you want to?"

"Longed to. The closest I got was in high school putting on kewpie-doll makeup and pantomiming Kay Starr records, forty-five speeded up to seventy-eight. It's pathetic."

She distills moments beautifully.

"I think it's terribly sweet. How old were you when you did that?"

"Much too old. When did you have an ulcer?"

"When Keith and I lived in Panama. I tried to cure it by eating ice cream and became so enormous I could no longer clothe myself so I spent one entire winter wrapped in a sheet. I didn't move about much. Before he left for the base in the morning, he'd get me the day's ice cream and hose me off so I'd stay cool. Very attractive . . . the watering and feeding of the wife. But the ulcer went away."

"Why did you marry him? I can never remember."

"Because he dared me to, to prove I wasn't a lesbian, and because I was in love with his sister."

"I can't think of a firmer foundation for a nuptial venture. Extraordinary, with all that going for you, that it went sour."

"Of course, in the eyes of the church, we are still one, a thought that makes my blood run cold."

"I should think so. I have to pee . . . will you order me another drink?"

"One more . . . and then dinner."

Evelyn felt rather unsteady when she got up and she remembered she hadn't eaten since morning. As she sat down on the toilet, she fished a small yellow tablet from her pocket and swallowed it with the spittle created by working her tongue and jaws together.

"Could you roll me some paper under?" The voice startled her.

"Sure. Here it comes."

"It really bugs the piss outta me when they don't keep up a john, ya know what I mean?"

"Ummmm. It's annoying."

Evelyn's flush covered the beginning of the next sentence but as the water stilled she heard the voice saying, ". . . takes me to dumps. I bet you don't run into no shortage of johnny paper at the Waldorf."

"Probably not."

" 'Course then there's some broad wants to be paid fifty cents for handin' you a square of it. Ya can't win, can ya?"

"Some days it seems that way."

"All days. Seems that way all days to me."

"Well . . . 'bye now."

"Bye-bye, and thanks for the paper."

When Evelyn got back to the table, Regina handed her an open book of matches.

"You look so beautiful in the instant of time that is to-night," she had written inside the cover. "I will worship and adore you forever."

Evelyn read it over twice, feeling the words as though they

were touches. She reached out her hand under the table and
found Regina's waiting for it.

"That is the loveliest thing anyone has ever said to me,"
she said, "or written to me . . . or probably thought about
me."

They fell into another long, silent gaze, straining to make
their eyes reflect every nuance of feeling.

"Is there such a thing as Mexican champagne?" Evelyn
asked eventually.

"I think not, but surely José can find us something from
another land. What a perfect idea. We must have it!"

José came immediately, his pad poised for the dinner order.

"Champagne? You wish to order champagne?" He looked
baffled. "I will see what he has."

"José, darling," Regina said, after looking at the list he'd
brought, "we wanted something very dry. I know your stock
is a bit low but I'm sure next door at the liquor store they
would have something *brut, muy brut,* on ice. Would they
even miss you if you were gone five minutes?" She held a
five-dollar bill loosely in her hand, smiling at him.

"My break is coming. I see what I can do." He pocketed
the five and took an additional twenty-dollar bill Regina
handed him.

"Pure genius," Evelyn marveled.

"Just practice," Regina corrected her.

As Regina rose to go to the john, Evelyn gave her a beatific
smile and floated along with the sensation washing over her.
She felt impervious to any external influence, except Regina.
Everything else had receded, leaving just the two of them
encapsulated in a universe the size and shape of a dinner
table.

"You are perfect," she wrote on a napkin, "and I love you
beyond words and outside of time."

Miss Girard's gift with language is dazzling.

She propped the napkin against the stem of Regina's margarita glass and floated off again. When Regina returned José was with her, carrying a bottle of champagne swathed in a towel.

"Keep on the towel, please," he said, pouring, "or they know it isn't ours."

"José, you are brilliant, *muy maravilloso,*" said Regina.

"Is nothing," he murmured, looking very nervous and moving away.

"We must have a toast," Evelyn said. "You propose."

"Will you marry me?"

"I didn't . . . yes, I will."

"To that."

They raised glasses, saluted each other, and drank, beginning solemnly but ending with laughter.

"And speaking of nuptials, how was your brother's wedding?"

"Lovely . . . and deeply depressing afterwards. I felt that the reception was being held for the sole purpose of giving every family friend a chance to ask me when I was going to take the leap, make the big step, tie the old knot, et cetera."

"God, how ghastly! One of the reasons I got married was so that I'd never be asked that question."

"By the end of the reception I would have traded vows with anyone just to gain silence."

"It's not worth it, darling. Believe me."

"With a little time and distance, I can see that would have been an exorbitant price."

"*Mas* champagne?" Regina poured until it bubbled over the edge of Evelyn's glass. Evelyn licked the champagne off her hand.

"Could you eat?" she asked.

"I'm not famished," said Regina. "I could easily just nibble away at the guacamole while we finish the champagne."

"Perfect," said Evelyn. "They do go rather nicely together, don't they?"

"Champagne goes with just about anything."

"It's the first thing I ever drank," said Evelyn. "It was in a punch, mixed with fruit juice or some such abomination. I was sixteen and had two cups and puked within half an hour. A wonderful omen."

"I began drinking Dubonnet when I was twelve," said Regina. "I started with the dregs in the glasses of my mother's luncheon guests."

"I swore I would never drink," Evelyn said. "I really didn't think I would . . . right up until the time I did. My mother, of course, urged all of us not to . . . if we never tried it, we'd never have a problem, et cetera, et cetera, and that made perfect sense to me. Now it seems insane; an incitement, if anything, a goad."

Evelyn mulled that over as Regina tried to get José's attention, hearing her words hanging in the air, wondering if they were true.

"You wish to order now?" José looked hopeful.

"Guacamole only now," Regina said, "and then we order dinner."

"Do you realize you're speaking with an accent?" Evelyn asked, as José walked off, shaking his head.

"That's an old habit of mine that appears every time I'm in contact with anyone speaking broken English."

"But you sound Chinese."

"That's part of the old habit. No matter what accent I'm hearing, mine is always Chinese."

"How curious."

"When I was in acting school, my brogue sounded Chinese."

"Do it for me."

"You just heard it."

"Oh, I see. That *is* serious."

As José slid the guacamole onto the table, Regina snagged him.

"Un vaso de hielo, por favor, José."

"You want ice?"

"Sí, hielo. La champaña tiene calor."

Regina's cigarette had fallen onto the tablecloth during this exchange, causing it to smolder. Noticing, Evelyn sprayed water from her fingertips at the widening brown circle. When Regina saw what was happening she upended her water glass on the offending spot. As the smoke disappeared, some of the water crept over the table edge and dripped onto her lap.

"Shit!" said Regina, dabbing at it with her napkin. "Well, I guess it's better than a burn. I go through periods when I burn holes in the front of everything at least once a day."

"Mine are usually in back," said Evelyn. "Sitting on burning objects."

"You can't fix holes in the front. If it's a skirt I wear it backwards. If it isn't, I have to throw it out."

"I throw things out even when the hole's in back," said Evelyn. "Things never seem the same once they're seared."

"Basically," said Regina, "I hate clothes. I've always had the idea that my body looked better without them. A few years ago, when I felt compelled to act on that belief, it was almost impossible for me to keep them on."

"A great deal of stripping?" Evelyn asked.

"A great deal of that, a great deal of dancing with chiffon scarves . . . I mean, I did not just tear off my clothes and blatantly display my nakedness. I was witty about it."

"I'm sure."

"The wittiest of all, I suppose, was stripping down at a party for Martha Graham and giving the guests a solid fifteen

minutes of some *real* interpretive dancing. Looking back, I
can see I may have overdone the cartwheels."

"Well, I think your body looks perfectly splendid both
ways," said Evelyn, "clothed or not."

"I'm so glad you think so."

"Did they ever turn up missing? Your clothes?"

"God, all the time! Ah, the merry pranks of my fellow
party-goers. I spent one entire winter traveling home at
night in my coat only."

"I assume that kept your subway riding to a minimum."

"Yes, it was strictly a taxicab winter, which is not to say that
my coat didn't occasionally blow open and arouse the curiosity of the cab driver. I remember one saying to me very
seriously, 'Lady, you forgot your dress.' "

"And the others?"

"Usually I told them I'd been robbed . . ."

"And your dress stolen?"

"I can't say, of course, how often they believed me."

"I love the idea of a dress thief stalking about the city," said
Evelyn. "Women are afraid to walk the streets in anything
attractive . . . they only come out in housedresses."

"Bergdorf's goes out of business and Korvettes' sales
boom," said Regina.

"And Babe Paley is seen haunting discount outlets and
army-navy stores."

"Oh, I love it, darling," said Regina, "a perfect urban fantasy. Why don't you write it and send it to *New York* magazine?"

"Maybe I will. And Cee-Zee Guest is discovered in A & S's
basement."

"You must. You just must do it." Regina poured the last of
the champagne into their glasses.

"Diana Vreeland buys her entire wardrobe at Gimbels,"
said Evelyn. "And the Bouvier girls appear only in un-

bleached muslin sacks. And the Duchess of Windsor outfits herself at Alexander's."

"Oh, perfect . . . absolutely perfect."

"And what happens, of course," said Evelyn, "do you realize what happens?"

"What?"

"The housedress look becomes the rage, the in thing.

"Oh, God, I love it," said Regina.

"A fable for our time."

"It's absolutely brilliant and you must begin it the moment we get home."

"That doesn't seem likely," said Evelyn, raising her glass, "but I'll shoot for the weekend."

"Do you have to work this week?" Regina asked.

"I am still employed there, yes, although my appearances become rarer and rarer. I've got to do the story from Maine tomorrow and I have an interview Thursday."

"Let's go home now. I want you terribly," said Regina.

Evelyn felt Regina's urgency and her own response. She pointed to the menu, questioning, although she already knew they wouldn't stay.

"Later, at Bickford's," said Regina.

"The kitchen is about to close . . ." José appeared suddenly, unsummoned.

"Just the check, José," said Regina. "We're in rather a hurry."

She glanced at the check when he brought it, handed him several dollars too much, and told him to keep it.

"You're an angel," she said, squeezing his hand.

"*Gracias . . . gracias,*" he said, stunned into Spanish.

"*De nada,* José . . . and *gracias* to you."

He watched them go, making a fairly straight line between two rows of tables. As they neared the door, the dark one slipped and he started forward. She went down onto one

knee but quickly bounced up with the light one's help and
they exited arm in arm.

It was three o'clock A.M. and they were both ravenous.

"I have two lemons, some truly ancient chopped liver, two
quite old crab legs, and three cans of Ken-L Ration," Regina
called out to Evelyn in the bedroom. "With a lot of hot sauce
and onions, the Ken-L Ration can be rather tasty."

"Do you have a beer?" asked Evelyn.

Regina opened two and carried them to the bed.

"I'm afraid Bickford's is the only answer," said Evelyn.

"I'll go and walk F.B.," said Regina, dialing the all-night
coffee shop on the corner.

"One rare cheeseburger, raw onion." She began Evelyn's
order. "A grilled cheese with bacon and tomato. Pastrami on
rye, extra mustard. An order of french fries. And a strawberry milkshake. And hang on, there's more. A rare cheeseburger, grilled onions . . . right, one grilled, one raw. Chicken
salad on white bread, not toast. You toasted it last time.
Chopped liver on rye with extra mayonnaise. Put extra on
the bread and also put in an extra container, will you? And
a vanilla milkshake with chocolate ice cream. Be sure it's
chocolate ice cream, vanilla syrup, and not the other way
around, okay? Thanks. I'll be there in fifteen minutes."

"It should get us through to morning," said Evelyn.

"God, how I hate leaving this bed." Regina pulled Evelyn
next to her.

"I hate you getting up and clothed," said Evelyn. "Can't
we devise a system to prevent one of us always having to go
out in the middle of the night?"

"Yes," said Regina, "I can think of two possibilities. One is
having food here . . . but, of course, it would never be what
we wanted in the middle of the night. The other is eating
dinner at the appointed hour. But even with that there's a

chance of awakening at three A.M. screaming for burgers and shakes."

"There's no foolproof system, in other words."

"None. We are in bondage to Bickford's."

"I want you all over again," said Evelyn.

"I know," said Regina. "I can't believe I'm getting up. And yet . . ." She untangled herself from Evelyn and swung her feet onto the floor.

"I'll go next time," Evelyn said. "Actually, I don't see why we couldn't keep sandwiches here. We'd have a pretty good idea about the cravings ahead of time. They're always the same. Of course, we'd still have to go out for shakes."

"You're raving, darling," said Regina, pulling a sweater over her head. "Whumph feened huffloy."

"What?"

Her head popped out and she drew the sweater down her body. "What we need is a houseboy. It's the only answer: a very tiny, nocturnal Oriental who could live in the front closet."

"Do you realize what that would do to your speech?"

"That would be a risk. But right now I'm absolutely sure it would be worth it."

"Oh, God, let me go."

"No," said Regina, "I'm dressed. But I have to go this instant or I'll never make it. C'mon, F.B. Be right back, darling. 'Bye."

The door slammed and the sound jostled Evelyn's memory. F.B. was at Eric's. She heard the door open.

"I'm not taking him," Regina called, slamming the door again.

The bed jiggled and everything on the bedside table rattled against its glass top. Evelyn burrowed down into the covers, her hand wrapped around the bottle of beer. She began reviewing each step of their lovemaking, annoyed that she could not bring it all back. There were gaps.

Miss Girard reveals an intimate acquaintance with the void, a knowledge of emptiness that is staggering in one so young.

She tried to force her mind up against the blankness, bullying it. She tried sneaking up on it, to surprise it into revealing something. Nothing worked. So she drank the beer and relished those things she could recall. She must have dozed because it seemed Regina was back almost immediately.

"They are such swine in there," said Regina, placing two large bags in the middle of the bed. "Such utter and complete swine! When I asked if they'd put in extra mayonnaise, the man at the counter gave me the filthiest look, as though I'd said something truly revolting, as though I'd said, 'I hope you put in extra mayonnaise because I'm going home to smear it all over my black-dyke-Jew-Communist-lover."

"You should have."

"They assume that every woman out in the middle of the night is a whore and they treat you as though you're a slug from the slime and you should pay double for the privilege of eating their revolting food."

"Sit and have a swallow of beer and please don't say anything else about slime until I've eaten something."

"I'm sorry, darling. They are just such leprous pieces of vileness . . ."

"Please. What are you going to start with?"

"It wasn't ready when I got there so I told him to put on a double portion of chicken salad. That means I'll have to eat that one in the tub."

"It has to be something you can eat in bed," said Evelyn.

"I'll have the cheeseburger, I guess."

"Please, get undressed and get in. You've been away far too long."

They ate voraciously. Evelyn finished everything but half a pastrami sandwich. She put that on the bedside table, to be grabbed the moment she woke up. They made love again and fell asleep just as the room was turning a soft gray from the beginning of morning light.

Five

"The land will be foreign to them but here they will come . . ."

Evelyn ripped the paper out of the typewriter, wadded it up, and tossed it toward the wastebasket, missing.

"Soon this lovely New England landscape will be peopled with urban young women," she began again.

"Christ," she muttered, "sounds like I'm beginning a fucking fairy tale." She tore it from the machine and put in fresh paper.

"A female job-training program is set to open here next week." She stared at the sentence for at least a minute, paralyzed by boredom. How could she possibly do this? She was still slightly loaded and the pills had not taken hold at all.

"A job-training program for disadvantaged urban young women, set in the Maine countryside, is unlikely but . . ."

But what? But so what? Evelyn crumpled it and hit the basket as she passed by on her way to the ladies room. She took two pills immediately, then held cold water cupped in her hands and lowered her face into it. She did that several times, feeling slightly better after each immersion.

Back in the office, she sent out for two large coffees with lots of milk and sugar and began again. By the time she got a decent first sentence, the coffee was there and the pills had begun working. Those two things, in combination with last night's tequila and champagne, induced a fuguelike state from which she emerged around noon with the story complete.

She was walking toward the elevator when she heard his hissing sound: "Eevee . . . Eevee."

"Carlos, I'm in a terrible hurry." She tossed the words over her shoulder, speeding up, hoping to jump in an elevator before he caught her.

"Please . . . one moment only." His footsteps were very near and the elevator doors had closed, so she walked past them and into the ladies room, his voice trailing after her.

Carlos Aguirre was an Argentine journalist of some stature who had been assigned to the United States for years. Three years ago, he and Evelyn had gone to dinner and then to bed. When she'd turned up pregnant, he'd urged her to have the child and live with it in an apartment supplied by him. The fact that he shared an apartment with his wife would prevent him from joining her there permanently but he'd certainly be available from time to time. Evelyn declined, paid for her own abortion, and made clear she wasn't interested in extending their relationship beyond the single unfortunate night. Carlos went berserk. This man of seeming intelligence and rationality became as one possessed, dogging her steps, ringing her phone, occasionally pushing her around a bit in the halls of their mutual office building, hounding her night and day. The harassment, in one form or another, had been going on for three long years and now, here she was, hiding in a public john like some cornered animal.

"Carlos, this is ridiculous." She burst out of the door angrily, finding the hallway empty except for a cleaning woman. "Oh, I'm sorry . . . I thought there was a man . . ."

The woman shuffled away rapidly, shaking her head.

"I didn't realize . . ." Evelyn began to call after her, then caught herself. "That bastard!" Evelyn hated him still more for causing her this embarrassment.

She waited nervously by the elevator, afraid he would reappear, but she was still alone when the doors opened. Walking through the lobby, she kept close to other people as though they were protection. She didn't see him until it was too late to stay within the revolving doors and churn herself right back into the building.

"Eevee . . . please." He took hold of her elbow. She didn't try to strain against his grip but just stopped and stared at him. He looked like a frog, eyes bulging behind his thick glasses, mouth working furiously. "It is important. We must talk."

"Carlos," Evelyn began, trying to control the quaver in her voice, "I have told you over and over that there is nothing to say. Please just leave me alone."

"I don't wish to hurt you, Eevee. You misunderstand."

"Well, you are." She wrenched her arm from him and began walking, taking extra-long strides. He panted alongside her, pleading.

"Just a few moments. If not now, any time you like. Please . . . it is important."

"It's not important to me. It couldn't be."

"But you are wrong, Eevee, so wrong. Please . . . just give me a chance to explain."

Evelyn tried to imagine what they looked like: she, striding along, eyes straight ahead; he, almost running beside her, neck craning to peer into her face. He made her truly hysterical, or frightened, or enraged, or consumed with loathing. Now she was hysterical.

"Carlos!" She screamed it, stopping abruptly so that he sailed a few feet past her. "Leave me alone. I'm warning you."

The sound she made froze him to the spot long enough for her to jump in a cab and holler, "Get me out of here."

"Anywhere special, honey?" The cabbie's voice and the feeling of motion soothed her. She looked out and saw they weren't far from Regina's hotel.

"Just around the block, I guess."

"You wanna ride around the block?"

"Yes." My God, she thought, I'm like something out of a B movie . . . I'm warning you . . . get me out of here. "I'm surprised I didn't say, 'Follow that car.' "

"What's that?" The cabbie looked over his shoulder at her.

"Nothing." Evelyn hadn't realized she'd spoken out loud. "Really nothing."

She sat as though in a trance while they circled the block. It took half an hour and cost five dollars.

"Money well spent, eh?" She grinned at the driver as she paid him.

"It's your money, sweetheart." She thought she heard contempt in his voice.

"That's right, buster, and don't you forget it." She was still doing it, that same lousy script. And don't you forget it—what did that even mean?

"Have a nice day and thanks for the ride." She wanted to erase any animosity between them.

"Yeah. Thanks, lady. You too."

She bought six peach-colored roses at a nearby florist and walked toward the hotel, all thoughts of Carlos pushed aside by a wave of anticipation. She was sure Regina would still be asleep. As she opened the front door, she felt the emptiness in the rooms. Then she felt it enter into her and the ache began.

"Fuck!" She shrieked it into the silence and immediately felt foolish.

She knew the bedroom would depress her but she wandered in anyway. It was littered with sandwich wrappings, straws, plastic packets of ketchup and mustard, half-full milkshake cartons, a handful of shriveled french fries, dirty silverware, beer bottles. It was depressing.

As she returned to the living room the hangover engulfed her. At this moment, the moment of onslaught, there were always two choices, presuming pills were available. The first was to give in: place near the bed some sweet and starchy food and drink, wash hands and face thoroughly, rinse with lots of cold water, strip and get in bed, and turn on the soaps. The second was to administer a massive dose of amphetamine, drink one cold beer immediately, shower and change clothes, and have at least two glasses of iced coffee with milk. Today, Evelyn chose the latter and by one o'clock she felt very much in charge of herself. The appointment with her therapist wasn't until three-thirty. She could at least begin to write about the dress thief.

"So here comes Jackie-the-K legging down the avenue in muslin . . . muslin? . . . woweeeeee . . . the Norellette and ten-best coming along unbleached as cool as you please . . . coming along with that chiffon stride . . . zsgads!!!!! What portends?

"And whispering . . . sibillating . . . 'It's just a simple little sack' to no one in particular and Seventh Avenue cracks open —eeeeerck—stock boys tumbling with their racks into the chasm . . . aaaarrggk . . ."

Evelyn sat back and looked at it. Why was she trying to sound like very old Tom Wolfe? She tore it out and put in fresh paper.

"Gloria Vanderbilt Cooper was knocked to the ground yesterday outside of Lutece and her dress taken by an assailant who fled, shouting, 'I've done it again, I've done it again.' He carried the garment aloft and waved it as he ran.

"Mrs. Cooper was the fifteenth victim of the thief who has terrorized this city's society women in recent weeks. Police have dubbed him the Dress Bandit.

" 'It was just a simple little French peasant derivative with Spanish overtones in the laced sleeves,' said Mrs. Cooper, weeping. 'I made it myself. I thought he only went for designer things.' "

Not bad, thought Evelyn, but it might pall during the

course of an entire article. She made another large iced coffee and began again.

" 'He got Bitsy's Balenciaga off her in the *lobby* of her building,' Anne Ford Uzielli was saying to her sister Charlotte, 'in full view of the doorman.'

" 'My God, it's not even safe to go for the mail,' said Charlotte."

Evelyn wadded that up and threw it away. Better not begin now when she wouldn't have the time to finish anyway. She felt acutely alone. She wanted to be with someone. Then she thought of who would be available at this hour of the afternoon and her solitude seemed less bleak.

She decided to walk uptown. It was about thirty-five blocks to John Selwyn's and the motion would do her good. She tried very hard to be leisurely, even stopping to sit in the park for a while, but she still arrived early and had to endure the terror of waiting in his hushed outer office. She didn't know why the fear was so enormous but the moment she sat down to wait her entire body began to shake and sweat, her heart raced, and she had difficulty sitting still. She was up and pacing, as a matter of fact, when his two-thirty patient emerged.

"Evelyn." He stood in the doorway, smiling.

She returned his smile with what felt like a simper. When she'd worn braces on her teeth she had developed a closed-mouth smile that recurred now when she was self-conscious. She hated it. She hated that her self-consciousness persisted with Selwyn. If she couldn't discard it here, where could she? Sometimes the pills helped to carry her past it but not today. Today, it seemed, nothing was working.

"It's good to see you," he said. "I missed you."

Evelyn made an unintelligible sound.

"How do you feel about that?" he asked as she sat down across from him.

"I don't know," she said.

"I thought we agreed that you'd try to avoid that phrase. I know it's your first instinct . . ."

"I thought we agreed . . ." Evelyn cut in, mimicking him. "How the hell am I supposed to remember everything we agree to?"

"You sound angry," he said.

"I'm not angry," Evelyn snapped. "I'm just tired and sick and disgusted . . ."

"And angry that I'm making demands on you when you feel so lousy?"

"Why should I be angry? That's what I'm here for."

"Should has nothing to do with it. You feel what you feel and whatever it is, it's okay."

"Well, that's just a dandy little theory," said Evelyn, "and it's just dandy for you to say it but you don't have to feel it."

"Feel what, Evelyn?" Selwyn asked.

"Whatever it is," said Evelyn. "I don't know. Anything."

"Anger?"

"Okay, anger. It'll do. It's easy for you to say, 'Go ahead, feel the anger.' But what do I do with it? Or the guilt? Or the fear?"

"Those are choices you'll learn to make," Selwyn said. "But you must begin with recognition and acceptance of the feelings themselves."

"I'd rather go back to repression," Evelyn said.

"Would you really? Would you rather not feel what you do for Regina?"

"No," Evelyn answered loudly.

"That sounds pretty definite."

"It is. I wouldn't want to be without that feeling . . . but it's very painful sometimes."

"You're on shaky ground when you begin selecting those feelings that you'll allow yourself and cutting off others.

When you shut off one part of your emotional system, the whole thing breaks down eventually."

"But I can't deal with everything all at once." Evelyn hated the whine she heard in her voice. "If you could just give me something . . . if I just didn't feel so scattered, maybe I could deal with some of this crap."

"I can't give you medication, if that's what you mean."

"That *is* what I mean."

"And if I could, I wouldn't."

"Thanks a lot."

"You can learn from the pain. It's necessary now. A chemical is just another vehicle of repression, another dodge."

"I suppose you think I shouldn't even be drinking."

"It doesn't help."

"Well, it's impossible for me not to right now," said Evelyn, "so let's not even discuss it."

"You sound angry again."

"You're goddamn right I'm angry." Evelyn's voice rose.

"Good," said Selwyn, enraging her further with his approval.

"You insist that I feel all this crap but you can't tell me what to do with any of it."

"I know it seems unfair to you now," he said. "You weren't used to feeling much of anything and suddenly you're inundated by emotions, nearly all of them foreign, and you're raw. You feel battered."

"And you won't tell me what to do about it," Evelyn shrieked.

"It's not that I *won't* tell you. It just doesn't happen all at once. Our first priority is to keep your feeling system operating, keep it from shutting down again."

"Swell," said Evelyn. "In other words, what we're doing here is keeping me raw."

"That's a necessary part of the process, I'm afraid. But

we're also trying to give you a chance to deal with whatever it is you're feeling today."

"Well, perhaps that just isn't enough." Now Evelyn was haughty.

"Perhaps you'll decide that it isn't," said Selwyn, "but it's all I have to give you."

"What's that supposed to be? A threat?"

"I didn't intend it to be," he said. "Do you feel threatened?"

"Oh, Christ," Evelyn moaned. "I don't know."

"You're dodging."

"So I'm dodging. That's what I'm feeling right now . . . like dodging."

"Is it the anger you want to evade?"

"How the hell should I know? I'm new at this. You tell me."

"It would be so simple if I could, wouldn't it?" Selwyn smiled ruefully at Evelyn.

"Couldn't you try?" she wheedled. "Just this once?"

Selwyn laughed now.

"I'm too tired to think," Evelyn said, feeling the onslaught of her hangover as the pills wore off.

"I'm not asking you to think. Just tell me what you feel now."

"I don't know."

"Right now."

"Pathetic."

"Can you tell me more about that?"

Selwyn kept at her the rest of the hour, prodding her gently, coaxing her along. And Evelyn tried but the effort left her exhausted and hopeless. There had been times when this sort of exertion made her feel positively buoyant but today was one of the days when she wondered why she bothered to go at all.

Six

Evelyn would know very few people at the party. In fact, when she and Regina were dressing she'd been able to think of just two: Teddy and Clarice. They were Regina's old and good friends and the only lesbian couple Evelyn had ever met.

"According to my best calculations," she said, "there will be two, count 'em two, people in this gathering I've ever laid eyes on before."

"At least three, darling," said Regina.

"Who?"

"Teddy and Clarice and me."

"I wasn't counting you."

"And you've met Hilton St. Onge."

"Oh, Jesus, will he be there? Then I need no others."

"He's unspeakably dreary, I know, but Clarice's faggots always are."

"Will there be lots of them?"

"Lots and lots. The last time one cornered me I heard about South American economics for one solid hour. Stupefying boredom! I don't know how she stands it."

"Why does she have them around?" Evelyn asked.

"God knows. As buffers . . . window dressing . . . slaves. I'm not really sure but they're always there. Teddy said the other day that the first summer she and Clarice were together they spent exactly one night alone at the beach house. One faggot-free night in the entire summer. One!"

"Doesn't it drive Teddy mad?"

"To distraction. But Clarice won't go anywhere without them."

"So it will be Clarice's faggots and the Dyke Mafia. I'm terrified."

"Darling, among those you persist in calling the Dyke Mafia are Anne Hart, whom I adore, Pat Nathanson, who's terribly funny, Edna Scott-Martin, who's divine if she's not dead drunk . . ."

"Allie Haliburton, who's magnificent if she's not insane."

"I suppose she might make an appearance," said Regina. "Well, curiosity should make you glad to see her, if nothing else."

"I loathe parties."

"God, darling, so do I. But this one might not be too bad. Since it's for Teddy, it just might be marvelous."

"It's different for you to say you hate parties than for me to. You can at least find some way to function at them. You are at least a speaking human being."

"And you're not? You're one of the most articulate human beings I know."

"You've never seen me at a party. You've never really seen me around other people. They make me nonverbal."

Before leaving the hotel, Evelyn took two German air force bombs and had iced coffee with brandy, instead of Scotch. Now, standing outside the door, hearing the party within, she felt she was a self-contained unit, capable of taking what was inside, if she chose, or leaving it alone.

"My darlings." Teddy wrapped her arms around them at the same time. "I'd about given up on you."

"We would have been here sooner . . ." Regina began.

"Spare me," said Teddy. "Please."

"Happy birthday, Teddy." Evelyn heard her own voice, sounding very far away.

"Hi ya, girls. Want a drink?" Clarice kissed each of them.

"Two very large Scotches," said Regina.

"One at a time doesn't do it anymore?" Clarice asked.

"Very amusing, Clarice," said Regina. "One is for Evelyn."

"I have great difficulty speaking when there are more than two people in a room," said Evelyn.

"She loathes parties and is particularly terrified of this one," Regina said to Teddy.

"Anyone in her right mind would be," said Teddy. "There are so many treacherous currents swirling around this room. I'm exhausted from trying to avoid them. Elsa just told me that Crissie threatened to show up here and unmask her, as it were . . ."

"As what?" Regina asked.

"As duplicitous and deceitful . . . and as a thief."

"She's going to come here and accuse her of stealing Diana?"

"No, no, no. My God, Regina! Accuse her of stealing money from the club and planning to run off with Diana."

"Is it true?"

"I haven't any idea nor do I want to know. I just hope Crissie has the decency to stay away tonight. I really can do without hearing her love-crazed denunciations which we all know by heart, having been treated to them so many times before. Twice a year, regularly, this madness besets her, with or without factual substantiation, and for a week or so she bursts into gatherings, hurls her charges, ruins the evening, and vanishes. And the next time you see her, she's all confusion and contrition and it's really too boring and I hope to God it doesn't happen tonight!

"And Evan Hughes just told me he'd heard from a friend at Columbia that they want me to rewrite Peter's script, totally, and he told me as Peter was standing there! And Shana and Barbara are seeing each other tonight for the first time in three months and have divided the room into two armed camps, separate and distinct. I've never seen anything like it."

"Hair-raising," said Regina.

Evelyn smiled at Teddy, grateful for the amount she talked.

"So you may be very grateful that you're not acquainted with any of the participants in these macabre little dramas," Teddy said to Evelyn. "You will be spared."

They stood now on the edge of the living room which was very large and very crowded. Clarice emerged from the mass, shoved drinks in their hands, and disappeared into it again. Teddy went off to answer the door. Evelyn could feel Regina looking around, recognizing people, smiling. She tried to compose her face in a mask of disinterest. She tried internally to strike the pose of casual observer. She felt very callow.

"Come over here, darling. You'll adore Pat Nathanson." Regina led her toward a long-legged blond woman who was moving aimlessly about one end of the living room.

"I'm searching for some decent light to sit in and wouldn't you know Clarice wouldn't have any," she said as they approached.

"Oh, how like you . . . seeking out your own little spotlight," said Regina. "This is Evelyn Girard . . . Pat Nathanson."

"Hello. I don't want a spotlight! My God, anything that isn't white and stark. Have you ever seen anything as atrocious as all this brightness?"

"I hadn't noticed until you mentioned it," said Regina.

"I want something pink and soft and flattering," Pat said. "Despite the silicon I had injected in my forehead last week, I'm feeling extremely wrinkled tonight."

"Well," said Regina, "you look smashing and unbelievably thin."

"I am. I just got back from La Costa where they tortured

away about ten pounds and I'm now on a maintenance diet that consists mostly of something like whey, which I drink, and melons, which I eat."

"Whey and melons? Where did you discover that?" Regina asked.

"One of my fellow sufferers at La Costa. She's been doing it for years and looks marvelous. It's supposed to be very good for the skin."

"And nothing else? Just whey and melons?"

"It's not exactly whey. Judging by the price, it has gold dust in it. And yesterday I spent a dollar and ninety-three cents for a melon at Gristede's."

"I hope she's not dipping into her face fund," Regina said to Evelyn. "She's been saving for years for the lift she plans to have the day she turns forty."

"God, no," Pat said, "I haven't touched a penny of it. The silicon may help me postpone it a bit beyond forty. I haven't decided about that yet."

"Do they hurt . . . the injections?" Evelyn asked.

"Just a small sting at first, like having your finger pricked for blood. I'm also thinking a lot lately about thighs and buttocks."

"What about them?" Regina asked.

"Having them lifted, tucked, whittled, whatever it is they do."

"If you continue living on melons and whey I shouldn't think there'd be much to whack off," said Evelyn.

"Perhaps not," said Pat, "but let's face it, I'll never be able to stick with that. Right now, for instance, I'm going to have a drink. That is definitely not included in the diet."

"See you later," said Regina.

"Nice to meet you," said Evelyn.

"She looks terrible," said Regina, as Pat walked away. "Her skin is the color of whey."

"I can't stand just following you around," said Evelyn. "I feel like a pet."

"Darling, don't be ridiculous. You're not following me. You're just with me. Let's get another drink and then perhaps you'd like to meet Haliburton. I see she's holding court over there."

"How do you feel about seeing her?" Evelyn asked.

"Like vomiting, as always. The summer after our parting I was working in California and starting to put on weight again. Every time I felt like eating I would call her in New York and just hearing her voice made me lose my appetite for days. I've always been very grateful to her for keeping me at one hundred and fifteen for three solid months. Wait here, darling. I'll get the drinks."

Evelyn had to fight not to move along with Regina. The panic as she walked away was immediate. You feel what you feel, Evelyn told herself. You must allow it. It's okay. It's good. As she murmured internally, the panic deepened and she became furious with John Selwyn. Her anger at him diluted the panic somewhat.

"Evelyn, isn't it?"

"It is." She looked up to see Hilton St. Onge descending. "How've you been, darlin'?"

"Just fine, Hilton. How about you?"

"Never better. I have just returned from Les Isles and three weeks in the sun and I feel like a new man. Seen any around?"

Despite his poking her in the ribs, Evelyn left the joke unacknowledged.

"You look brown," she said.

"Darlin', you should have seen me. I was black! I mean black! *Noir . . . negro . . .* pitch."

"Dark?"

"Very, very dark. Could I sweeten your drink?"

"Regina's sweetening."

"Oh, how I long to see her. I met a friend of hers in the islands, an adorable boy, Jason Metzger."

"Oh, yes . . . Jason." If Regina had stopped to talk Evelyn would kill her.

"What've you been up to, darlin'?"

"Oh, the usual. This and that."

"B.A.U.?"

"What's that?"

"Business as usual, darlin'."

"Yes," said Evelyn, "that is exactly what I've been up to."

"It's an expression we use around the agency."

"Ah, something from the P.R.B."

"P.R.B.?"

"Public relations business." Evelyn was embarrassed for herself but he showed no sign of moving. "Is it your agency, Hilton?" Where the fuck was Regina!

"With two partners, Elwyn Soames and Harrison Meade. Harrison's over there with Dolly Kinross. I started it myself about twelve years ago just after leaving B.B.D.&O. and retained sole control until . . ."

Evelyn continued looking at Hilton St. Onge, nodding and smiling, but his words streamed together, indistinguishable from one another. He sounded to her as though he was humming.

Her grasp of the telling detail, the microscopic specific, is sure and deadly accurate. She can conjure an entire world in a single word or phrase.

"Deadly dull," she said.

"What's that?" He looked startled.

"Starting a new business . . . a lot of the work it takes must be deadly dull."

"Can be, can be. But it needn't. We had some real good times at the beginning, as a matter of fact. We were located at first in a big old loft . . ."

"Ah, here she is," said Evelyn. "At last." She dug her nails into Regina's arm for a second before taking her drink.

"I'm sorry it took so long . . ."

"At last you are here." Hilton embraced her tightly, then held her at arm's length. "And lovelier than ever . . . a vision."

"Hilton, you're too kind . . . and very suntanned."

"He was *noir*," said Evelyn.

"Just back from Les Isles, my love, where I met and adored Jason Metzger who loves and adores you more than anything on earth."

"Oh, God, how is he? And how much longer is he staying?"

"Well, my pet, since he was taken, as they say, I suppose he'll be back when the taker returns and I have no idea when that will be. And he's fine. He sends you love."

"I hope he's taking full advantage of being removed from the horrors of his poverty-ridden life in the city."

"*Full* advantage, my sweet, I can assure you of that."

"Darling," Regina bent toward Hilton confidentially, "you will surely understand if we go over to pay our respects to the lovely Miss Haliburton."

"I wouldn't dream of keepin' you from that pleasure." Hilton winked at Regina. "I've got to go sweeten up anyway."

"My God," Evelyn hissed at Regina, "where were you?"

"Edna Scott-Martin accosted me at the bar and raved on about a play she wants me to produce for her. The characters are all ninety years plus and are to be played by children, to indicate the shrinkage of age, I suppose. She didn't say. She was so drunk she forgot to put vodka in her glass but stood there drinking it anyway. Does that tell you something?"

"It tells me she sounds like delightful company compared to Mr. St. Onge. How does anyone get to be so boring?"

"Years of practice. Never deviating for one instant. Never, never saying anything that isn't an immediate inducement to sleep."

"Who are these people?" Evelyn whispered as they stopped at the edge of a circle.

"The faithful," said Regina. "Those who have been neither destroyed nor repelled by Haliburton. You will notice there aren't too many. Ex-lovers usually won't have anything to do with her and the friends of ex-lovers even less. That leaves this little knot of folks you see here."

"Hey, Reggie." Allie Haliburton rose and came toward them. "Where ya been keepin' yourself?"

"Out of your way, my treasure," said Regina.

"Now why would ya want to go and do a thing like that?" Allie threw her head back and laughed, a series of staccato snorts. "And this is it, I presume?" She gestured toward Evelyn.

"Evie," said Regina, "meet the always gracious and charming Allie Haliburton."

"Yes, I'm it," said Evelyn. "You can't know how I've longed to meet you."

"Oh, yes I can, sweetheart." Haliburton's head snapped back again into that laugh. "Young meat, my sweet." She nudged Regina.

"That's disgusting," Regina said.

"Think so? I just calls 'em as I sees 'em."

"And the way you sees 'em is as revolting as ever," said Regina. "Did you get the license for the bar?"

"Jesus, no. Ya wouldn't believe the way these bastards are hanging me up. Ya'd think I was trying to stuff hookers in a nunnery. I been on the horn all day to Albany just to set up an appointment to go before the fuckin' commission."

"I'm sorry it hasn't come through," Regina said.

"So if it doesn't I'll head for sunny Spain with Alfonsa over there."

"Alfonsa?"

"My Spanish princess . . . the broad with the long feet on the end of the couch."

"Well, I hope you get the license," said Regina, by way of setting up an exit. Evelyn felt it had suddenly become quite painful for her.

"You betcha, baby," said Allie, touching Regina's cheek. "Later." She returned to the couch, sliding down next to Alfonsa and kissing her on the neck.

"Is that for your benefit?" asked Evelyn, as they turned away.

"God knows! It's all too depressing. Let's get another drink."

"Reg . . . Reg . . ."

Evelyn heard the voice but couldn't see where it was coming from.

"Reg . . . over here."

"Oh, shit," said Regina, "it's Edna again. Well, you might as well meet her." Regina steered Evelyn toward a spot where she still didn't see anyone.

"I'm taking refuge."

Now Evelyn saw her, sitting in a deep armchair, turned so that it was facing almost directly into a corner. She was a very small person. Her legs hung down from the chair without touching the floor and she was dressed entirely in tweed— trousers, jacket, vest, cap.

"I'm taking refuge from the tall ones. You don't know how grueling it can be just to stand among people who are half again as big as you are. And to *talk* to them is completely exhausting. Do I know you?" Edna squinted up at Evelyn.

"I'm Evelyn Girard." She stretched out her hand and Edna grasped it eagerly.

"Reggie's not like the other tall ones," said Edna. "You're very lucky."

"I think so." Evelyn smiled at Regina, feeling a little foolish. "Regina's just been telling me about your play."

"My what?" Edna's voice squeaked. "My what?"

"The ninety-year-old children," Regina prompted her.

"I am calling that an event for the stage," said Edna, "not a play. It will in no way be a play."

"Darling," Regina began, "we were just on our way . . ."

"Don't let me keep you," Edna interrupted her.

"Can I bring you a drink?" asked Regina.

"Tonic and lime, when you get a chance. I don't drink," said Edna. She stared straight ahead into the corner and didn't appear to notice their leaving.

"Is she . . ."

"Starkers," said Regina, "whenever she drinks."

"I have to go to the john," said Evelyn.

"Down the hallway to the right."

"Where will I find you?"

"I won't go far, darling."

Evelyn stopped on the way to get a drink. Standing at the bar, she took her first close look at the room and couldn't find anyone who looked uncomfortable.

Immediately after closing and locking the bathroom door, she opened the medicine cabinet. It was a big one, running the length of the counter and basin, and the entire top shelf was lined with pill vials. Evelyn grinned at herself in the mirror.

The vials appeared to be arranged according to type: all the sleeping pills together, the tranquilizers next, then a stretch of amphetamines, then antibiotics, pain killers, and finally miscellaneous. It was like being turned loose in the stockroom of a pharmacy.

Evelyn took a very large swallow of Scotch. She was stunned that someone who had so many pills, and took such obvious care with their storage, wouldn't have them under lock and key. If they were hers—if they were hers they wouldn't be sitting in the medicine cabinet. They would be hidden. But if, for some unimaginable reason, they had to be in the medicine cabinet, she would put a Pinkerton in the john for the duration of the party—armed.

She took two of each of the tranquilizers and sleeping pills and wrapped a tissue around them. Then, one by one, she took down the amphetamine bottles and helped herself more generously to them, the first two going into her mouth, the rest into another tissue. She put a packet in each of her jacket pockets before sitting down on the toilet. A very good haul. It made her feel more kindly about the party itself.

She sat, sipping her Scotch, and when she finally noticed the knocking, she had a feeling it had been going on for some time.

"Just a minute," she called out, suddenly remembering she'd forgotten to take any pain killers. She waited to flush the toilet until she was ready to slide back the cabinet doors. The flush was unusually long and she felt sure it covered the sound of pills pouring.

"I'm awfully sorry," she said to a woman pacing the hall outside. "I seem to have slipped into a trance."

"Trance, shmance. I was about ready to piss in the hall." She slammed the door so hard Evelyn felt herself reverberate.

"You have just met the lovely Letitia," said Teddy, passing by. "All charm and manners."

"So I see," said Evelyn, swallowing Scotch and moving shakily down the hall. She thought she heard the pain killers knocking together as she walked. She took a napkin from the bar and stuffed it in her pocket to muffle them. She also ordered another drink and looked around for Regina while she waited. She found her talking with two men near the doorway.

"I've just had a run-in with a terrifying creature called Letitia," Evelyn announced as she walked up.

"Ah, our adorable Letty," said one of the men. "Did she raise her voice by any chance?"

"Raised voice and slammed door," said Evelyn.

"Were you in the door when she slammed it?" he asked.

"God, no," said Evelyn.

"Then, my dear, you got off easy," he said. "She slammed a door *on* a friend of mine last fall and he just got out of his cast last week."

"What set her off?" asked the other man.

"I stayed too long in the john," said Evelyn.

"And she was pacing up and down and threatening to piss in the hall?"

"Right," said Evelyn. "Said she was about to."

"Happens all the time. She has a hair-trigger bladder, or so she'd have you believe. I personally think she just cannot tolerate the sight of a closed door when she wants to be on the other side."

Regina introduced Evelyn to the men, Gabriel Finch and Ira Hawkins.

"Who is she?" asked Evelyn. "And why is she allowed to run loose?"

"The only child of a very wealthy southern publisher who wanted a son," said Regina. "She was raised to be a perfect southern gentleman and somewhere along the line it went awry. When I met her years ago, she *was* a perfect southern gentleman. She dressed in ice cream suits, cravats, carried a walking stick, drank mint juleps, and spoke softly."

"When the girl back home refused to marry her, she went to pieces," said Gabriel.

"That'll do it," said Evelyn.

"I'm serious," he continued. "Letty referred to her as 'my intended' and had some idea of getting established here and then sending for her. It's a real fairy tale, I tell you."

"What happened?"

"I don't really know," said Gabriel, "but she went back home for a visit and ever since her return she's been on the rampage. That's almost ten years. Went home for a visit a perfect gentleman and came back slamming doors and threatening to piss in the hall."

"Is there anything redeeming about her?" asked Evelyn.

"M-O-N-E-Y," said Gabriel. "Amazing what people will put up with if that's involved.

"How awful." Evelyn felt consumed by sadness for the creature called Letty.

"Save your sorrow," said Gabriel. "She absolutely adores being outrageous and knowing she gets away with it because of her money. She refers to herself as Letty the Loot."

"I think she can be terribly funny," said Regina, "in a macabre sort of way."

"That is a facet of her I have missed," said Gabriel.

"I need a drink," said Ira.

"Until later, my pets." They walked off and Evelyn turned to Regina, grateful for a moment alone.

"Gabriel Finch is so unbelievably bitchy and so deeply envious of anyone with money," said Regina. "He can't even say the word. He has to spell it out. He used to tell people I'd gotten a million-dollar trust fund when I turned twenty-one."

"Untrue, I assume."

"Deeply untrue, and I told him if he didn't stop telling hateful, vicious lies about me, I'd tell everyone his real name was Swineflinck, which it is. He tries to make people think he's shabby gentility, father lost it in the crash and all that. Father lost it, whatever it was, in the bilge water of the boat coming over from Latvia. I can't stand his pretensions!"

"So," said Clarice, approaching a bit unsteadily, "how's it going?"

"Evelyn's just crossed paths with Letitia for the first time," said Regina.

"Old piss-in-the-hall?" Clarice asked.

"That's exactly what she said," said Evelyn.

"Snores," said Clarice, her voice rising. "That's all I got for her . . . snores."

"Did you ever see that room she papered completely in Colonel Sanders boxes?" Regina asked Clarice.

"God, darling, she thinks she is Colonel Sanders," said Clarice.

"I thought she'd passed beyond that."

"Old ideas die hard. She still turns up in her whites every once in a while."

"Regina Ross . . . I do not believe my eyes." A tall, thin woman with auburn hair and a drawl flung her arms around Regina. "I thought you had left us, disappeared off the face of the earth."

"Maybe that's wishful thinking after our last encounter," said Regina.

"It was A.O.K. from my P.O.V., sweetie, but you did have a bit of a fracas with Reuben, if memory serves."

"I took his necktie . . . ripped it off him as we were sitting in the restaurant," said Regina.

"You said you'd been lookin' for that color all your life . . . said it was a perfect match for your eyes."

"That is revolting," said Regina. "Anne, this is Evelyn Girard . . . Anne Hart."

"Pleased to meet ya."

"Did I give his tie back?" Regina asked.

"After runnin' it through your vichyssoise."

"Well," said Regina, "it's so embarrassing I can't even be embarrassed. What have you been up to?"

"I'm still reviewing and doing interviews every so often. I just finished a series on famous women that's been runnin' in the papers here."

"You will realize then," said Regina, "that, of course, I haven't read it."

"I do remember somethin' funny about you and newspapers . . ."

"I can't touch them unless I'm wearing very heavy gloves and I can't stand *them* except in the dead of winter."

"Well, honey, let me assure you that my series is not really worth waitin' for till next winter."

"I'd have to agree with that," said Evelyn.

Anne and Regina turned toward her, startled.

"I just mean that it could have been so much better," said Evelyn.

"In what way?" Anne tried to sound politely curious but her voice shook slightly.

"It was so superficial. I think it would have been more interesting . . ."

"Do you have any idea of the limits that go with newspaper writin', particularly anything that's gonna be syndicated?"

"I write for one," said Evelyn, "a newspaper, that is."

"Aaah . . . and you found it superficial."

"Somewhat." Evelyn suddenly didn't want to continue, felt she should stop, but couldn't. "I'd like to have known more than what you'd find out glancing through a file from the morgue."

"Well, let me tell ya, sugar," said Anne. "I did a lot more than copy old clippins." The quaver in her voice was very evident now.

"Well, let me tell you," said Evelyn, "that if you did, it didn't show. That series was a perfect example of a kind of writing I abhor. It purports to be 'in-depth' and is about as deep as the paper is thick."

There is never a false moment.

"Sweetheart, it is your privilege not to read it. Reggie, I'm gonna make my way over to Teddy. I haven't seen her forever. Take care." Anne brushed a kiss against Regina's cheek and turned away without even looking at Evelyn again.

"What the fuck are you doing?" Regina hissed at Evelyn.

"Well, it's all true. You'd agree if you read it."

"I don't give a shit if it's true. Is that any reason to attack her?"

"She's a dreadful writer and I don't see why I should have to say otherwise."

"You weren't called upon to say anything."

"I never am with you around."

"Oh, Jesus. I'm getting another drink. I don't know if you should."

"Are you trying to tell me . . ."

"I'm telling you you're getting drunk."

"You're telling me that? *You're* telling me?"

"You heard me." Regina turned and walked toward the bar.

Evelyn's rage seemed to begin in the hand holding her glass. It shook so severely the Scotch spilled over the edge and the ice banged loudly against the side. Then she felt it at the bottom of her stomach. It spread from there throughout her entire body. By the time she walked out, apparently unnoticed, she was shaking so hard the pills in her pockets were rattling in their tissues. While she waited for the elevator, Hilton stuck his head out the apartment door.

"Do you have to rush off so soon?" he whined.

"That's exactly what I have to do, Hilton . . . rush off."

"We must have dinner soon, love. Just the three of us."

"Just love to," said Evelyn, stepping into the elevator. He returned her wave by waggling his fingers beside his cheek and winking.

Down on the street, Evelyn found a cab right away and gave him the address of her apartment, downtown and crosstown.

"I was hopin' you might be goin' up," said the cabbie, a young man with lots of pitch-black hair and a thick Brooklyn accent.

"Sorry," said Evelyn.

"My garage is up and I'm about ready to knock off."

"Well, I'm not. I'm going down, pardon the expression."

"You're pardoned." He gave a slight smile and screeched into a violent U-turn. Evelyn fell onto her side in the back seat.

"You're in that big a rush?" she asked crossly, pulling herself up and smoothing out her clothes.

"When you been locked in here for ten hours, you hurry at the end, believe me."

"I can see that." The rage vanished suddenly and Evelyn felt desolate. She wished she hadn't left. She wished she had a drink.

"On second thought," she said, "let me off at one of these bars along here. It's too early to go home."

"Any particular one?"

"You pick one . . . and I'll buy you a drink."

He didn't respond but about three blocks later he pulled up in front of a bar and got out.

"Do you know this one?" Evelyn asked.

"I been here." He held open the door and she walked into a very long, dark room. By the time her eyes adjusted, he'd steered her to one of the four small tables at the far end of it.

"What're you drinkin'?" he asked.

"Dewar's . . . double on the rocks," she said.

Watching him walk to the bar, Evelyn saw he was shorter than she'd expected. He moved with a slight swagger, his hands resting lightly on his hips.

"That's very generous," said Evelyn, as he placed a tumbler of Scotch in front of her.

"Bartender's a friend," he said.

"You've literally been in your cab for ten hours straight?" she asked.

"That's right," he said, "which reminds me . . ." He got up and disappeared into a narrow, black hallway behind them.

Peering through the murk toward the bar, Evelyn saw only four or five people. Each was alone and silent.

"By the way," he said when he came back, "my name's Johnny."

"I'm Evelyn."

His look was meant to be a smile, she knew, but the hardness around his eyes changed it into something else.

"You don't stop to eat?" she asked.

"I only eat once a day," he said, "very late at night."

"And drink very little," she said, nodding toward his glass.

"Wine only," he said. "There's no percentage in the hard stuff."

"No percentage in the hard stuff," she repeated. "You have a way with a phrase, Johnny."

"You really pack it away, huh?"

"I wouldn't put it quite like that." Evelyn had meant to be ironic but snapped at him instead.

"I bet . . . but you do, don't you?"

"I will say that I've had a great deal to drink tonight. That is absolutely true."

"Drinkin' alone?"

"Hardly. God, I wish I had been."

The silence of the rest of the room reached out and enveloped them. Johnny's eyes never stopped moving. Evelyn stared down into her drink. She'd drunk more than half of it when she felt his hand grip her wrist and pull her to her feet. He stepped into the hallway, turning her around and flattening her against the wall. He did it all in one motion, gracefully. She heard the sound of a zipper as she felt the wall behind her.

"You want some a' this, baby?" Through her clothes, she felt him rubbing up and down against her. She said nothing.

"Pull your skirt up." She did and felt him inside her almost immediately. He pushed himself in and out rapidly, several times, and then withdrew.

"Now pull it down and let's get outta here." He moved away but kept his hand on her wrist.

Evelyn reached for her drink as they passed the table but he pushed it aside.

"You had enough a' that," he said.

"Fuck off." She wrenched her arm from his grasp and drank down the remaining Scotch.

He took her arm again and they walked out. He opened the front door of the cab for her. She began to stumble but caught herself by splaying out her hand against the edge of the roof. As he got in, he reached for her and pulled her over beside him. Once again, his zipper sounded and he placed her hand around him. As he drove, he kept his hand on hers, moving it where he wanted it to go. They said nothing to each other.

He remembered the address and parked directly in front of it. Evelyn went into the apartment first, walked straight to the bar, and poured a snifter of brandy.

"You got a candle?" he asked.

She didn't answer but went to the kitchen and got a candle and holder, carrying the Cognac with her and drinking it along the way. He took the candle and walked toward the bedroom, as surely as though it were his. Evelyn followed him.

He lit the candle and placed it on the bedside table. Then he began to undress slowly, conscious of the light playing over his skin, turning so it shone on every part of him. Evelyn watched from the doorway. When he was naked, he came toward her and took the glass away. Then, without hurry, he undressed her. Their breathing was the only sound in the room.

He took her hand and led her toward the bed. When they reached it, he pulled her against him so that she felt him all along the front side of her body and the bed against the back of her legs. Then he pushed her down across the bed, her feet remaining on the floor, and stood over her, masturbating.

"You want some, don't you?" It wasn't really a question and Evelyn remained silent. "You're gonna want it more before you get it." He gave his imitation of a smile.

"You don't usually see 'em so big, eh?" It lay in his hand, displayed like a choice cut at the butcher's. "It was always the biggest. Cassie Scapesi was the only one come even close."

"Cassie Scapesi?" Evelyn suddenly felt she should say something.

"You usually see 'em all shriveled up by booze, I bet." His hand was moving rapidly now. "Isn't that right? Usually all withered up by booze? Too much whiskey'll make it lay there like a dead fish. Isn't that right?"

Evelyn stared, mute, as his hand flew up and down. Then he stopped, placed his hands behind his hips, and curved them outward toward her.

"Tell me how much you want it," he said.

When she was silent, he slapped her. She kept her head turned to the side as he began to parade around the room.

"Maybe you'll hafta come and get it. I can keep it this big and this hard for hours, baby, 'cause I got no whiskey in me."

"Your idea of cabbie as natural man . . ."

"Shut up! Just answer my questions. No other talkin'. Don't you wish you could have it now? Right now?" He approached the bed and pulled Evelyn into a sitting position. Then he wrapped her hands around him and began pumping up and down.

"It was always the biggest. It's the biggest you've ever seen. Right, baby?"

"Yes," Evelyn said. She didn't want to be slapped again.

"Everybody'd beg me for it . . . broads, guys, everybody. Feel like beggin', baby?"

He thrust himself into her mouth so she couldn't answer. He pulled her mouth back and forth on him by yanking her hair and pushing on the back of the head. The hair-tugging stung and made her eyes water. Then he raised his knee and pushed it into her groin, leaning heavily on it. It hurt but she remained silent.

"You want me so bad now, don't you? Don't you?" He pulled back on her hair until she was staring straight up at him. "It's bad now . . . so bad. Ain't it?"

As she nodded, he shoved her mouth down on him again.

"You're always so thirsty, I'll give you enough to drink so you'll choke." He laughed, pulling her head back and forth, back and forth.

"Spread your legs." It was a command. "You feel so horny, you want it so bad, give it to yourself." He pushed her so she fell back across the bed. Then he took several steps backwards and stopped, staring at her.

"I said give it to yourself." His voice matched the sneering look on his face. "To yourself." He rubbed his hands quickly up and down himself as if to demonstrate.

"Do it." Now Evelyn heard menace and lowered her hand as he ordered.

He stood, vehemently erect, hands on his hips, staring at her. "You'll be beggin' in no time . . . hollerin' for this . . . beggin' and cryin'." His voice fell into a sing-song pattern and he touched himself again, matching the rhythm to his words. "Beggin' and beggin' and cryin' and beggin' . . ."

His voice hypnotized Evelyn and she moved in time to it also, everything else falling away but the sound of his voice.

"Beg me." It tore through the haze harshly. "I said beg me."

She felt the slap on her face though she hadn't seen his hand coming. "Please." She exhaled it after gasping with the slap.

"Again."

"Please."

"More."

"Please."

"More. More."

"Please . . . please . . . please." She moved her head from side to side, her eyes closed.

"Keep saying it."

"Please . . . please . . ." He entered her, moved inside her fiercely, then withdrew. He turned her over, raised her to her knees and came at her from behind. His stabbing motion sent ripples of pain spreading out from her center. Then he pulled away and lay on his back. He raised her above him, his hands on her waist, and pulled down, impaling her.

"Please . . . please . . . please . . ." She never stopped murmuring.

Then he raised himself and placed her beneath him. He moved up and down, his hand flicking out, crossing her face, back and forth. As the fury of his movement inside her grew, his hand opened and she felt the full palm against her cheek. With each thrust, he hit her, until she could no longer distinguish one impact from the other.

"Please . . . please . . . please." Now it had risen to a scream but the sound ran together with his noises and she no longer heard it as her voice.

At the end, the words were gone. When he stopped, she heard the echo of a wordless scream hanging in the air. She heard it as she watched him walk to his clothes and carefully put them on, as he glanced in the mirror and pushed his hair into place, as he came toward the bed and snuffed out the candle, leaving her in darkness. She heard it until it was obliterated by the door slamming behind him as he left.

Seven

A bell was ringing but when Evelyn flung open the door the hallway was empty. She went to the phone.

"Where are you?" Regina's voice was blurred around the edges.

"What time is it?" Evelyn asked.

"Four-thirty. Why aren't you here?"

"I seem to be at home."

"Why did you go there?"

"I had a little light entertaining to do . . ."

"What do you mean?"

"Well, the cab driver was so unusually nice . . ."

"What happened?"

"I don't think we want to get into this now, do we?"

"Get in a cab and get up here."

"I don't know if I should chance another cab tonight."

"Get one and get up here." The sound of Regina slamming down the phone made Evelyn jump. Something in Regina's voice made her move quickly and she was dressed and on the street in less than ten minutes. She stood on the curb, her arm raised, forgetting why she was there. The squeal of the cab's brakes reminded her.

Miss Girard reaches for fictional experience that is beyond the grasp of most of our younger writers. And she treats that experience with unrelenting honesty and supreme elegance of style, the rarest of combinations.

"Honesty and style," Evelyn muttered. "That's it. That's what it takes."

"Speak up. I can't hear ya."

"I said honesty and style." Evelyn, hearing herself, realized she was still drunk. "Honesty and style."

"Yeah, I heard ya."

She began to notice now that she felt bruised, lacerated, inside and out. Her entire body ached. She let her head fall back against the seat, feeling tears begin. If she kept her chin tilted up, she could contain them, keep them from running down her face. Very soon, however, the angle of her head made her nauseous and she had to lower it, causing the tears to spill.

"Can I do anything, lady?" The cab driver looked genuinely concerned as he pulled up in front of Regina's hotel.

"No," said Evelyn, trying to read the meter through the watery film covering her face. "No, thank you. I'm allergic."

"Some allergy." She was surprised to realize he wasn't being sarcastic. "It's three seventy-five."

She handed him a five and got out, leaving the change. She hadn't the stamina to plow through her purse looking for the key so she knocked on Regina's door. F.B. began shrieking inside but the door didn't open. She knocked again, three long, two short. The door opened slightly and Regina peered around its edge. When she saw Evelyn she threw it open and pulled her inside.

"My God, darling." Regina held her at arm's length, staring. "What's wrong?"

"What do you mean?"

"You look terrible."

Evelyn made a sound in the back of her throat. As it pushed forward and emerged in a wail, she pulled Regina to her, wrapping her arms around Regina's neck, burying her face in Regina's shoulder, holding herself against Regina hard enough to quiet the shaking. And she wept. She felt each cry begin deep within her, gathering momentum as it rose, finally tearing loose in an explosion of sound. Then she shuddered silently until the next cry began.

"Oh, baby . . . oh, my darling." Regina stroked her head, purring the words over and over.

Evelyn couldn't stop. She felt Regina leading her toward the bedroom but even walking didn't break the rhythm of her cries. She couldn't speak. There was no space for forming words. The weeping filled her.

"Poor, sweet baby . . . poor darling." Regina murmured continuously as she stripped off Evelyn's clothes and wrapped her in a soft cotton nightshirt. Then she helped her into bed and slid in beside her, never letting go. She wrapped herself around Evelyn, entwining their legs, making a sheath of her arms that fitted Evelyn's back and shoulders. She held her, unmoving, for a long time. Evelyn's cries grew weaker and, finally, turned into sighs.

"Can you tell me?" Regina asked when Evelyn was quiet. "Please try to tell me."

"Can't you guess?"

"Try to tell me."

"The old cab driver routine . . . only this one was nasty. I guess that was bound to happen. Should have quit while I was ahead."

"Did you fuck with him?" asked Regina.

Evelyn nodded.

"Oh, Christ . . . I'm so sorry. What else?"

"He hit me around a bit."

"Oh, God." Regina pulled Evelyn tight against her. "Are you hurt?"

Evelyn drew away just far enough for her hands to reach her face and touch it gingerly. "This cheekbone is tender." She continued running her fingers over her face, stopping whenever she hit a sore spot.

"Why do you think you did it?" Regina asked.

"I don't know." Evelyn turned away in self-disgust. "Old

habit . . . punishing you . . . pure drunkenness . . . I don't
know."

"Punishing *me?*"

"I realize it doesn't work out that way. That's something
I've had difficulty with all my life. I've never quite gotten it
straight."

"Darling." Regina drew Evelyn back to her. "I can't bear
to think of you hurt."

"At this moment," said Evelyn, "neither can I. Earlier, it
didn't seem to matter. Or, by the time it mattered, it was too
late. Or something. I don't know."

"Where did you find him?"

"In his cab . . . the usual spot. And then we had a drink,
making it all proper. I wouldn't want you to think I just met
him and immediately dragged him home to bed. No, no. We
had a lovely drink in the bar of his choice and then went to
my place . . . for the debacle."

"Do you want to tell me?" Regina held Evelyn's face between her hands and kissed her eyes.

"It took place by candlelight," said Evelyn, "a nice touch,
I thought. The lighting was the best part, believe me."

"His idea, I presume?"

"His. Just another incurable romantic."

"Did he hit you right away?"

"No. First he masturbated, then he invited me to do same,
then the fucking, then the hitting."

"Were you terrified?"

"Eventually, yes. At the beginning . . . I don't know . . .
drunk . . . enraged . . . I can't sort it out. Please touch me."

As she spoke, Evelyn took Regina's hand from her face and
placed it between her legs. She put her other hand behind
Regina's head, bringing her mouth close. When she enclosed
it with her own mouth, she felt relief and desire radiate
through her body simultaneously. After several minutes,

Regina brought her mouth down to Evelyn's breast. She sucked in time with the motion of her hand. Evelyn moved with the rhythm. Her moans became regular, accompanying her movement. She felt all her boundaries blurring, spilling over Regina's, mixing together, merging. When she went beyond herself into the moment of orgasm, she stayed suspended there for what seemed a very long time.

Evelyn slowly became quiet as Regina held her, murmuring softly against her cheek. Sleep began to seep into her as though it were coming from Regina's skin onto hers. Just before it filled her entirely, she saw herself, floating in midair, her face smoothed and softened by contentment. Then the chasm opened and she slid gently down its side.

Evelyn awoke to the sound of the running shower.

"Regina." She shook her ferociously. "There's somebody in the shower."

"Jesus Christ." Regina sat straight up, staring wildly at the bathroom door. "Jesus Christ."

"What'll we do?" Evelyn asked, still shaking Regina but unaware of it.

"Darling, stop shaking me. Pay no attention." Regina sank back onto the pillow, snoring as she went.

"Pay no attention!" It was a whispered shriek. "Are you insane?"

"It's Olive," Regina murmured.

"What do you mean?" Evelyn was no longer whispering.

"Olive's in the shower. Go back to sleep, darling."

Evelyn lay back, shaking. Her fear had given her a few moments of adrenal energy but now it was spent and she was weak.

"Olive's in the shower." She said it softly to herself. "Olive Duffy's in the shower."

As the water stopped running, Evelyn heard a heavy thud. She sat up and listened carefully until she heard Olive mov-

ing about. Much later, after a series of crashes, Olive peered
around the corner of the bathroom door, trying to see
through the escaping steam.

"Is anyone there?" she hissed.

"Yes," Evelyn answered.

"Is there a pill that can keep one from staggering?" she
asked solemnly.

"If there were, I'd have it," said Evelyn. "Believe me."

"But you don't?"

"Alas, no."

Olive disappeared back into the steam, closing the door
behind her. Evelyn dozed and didn't awaken until she heard
Olive hurling herself at the bathroom door, which was stuck.
Evelyn was just rising to give it a tug from the outside when
Olive squirted into the room, looking very surprised.

"How do I look?" she asked, weaving in place and panting.
Her hair was still damp, its pixie cut brushed down flat,
topped off by a red plaid tam. Although Olive was thirty-five
years old, she still bought her clothes in the young miss department. The dress she wore now was a long-sleeved, high-
necked, very short shift covered in appliquéd daisies. She
had on black Mary Jane shoes and white stockings that looked
as though they were made of chenille.

"What happened to your legs?" Evelyn asked, staring at
their bumpy surface.

"A few little shaving nicks that I covered with Kleenex,"
said Olive. "Are they noticeable?"

"Where are you going?"

"I have to meet Joel at Sardi's for lunch . . . to discuss the
particulars of our separation."

"Jesus, Olive. You had a rather late night, I gather?"

"Had no night . . . not in bed, that is. Haven't been to bed
and now I must go to lunch. What time is it?"

"Quarter of twelve."

"I promised Joel I'd be on time." Olive began to move

toward the door but veered off into the wall, softening the thud by letting her hand hit first. "You see why I wanted the pill," she said. She straightened herself up and walked with great deliberation through the doorway into the living room.

"You look just fine," Evelyn called after her, her words obliterated by the sound of a lamp hitting the floor. "You look just fine," she called out once more, this time into silence.

After a few moments, she heard Olive's tread again. It moved, without further interruption, to and through the door and then was gone. Evelyn got up to make sure the door was closed tightly and only then remembered her own appointment. She had an interview at two-thirty.

She has captured here the quintessence of a unique personality, given it voice, and made it come alive.

She went immediately back to bed and wound herself around Regina, feeling the cadence of her sleep, hoping it would muffle the beginnings of panic. She tried to breathe in time with Regina. She tried, for an instant, to become her. Then everything began to slide away. She was totally separate, surrounded by impenetrable barriers, besieged. Nothing could enter and nothing escape. She lay very still, trying to go blank, trying to get her insides synchronized with her quiet surface. Finally, it happened. She savored the emptiness, unable to remember why she sometimes considered it the enemy.

"Is Olive gone?" Regina murmured, her voice fuzzy.

"What a perfect choice of words." Evelyn turned Regina over and held her tightly.

"Still a mite tipsy?"

"She left here literally bouncing off the walls. Her legs were covered with little bumps where she'd shoved Kleenex in her stockings to stop the nicks from bleeding. And she wanted to know if I had a pill that would keep her from staggering."

"Oh, Jesus. What about you? How do you feel?"

"I can recall better mornings."

"Oh, baby." Regina extricated herself from Evelyn's arms and wrapped hers around Evelyn. "My poor baby."

Evelyn felt herself already beginning to turn the previous night into a drunk story . . . The Case of the Candlelight Cabbie. Making it a tale removed it from her and made it bearable. She had for so long insulated herself from her own experience that even when she recognized what she was doing, she was powerless to stop it.

"Let me put it this way," she said. "I wouldn't want to spend every night with him. I mean, it saves on cab fare but the wear and tear in other areas . . . can it be worth it?"

They lay locked together, quietly. They drifted. They wove in and out of a dozing state, murmuring against each other's skin. And when the alarm went off at one, it was a harsh intrusion that left Evelyn shaking. Next to her, Regina was scratching furiously.

"Middle left, darling, hard," she muttered, flipping so that her back faced Evelyn. "Oh, yes . . . perfect . . . perfect. Now over, no, other way . . . there. Oh, yes . . . yes."

Her back was covered in welts of varying lengths and widths and the welts were criss-crossed with angry red scratch marks. She looked as though she'd been flogged.

"My God, baby," said Evelyn. "What can I do?"

"Harder."

"Family hives?"

"Exactly." Regina thrashed in a spasm of itching, then leaped from bed and ran toward the bathroom.

"Where the fuck is my itch spray?" she screamed, flailing about in the medicine cabinet.

"It's in here." Evelyn saw its red cap poking out from beneath old sandwich wrappers on the bedside table.

"Oh, God, spray me." Regina raced out of the bathroom and presented her back. "God . . . feels so good. Yes . . . lower right . . . that's it. Oh, God, thank you."

"Which is it?" asked Evelyn.

"Venomous aunt for lunch," said Regina.

"What form does it take . . . the venom?"

"Indiscriminate spewing." Regina lay down on the bed, still breathing rapidly from her frenzy. "Her monstrousness is truly beyond the pale. She's viperous. What she's spreading at present is that her sister's husband isn't the father of her sister's child . . . and the child is twenty. This particular vileness has been around for decades, and she drags it out whenever current poison dries up."

"Lovely."

"God . . . I really can't talk about it. I really can't or the hives will start all over again."

"I have the internal equivalent of hives at the thought of this interview today."

"Alice Bennington?"

"Mmmnnn. How will I talk to her?"

"Oh, darling, you do interviews brilliantly."

"Not when my tongue is so thick it fills my mouth and I'm shaking so violently I can't hold a pencil."

"My God. We're a mess, aren't we? Maybe we should take a vacation."

"Where? How? Oh, Christ, I think I'm going to be sick."

Evelyn reached the toilet just as the hot stream shot out of her mouth. Some spattered on the seat and the floor but the bulk of it went into the bowl. The results of three successive retchings all hit the mark. When it was over, she rested her head on the toilet seat, crying softly. Then she slid onto the floor, welcoming the feel of cool tiles along the length of her body.

"Are you all right, Evie?" Regina called through the door.

"Tip-top. Just freshening up a bit and I'll be right out."

When she emerged, Regina shoved into her hand a cup full of strawberry milkshake.

"And I thought there were no miracles!" Evelyn took two

enormous gulps. "Where did it come from?"

"Where else? I got it last night on my way home but we never quite got to it. There's pastrami, too."

"It's the nicest thing that's ever happened to me." Evelyn hugged Regina tightly and then walked toward the living room, gulping as she went. By the time the first bite of pastrami reached her stomach, the shaking had begun to subside. When she finished the sandwich and milkshake, it was down to a tremor.

In the cab, riding downtown to her appointment, Evelyn prayed the pills would take hold by the time she reached Alice Bennington's apartment. The door opened soon after Evelyn rang the bell and there she stood, in old gray sweater and slacks, no makeup, looking devastating. Evelyn had seen her in films and on stage and always thought her vastly talented. Now she was here to question her. It was a moment Evelyn had never gotten used to.

"Alice Bennington?" she said, ridiculously.

"Yes."

"I'm Evelyn Girard. We have an appointment."

"Of course. Please come in." She smiled warmly while Evelyn passed through the open doorway. "Just go straight ahead into the living room. It's another hideous day, isn't it?"

"I hadn't noticed," Evelyn murmured.

"You're just getting used to it . . . and why not? It's been ghastly for days."

Evelyn made a small, amorphous noise, trying to remember what it had felt like outdoors.

"Ghastly to me is in-between," said Alice Bennington. "I'd rather have it raining bloody murder. It seems to me it's been weeks of a little gray, a little bright . . . am I wrong?"

"I don't think I've been very in touch with the weather," said Evelyn.

"And I had to go and point it out and now will it make you

miserable, right? God, I'm sorry. Sometimes I talk too much."
She laughed ruefully as she slumped into the corner of a large
overstuffed sofa.

"You can't, as far as I'm concerned," said Evelyn.

"How so?" asked Alice Bennington.

"Interviews are very difficult when someone speaks spar-
ingly."

"Oh, my God, of course. Well, that's not my problem."

Alice Bennington took a cigarette from a glass dish on the
coffee table and lit it. Then she looked at Evelyn expectantly.
Evelyn felt the look even though her head was lowered while
she fumbled in her purse for a notebook and pen. She also felt
the silence grow, its weight increasing every instant.

"No, that's certainly not your problem," she murmured,
repeating the words simply to fill space. When she raised her
head, Alice Bennington was still looking at her, still expectant.

"So . . ." said Evelyn. She gave a small, nervous gasp that
could have passed for a laugh if there'd been any other sound
in the room. As it was, it hung, quite clearly a gasp, frozen
in the silence. Evelyn looked straight at Alice Bennington,
willing herself to speak. Alice Bennington smiled encourag-
ingly. Nothing happened.

Evelyn shifted in her chair, trying to look as though she
were thinking, hoping the movement would jar something
loose. Alice Bennington continued to smile.

*Miss Girard has a keen eye for the patterns implicit in all
human experience.*

Evelyn was as blank as the notebook page before her. She
felt time, as an active presence, passing noisily through the
room.

"So . . ." This time the word was full of resignation. "Alice
Bennington . . ." Evelyn realized she used the full name as
one in her head and that's the way it had come out.

"How embarrassing," Evelyn murmured. "Miss Bennington . . ."

"Please call me Alice." The actress leaned forward and Evelyn responded in kind.

"I have been having a nervous breakdown, the walking around sort," said Evelyn, "and one of the things that happens to me is that I go completely blank. That has happened now. For instance, I can't remember why I've come here. I can, however, still write. So why don't you just tell me whatever you think I should know and I'll take it down. If you could do that, I would appreciate it more than I can possibly say."

"My God," said Alice Bennington, "can't I get you something?"

"No, nothing," said Evelyn. "Just your words."

"Poor baby. Please let me know if you change your mind. To the best of my recollection, which isn't so hot either, you're here to talk about this one-woman TV show. Ring any bells?"

"Sounds possible," said Evelyn, writing "TV special" in her notebook.

"I do all different sorts of things that I can't believe you'd want to hear about now," said Alice Bennington.

"Please," said Evelyn, "I do."

Alice Bennington talked for fifteen minutes, interrupting herself several times to ask if she should go on, to ask if Evelyn wanted anything. Evelyn scribbled mechanically, recording her words.

"In one sense, I enjoyed the dance sequences most . . ." Alice Bennington broke off and put her hand on Evelyn's arm. "Are you cold? You're shaking terribly."

"Not cold . . . just shaking," said Evelyn, her pen skidding off the page.

"Just sit still a minute, if you can. I'll be right back." Alice

Bennington got up and started out of the room. Then she spotted the afghan on the sofa, picked it up, and wrapped it around Evelyn before leaving. Staring after her, Evelyn noticed a mirror on a wall straight ahead. Pushing up on the arms of her chair, she brought her head to its level. Even at a distance she could see that her bruised cheek wouldn't pass for an under-eye fatigue circle, as she'd hoped. She sunk back in the chair, wondering what Alice Bennington thought of it.

When she returned, she was carrying a tray. On it was a fresh doily and on the doily were two small paper cups containing pills, a decanter of rich brown whiskey, a glass, a pot of tea, gently steaming, and a teacup.

"I've died and gone to hospital," said Evelyn.

"And there are no angels, just nursies," said Alice Bennington, setting the tray on a table beside Evelyn. "What looks good to you?"

"Absolutely everything," said Evelyn. "How is it you know all my favorite things?"

"I've been there," said Alice Bennington. "Please, help yourself."

"How can I thank you?" Evelyn was stunned.

"You needn't. I'd suggest a yellow Valium to begin with and a small glass of whiskey. Or whiskey in the tea, if you like. I know this is lousy as a steady diet but we've got to stop your rattling."

"If I can keep from flying apart until four-thirty, I see my doctor and that should help."

"Flying apart really says it, doesn't it? It happened to me at about one in the morning at the end of my Hollywood period. I was out of L.A. by four, came directly to my mother's house in the Bronx, and didn't leave it for two years."

"Did you experience the blankness?" Evelyn asked.

"What do you think I was doing in the Bronx for two years!" Alice Bennington threw her head back in a full laugh.

"There was no rich, inner life, believe me."

"It hit you that suddenly?"

"You mean one in the morning, bang, out of nowhere?" She reached toward the tray to pour some tea, put whiskey in it, and handed it to Evelyn. "God, no. It had been coming on for years. Every minute I was in that lousy town added to the disturbance."

"It was dormant?" Evelyn sipped the tea with whiskey and felt herself steadying as it traveled downward.

"More or less." Alice Bennington poured herself a glass of whiskey and took a swallow. "But when it hit . . . sweet Jesus! I not only felt like I was drowning and watching my life pass in front of me, I also saw every frame of every crummy picture I'd ever made. Oh, God, it was awful."

"You hated all of them?"

"All. Every last one. And seeing them again, running through my head, was the ultimate nightmare. There were so many! They lasted all the way from Sunset and Doheny to the Bronx."

"I hope you didn't keep rerunning them for two years," said Evelyn.

"Christ! I wouldn't be here if I had. No, just the one time, en route to Mama's. And, I hope, the last time."

"I hope so . . . although I don't think they're that bad."

"Neither does Mort. He's mad for them, makes a big point of scanning the fine print in *TV Guide* every week and usually manages to find at least one. He'll set the alarm for four in the morning to get up and see one. Those are the nights we sleep apart."

"You've never seen any of them, except in your head?" Evelyn asked.

"I can't even stand to hear the sound. I once walked in on him, not knowing what he was doing, and I heard myself saying, 'For my sake, emperor, please spare him.' I was sick for days."

"I sincerely hope I can get through this without shutting myself up for two years," Evelyn said.

"No question." Alice Bennington reached across to Evelyn and squeezed her arm. "You're going to make it. I can tell. God, at least you've got yourself a doctor. I didn't even do that. Mama thought what would help most was listening to opera and holding my face over a steaming kettle."

"Exactly how was that supposed to work?"

"The opera was to soothe, the kettle to dispel vapors. Actually, it didn't do any harm and probably helped as much as anything could have at that point, short of professional help. The opera *was* soothing and the steam *did* clear my head, occasionally."

"Did you finally get to a doctor?"

"Sure, for seven years. It's not as though I didn't know such things existed the two years I was hiding at Mama's. I just wanted total retreat. I think I wanted emptiness . . . the blankness, as you call it."

"I really don't," said Evelyn, "except, of course, as respite every once in a while."

"Then you won't have it for long. I believe that. You probably need it now, for protection."

"I certainly don't need it in an interview."

"Do you have enough?" Alice Bennington took Evelyn's notebook and glanced through it. "If you find you need more, just call me."

"You're very generous," said Evelyn. "Again, how can I thank you?"

"No need. Just feel better. Now I'd better stuff you in a cab or you'll be late for the doc."

"I can find a cab . . . really." Evelyn rose and carefully folded the afghan. "You've done more than enough."

"You're sure?" Alice Bennington stood up and walked beside Evelyn to the door. "There are usually plenty at the corner."

"You're an extraordinary woman," said Evelyn, extending her hand.

Alice Bennington placed it between hers. "No. I just know how you feel. And let me tell you something. To this day, when I feel lousy, I listen to opera and hang my face over a kettle and it helps. Don't give up your doctor for it but try it sometime . . . like when you're depressed by a session."

"I will," said Evelyn. "Thank you, I will. And when I do, I'll think of you."

"Good enough. Take care." She squeezed Evelyn's hand.

"I think you're absolutely splendid," Evelyn said, smiling. "You really are."

Alice Bennington remained in the doorway while Evelyn walked to the stairs. When she reached them, she turned and looked back. She wanted to say something else but the words never came. Instead, she just stood for a moment, returning Alice Bennington's smile. Then she raised her hand, palm open, and cupped it shut in an abbreviated wave as she started down the stairs. Behind her, after a few moments, she heard the door close quietly.

The phone was ringing as Evelyn came through Regina's door.

"Eevee." There was a pleading whine in his voice. "Eevee, please listen a moment."

"A moment is exactly what I have," said Evelyn.

"Eevee, I must see you. It is important."

"Carlos, I beg of you. Just leave me alone. Your moment is up." Evelyn slid the receiver into its cradle and lay back on the bed. The phone rang again almost immediately.

"They cut us off," he said.

"No, Carlos. I hung us up. And will again."

"Please . . . just one moment. Do not be so foolish. Do not throw this away."

"Throw what away, for God's sake? What are you talking about?"

"Eevee, we are important for each other . . . I know it."

"Speak for yourself, Mac!" This time Evelyn slammed the receiver down.

Miss Girard's idiom is unique, fiercely individual, charmingly idiosyncratic. Her voice is indelible.

When the phone rang again, she grabbed the receiver and began hollering.

"All right, you bastard, if you still don't get it . . ."

"Evie?" The voice on the other end was tentative. "Ev . . . is that you?"

"Mom? Sorry. I thought you were someone else . . . obviously."

"Is this a bad time? I tried you at the apartment and when there was no answer I remembered you'd given me another number and you said I could reach you there if the apartment didn't answer so . . ."

"No," said Evelyn, "the time is fine. How are you?"

"Real good. I just got back from a weaving workshop at Flossine Dauntz's that was real interesting and . . ."

"Flossine Dauntz?" Evelyn could not contain her incredulity.

"She's the little gal from Leamington I told you about who's . . ."

"Why do so many weavers have such peculiar names?"

"It is quite a name, isn't it? Well, the workshop was real interesting and then afterwards she served a kind of high tea which was real nice. She had the best little cakes . . . kind of pfeffernussey but rolled in finely ground hazelnuts. And so nice because they weren't at all heavy. I hate to eat something at that time of day that fills me up."

"Sounds good." Evelyn stood at the end of the fully extended phone cord and strained toward the refrigerator, just able to reach a beer with her fingertips.

"How are you, hon?"

"Fine. Real good." Evelyn tucked the phone between her cheek and shoulder and tilted her head back for a swallow of beer as she walked back toward the bedroom.

"How was the assignment?"

"Went pretty well, I think."

"That's good."

"How's Dad?"

"I think he wants to say hello. Just a minute."

Evelyn poured a generous amount of beer down her throat as she waited.

"Hi there." His voice was small, the words quick. He was fighting the slowdown and his greeting was a victory of sorts.

"Hi, Dad. How are you?"

"Just fine, dear. And you?"

"Fine." Evelyn tried to think of something to ask. She couldn't.

"Evie . . ." She felt him suddenly beginning to lose ground.

"Yes," she said finally.

"Evie . . ." He snuffled. Evelyn took another large swallow of beer.

"Did you ever . . ." She could feel him shaking his head, rubbing his hand across his eyes. "Did you ever see a more beautiful bride than Joycie?"

"Not recently."

"Dear . . . are you kidding?" The pause, Evelyn knew, did not indicate that he was waiting for an answer. "There has *never* been a more beautiful bride."

"So why did you ask?" Her tone was astringent.

"Well, good to talk to you, dear. Here's Mom." One thing he never lingered over was good-byes.

"Okay, Dad. You too."

"So . . . real good to hear your voice, hon."

"You too, Mom."

"This number . . . is it best to get you there in the daytime? I suppose you're at the apartment at night."

"You can always find me at one or the other."

"Uh-huh . . ." Evelyn felt her mother waiting for more. When it didn't come, she rushed at the pause, trying to erase the impression that she'd been waiting at all. "It was just so good to have you home, Evie. I can't tell you how much it meant to everyone for you to be here."

"Well, I certainly enjoyed it."

"Okay, hon. Real good to talk to you."

"You too, Mom."

"Okay. Bye-bye."

Evelyn sat staring at the phone after she hung up, pieces of the conversation echoing in her head.

"Oh, Jesus Christ." She felt a cry begin. "Jesus fucking Christ!" She wrenched herself from the bed as though she were attached and had to tear away from it. She paced up and down the living room, moving as though she were caged.

"Christ all fucking mighty." She slumped into a corner of the sofa, threw back her head, and closed her eyes.

"My, my, my," she murmured, "aren't we dramatic?" And following that thought she strode to the bar, poured a large brandy, carried it to the window, tossed some down, and glowered out.

She constructs each scene with a sure sense of its inner logic.

She was still standing there when Regina came in.

"What are you doing?" She peered at Evelyn through the fading light. "You look like a bad movie."

"I am a bad movie," said Evelyn.

"What is it, darling?"

"Chat with the folks," said Evelyn. "Guaranteed to depress."

"How was the interview?"

"As I entered her apartment, I began to go around the bend. But she saved me. She's an incredible woman. I'll tell you more later."

"As I sat having lunch with my aunt, I *went* around the bend and she didn't even notice. She is a truly despicable woman.

"Evil, vicious gossip?"

"Vile filth! She now insists that the father of the sister's child is the husband's oldest best friend."

"New evidence?"

"Fresh poison. She now calls the child a bastard to its face and claims the liaison is still going on . . . although the husband's oldest best friend has not set foot in this country for three years. He lives in Hong Kong."

"How can she make a case?"

"She says he sneaks in and meets the sister when she claims to be at one of her health spas."

"So, all in all," said Evelyn, "it was a pleasant lunch."

"Absolutely perfect." Regina had been making a drink as she spoke and now she carried it to the sofa, collapsing onto it. "And by the end of lunch I was so covered with hives and burgeoning eczema that I nearly turned the table over with my scratching."

"Did she notice?"

"She said I seemed a little restless. Oh, God, never again."

"Don't you always say that?"

"This time I mean it. I really mean it, darling."

"Regina, every time you make a pronouncement . . ."

"And to that end," Regina held up her hand to silence Evelyn, "and to that end, I went after lunch to see Alan Hughes, who's an old friend, and I'm going to be his assistant when he does the Ibsen play in Los Angeles this summer."

"My God, Reg . . ."

"Take a leave of absence and come with me."

"God, I don't know . . ."

"We both need to get out of here. That's obvious."

"All this because of lunch with auntie?"

"My darling, I once fled to London for six months to avoid having dinner at her apartment."

"That's power," said Evelyn. "I don't know if they'd give me a leave of absence . . ."

"Work for them out there. Couldn't you do that?"

"I'll quit," Evelyn said.

"Oh, darling, I don't know . . ."

"No more vomiting before interviews, no more screaming fights with the copy desk, no more Carlos, no more Barbara Eden and Lorne Green. Oh, God! What a perfect idea!" Evelyn leaned over Regina and gave her a noisy kiss. "I feel free just thinking about it. Really free."

She took Regina's glass, filled it to the top, and poured another for herself.

"Are you sure, darling?" Regina was hesitant.

"Absolutely," said Evelyn, taking a gulp of Scotch. "Absolutely . . . one hundred percent . . . no question. When do we leave?"

SUMMER

Eight

"Isolation is a fact. We all know that. The degrees and colors are what amaze me. It's never quite the same. Now, it's almost soothing. I see my surroundings, hear Regina's laugh rising from the pool, know it's the sound of someone I love more than I thought I could—and I'm nowhere near. I wonder if it's cowardly to wallow in such suspension—a variation on the theme of I-don't-feel. It helps to write: I sort, I order, I shore up somewhat my sagging internal reality.

"And there is always, always, the temptation to wonder when the end will be. What perversity keeps that focus sharp? I see, or think I see, bits and pieces of ending every day. Perhaps they just add up until the total's reached. The ending formula."

Evelyn put down her pen and stared out the window. She stared until everything blurred, sound as well as sight. Naked, covered in a light sweat, she wrapped the blur around her like a cocoon. When Regina, dripping wet in the doorway, said her name, it took her a moment to focus.

"A towel, darling . . . please. I left the elevator awash. Don't want to do the same to our room."

Evelyn got a towel from the bathroom and brought it to her.

"Did I interrupt you?" Regina asked, noticing Evelyn's silence and the open notebook. "I'm sorry, sweetheart. Please go back. I'm just going to jump in the shower and run."

"No," Evelyn murmured, "not really. It's okay."

Regina brushed a kiss against Evelyn's cheek as she moved quickly toward the bathroom.

"Supposed to be *at* the theater now," she called over the running water. "But God, I'm glad I took that swim. So marvelous."

The bathroom door slammed and Evelyn went back to her desk near the window. If she stood up at the desk and looked down, she could see the pool, three stories below. If she looked straight out, she saw Ann-Margret spilling over the edges of a giant billboard. If she looked to the right, across the living room and through the bedroom to its window, she saw pieces of a very buxom wooden woman twirling forever atop a nearby building. And to the left she could see into the small one-way street that bordered the back of the hotel.

Instead of looking at any of those, she went to the bed, lay down, and closed her eyes. There was no movement in the air and the heat pressed on her like a woolen blanket. She moved as though to shrug it aside but the action only made her sweat more.

Miss Girard does not give herself simple problems to solve but she makes the solutions appear effortless. Her wizardry, in this regard, is dazzling.

She was lying very still, trying to stop the sweat with her mind, when Regina burst from the bathroom.

"Time, darling?" She brushed her damp hair as she moved toward the closet.

"Four-fifteen," said Evelyn.

"I'll be dead center in the rush hour. I don't believe it." She continued brushing her hair with one hand while she skipped along the rack of clothes with the other. She pulled out two hangers, dropped her brush, slid into pants and a shirt which immediately stuck to her skin, picked up the brush and gave her hair a few more strokes, grabbed a satchel, blew Evelyn a kiss, and was gone. Now Evelyn was sweating profusely just from watching her.

They had been in California almost a month. Regina's time

was consumed by Ibsen. She was either in rehearsal or with the actors elsewhere, interpreting for them the vagaries of Alan Hughes, consoling, calming, bolstering. She drank while she did this and it usually lasted until at least three or four in the morning.

Evelyn spent the first two weeks getting acquainted with the peculiarities of that part of Southern California in which she found herself—Hollywood. She took it as a microcosm of the region and tried to be analytical in her approach to it—without, of course, sacrificing the poetry. She walked the Sunset Strip, noting carefully. She immersed herself in the world of the all-night supermarket. She sat on a stool at Schwab's counter and ran fantasies of discovery over and over in her head. She prowled the residential streets where pastel lights played over the fronts of apartment buildings and all of the greenery looked counterfeit. She spent long hours at the hotel pool watching celebrities, and others, at their relaxation.

She then spent several days getting ready to write about what she'd seen. She sent free-lance queries to several outlets back East and received favorable replies: they'd be glad to see anything she sent along. She made copious notes and clipped items from the local papers. She opened a bank account with her severance pay, bought abundant supplies, and set up her desk near the window. Now, at last, she was free to write what she wished.

"Surely it is significant that in Hollywood none of the flowers smell. Surely it says something not only about the California soil but also something about the landscape of the California mind."

She'd get at least one free-lance piece out of the way, Evelyn thought, and wrote those sentences in mid-insight one morning. Three days later she still had not been able to define what it was they said about the California mind.

Guessing that she'd been paying attention to the wrong
muse, she began a poem.

> Sleep is, for us, the perfect metaphor.
> When you leave me each night I know
> The vacancy a final exit will evoke.

Through long afternoons at the pool, evenings in the room,
mornings lying in bed, she tried to go on but couldn't. She
turned to fiction but got down just a paragraph—no more.
Everything was abbreviated, fragmentary. Things occurred
to her in tiny pieces, tips of icebergs only. She could not get
beyond beginnings. Increasingly, as she confronted the opportunity to write for herself, and responded with paralysis,
she turned to her journal.

She reached for it now on the bedside table but it was in
the other room. She didn't want to move until the sweating
stopped. The sun would stop beating in in about half an hour
and then there would be a chance to dry.

She took a couple of pills from Regina's bedside bottle, glad
not to have to use her own, sure Regina wouldn't notice that
two were missing. These didn't count, Evelyn felt. They
were just the foundation, the underpinning for what would
come.

She was to spend the evening with Stuart Sands, a former
New York actor she knew slightly through mutual friends.
He had become the star of his own TV series, *Mr. Stupendous,* by appearing relentlessly on game shows and cultivat-
ing an image of boyish irresistibility. He was actually forty-
two years old and wholly charmless. Evelyn could not
remember why she was seeing him.

By the time he arrived to pick her up, her equilibrium was
solid. She'd hit the perfect balance point: yesterday's hangover was gone and two Scotches had taken the harsh edge off
the pills. She was mellow and sharp, at once.

"Stu . . ." She held out her hands as she glided toward him across the lobby. "So good to see you." She brushed a kiss against his cheek, congratulating herself on her entrance. Perhaps a bit too much Loretta Young, she thought, but nice nonetheless. Very nice.

He stood silently, as though he were posing. Then he smiled, his irresistible smile. It reminded Evelyn of a very old cereal ad.

"My place for drinks?" He added a wink to the smile.

"Sounds perfect." And sounds like someone else, Evelyn realized, hearing herself.

Stuart put his hand under her elbow and began guiding her toward the door. She could feel that he held his upper body completely still, all of his walking done from the hips down. Outside, he directed her to a dark green sports car so low it only came to Evelyn's waist as she stood on the curb beside it.

"How terribly Hollywood *this* looks," Evelyn exclaimed as he bent from his waist to open the door.

"Little runaround," he murmured. "Gets me where I want to go."

"I betcha." Evelyn thought her reading might elicit at least a grin but when she turned to look at him, his face was blank.

He got in and spent what seemed an unnecessarily long time fiddling with buttons and knobs on the dashboard. Evelyn scrutinized him closely. He looked as though he'd been covered with spray net—all over. Everything about him appeared to have been set, just so, and then sprayed to a standstill. His hair was a mass of immobile dark curls. The scarf knotted at his neck didn't move but remained frozen in its casual position. There was no line anywhere on his pants except the razor-sharp crease down the middle of each leg. His eyebrows formed a perfect arch, not a single stray hair spoiling the line.

"Off we go," he said, pulling away from the curb with a roar and squealing ostentatiously around a corner. He had to slam on the brakes almost immediately to avoid hitting a woman crossing the street.

"California pedestrians," he muttered, embarrassed but trying to shift the onus onto the state laws. "They're murder."

"Almost," said Evelyn brightly. She checked him for smile indications but there weren't any.

"Agent's pad is up there." Stuart jerked his head toward the right. "You can see the turrets if you look up at the next cross street."

Evelyn gazed up dutifully. "I think I saw a piece of one," she said when they'd passed the street, wondering why she felt it necessary to lie.

"I'm in a little town house at the moment," said Stuart, shifting gears flashily.

"I didn't know they had them here," said Evelyn.

"They're not like Georgetown town houses," Stuart explained. "They're actually rather similar to apartments back East."

When Stuart opened the door to his, Evelyn said, "I can see the similarities. In fact, Stuart, you could have fooled me. I would have thought this *was* an apartment."

When she turned to include him in the joke, and realized he wasn't laughing, it hit her. He was absolutely devoid of humor.

"I'm not quite ready for a house yet," he said, moving silently across thick carpet to a wall of windows and pulling drapes across them. "This serves . . . for the moment. And it's so much more attractive than an apartment, don't you agree?"

He turned on that line and looked at Evelyn expectantly.

"Much . . ." she murmured. "Much."

"Like to have a look-see?" Stuart asked, not expecting an

answer. "Please do. I've got to make a call."

Evelyn still stood, rather uncertainly, on the edge of the living room, wanting only a drink and a place to sit.

"Don't be shy. Help self." He gestured grandly toward a small, dark hallway. Evelyn smiled—rather hideously, she felt—and moved into it.

The first door she opened was a bathroom which she entered gratefully, locking the door behind her. She quickly checked the medicine cabinet but found only sleeping suppositories and facial creams. Typical, she thought. Perfect. She ran the water until it was icy and took one of the pills she'd tucked in her pocket.

When she came out he was still talking on the phone and she moved down the hall toward the bedroom. It looked as though it was set up for a photo layout: Mr. Stupendous at Home. Everything was elaborately casual. The trades were "strewn" on a large bedside table, forming a perfect fan. Mr. Stupendous's p.j.s were "flung" across the end of the bed, their lavender falling against a matching swath in the bedspread. Camus lay open, face down, on a table across the room although when Evelyn touched it it crackled with newness. Evelyn shuddered and returned to the living room.

"What about Kupcinet? What about Douglas?" Stuart gestured toward a small bar built into the wall and Evelyn gratefully helped herself.

"Christ, Abe! One more motherfucking supermarket opening . . ." He realized Evelyn could hear and dropped his voice. It became a low hum in the background until he was ready to ring off. Then it came up again.

"That's cool, baby. Sounds real good. Confirm with me tomorrow."

He put the phone down and turned to Evelyn. "Bookings for the eastern trip," he said, trying to throw the line away but hitting it a little too heavily.

"Ah," said Evelyn, saluting with her glass and drinking.

"Sorry about the phone. Got just one more to make. You understand." As he spoke he poured himself a glass of soda.

"Certainly," said Evelyn. "Absolutely." She settled herself in the corner of a sofa across the room from him.

Her observations are remarkably acute.

"Babette." His voice was cross. "Stuart. May I ask what happened to the *Cosmo* picture story?"

He rose and carried the phone with him as he paced back and forth. Evelyn watched and wondered why she felt he was faking. She was sure if she were closer, she'd hear the time being announced on the other end of the line.

"It was not to be decided. It was a rock-hard commitment, to coincide with the resumption of shooting. I want an answer by morning . . . no maybes, Babette . . . tomorrow morning." He sat, the phone in his lap, and sipped the soda. "I don't care who objects. Do it."

He hung up, shaking his head disparagingly. "If you don't ride herd," he said, "nothing gets done. Nothing!"

He came across the room and sat at the other end of the sofa. "What do they think I pay them for?" he asked rhetorically. "Agents, managers, secretaries . . . more trouble than they're worth."

He slumped slightly, as though the weight of his retinue were literally pressing on him.

"Life at the top, eh, Stu?" Evelyn watched him closely. If he didn't at least smile, there was no hope.

"It's not easy, believe me." He swiveled his head around, trying to release some of the tension of celebrity from his neck.

"Hopeless," Evelyn murmured.

"Sure, sometimes . . . like now, for instance," said Stuart. "But don't let anyone kid you. There are great times, too."

"Could I have another drink?"

Although he looked somewhat disapproving, Stuart rose to get it.

"Do you *not* drink?" Evelyn asked, as he stood carefully pouring a jigger of Scotch.

"Wine with meals, occasionally." He held up the jigger to eye level to make sure it was exact before he poured it in her glass. "Part of the discipline of the business."

His tone made it clear that he considered anyone who was not disciplined of a lesser order. "It's not just the public image," he said, handing her a pale beige drink. "Booze interferes. It's an encumbrance, a distraction."

Evelyn couldn't be sure but she thought, when he stood over her for an instant, that she saw a makeup line on his throat.

"Don't you occasionally long for distraction?" she asked.

"I relax on the handball court," he said, settling back on the sofa where the light bathed him in a soft pink glow. "So . . ." He swept his hand in an arc in front of him. "How do you like the place?"

"Just super," said Evelyn. "Really stupendous."

He chuckled tolerantly and gazed about as though he were seeing it for the first time. "Of course, it's too small. I need much more space. But it is attractive, isn't it?"

"Stupendous . . . as I said."

A silence descended on them that made Evelyn terribly uncomfortable until she realized Stuart was unaware of it. He was still looking around the room, confirming its appeal.

"Your name's certainly a happy accident," said Evelyn.

"Hmmmm?" He seemed startled by her voice, as though he'd forgotten there was anyone else there.

"Your name . . . I said it's a happy accident."

"Oh. You mean Stuart Stupendous? Yes, that gets a lot of play."

Nobody talks like that, Evelyn wanted to say. Instead, she slumped down a bit so she could see him from another angle and determine if he was, or was not, wearing makeup.

"I thought we'd go to Fabrizio's," he said, glancing over to catch Evelyn's reaction. She felt him looking and wondered what he expected.

"I have no idea what that means," she said, hoping to deflate him.

"Ah, what a treat you have in store." He puffed up instead.

"Are you going to keep it a mystery?" she asked.

"I think that's exactly what I'll do. All set?"

Evelyn had drunk the drink he'd made her in two swallows and, even so, was unable to taste more than a whisper of Scotch. There was no point in having another here.

"All set," she said.

On the way to the restaurant, Stuart dropped names that went with places they were passing. Evelyn murmured after each one. When he pointed to a long stretch of black iron fence on her side of the street, Evelyn turned toward it with her upper body, fished a pill from her pocket, and tucked it alongside her tongue. She made several fishlike motions with her mouth, conjuring saliva, and swallowed.

"Real eye-popper, that one," said Stuart.

As Evelyn turned back toward him, the pill lodged halfway down. She gave her head a shake to get it moving and her eyes rolled back slightly in their sockets.

"Leaves you speechless," he stated.

Evelyn nodded and made two rapid fish gulps.

"Takes your breath away?"

"I'll say," she croaked, as the pill finally slid downward.

"*Et voilà!*" Stuart just missed Evelyn's cheek as he flung out his arm toward the large brick building they'd screeched up to. Evelyn murmured again, wishing the pill would take hold.

"Part of the charm of Fabrizio's is that you'd never think it was anything," Stuart explained.

"Aaah," said Evelyn.

"I mean from the outside," he said. "In the garage, Pete."

He flipped the keys at the parking attendant. Evelyn wondered why he'd bothered taking the keys from the car. Then she realized how he loved the flipping gesture. It was an essential part of his movement around the car to her side.

"Eh, Stuarte!" The sound came at them as they entered, although Evelyn couldn't distinguish the speaker in the darkness.

"Eh, Giusep!" She recognized Stuart's voice and then heard the sound of bodies slamming together.

"Evie Girard, the columnist." Stuart's voice again and she smiled and extended her hand. I've gone blind, she thought, when it encountered nothing. She moved her hand right, then left, and finally felt flesh. As her arm was pumped up and down she began to discern an outline in front of her.

"Such pleasure . . . my pleasure," the outline boomed. "Come, please . . . we have saved for you the best, the very best."

Evelyn felt Stuart's hand beneath her elbow and allowed herself to be propelled forward. By the time they reached the table she could see full silhouettes. Giuseppe's was enormous.

"For Mr. Stupendous I know," he said. "And for the lady?"

"Scotch," Evelyn said, "on the rocks . . . double."

As the figure moved off, she turned toward Stuart and saw he was straightening his scarf and smoothing his hair.

"Nothing like an Italian greeting to rumple a man," she said, feeling the chill of Stuart's look cutting through the darkness.

"It's a good crowd," said Stuart, after glancing around.

"How can you tell?" Evelyn asked.

"You'll adjust," he said curtly. "If it were any brighter, it would change the whole room."

"No question of that," said Evelyn, patting about the table until she felt an ashtray. "I can already see my hand in front of my face." She raised a cigarette to her lips. "Pretty soon I'll be able to find you."

A flame leapt up in front of her. "Ah, there you are now . . . part of you anyway." She lit her cigarette and the flame vanished. "Now you see him, now you don't."

Her vision goes far beyond mere documentation of sightings by the naked eye.

"I don't believe it! I don't believe it!" A shape appeared beside the table and cut into the silence. Stuart rose.

"*You* don't believe it," he said. "Incredible!" Their forms merged for a moment.

"Evie Girard, the columnist," said Stuart. "Susie Parent, from the series."

"I don't believe it either," said Evelyn, smiling up at the voices.

"Is Freddie in attendance?" asked Stuart.

"He most certainly is," said Susie, "and I'll get him this instant. You have saved my life, Stuart. Or at least my evening, you know what I mean? He ran into some agent and they're talking you-know-what."

"Of course, I know what. Disengage him and join us."

"What?" asked Evelyn, as Susie moved away.

"What?" echoed Stuart.

"What is you-know-what?"

"Business. Freddie's her manager, among other things."

A hand set Evelyn's drink in front of her and she took a large swallow immediately.

"Susie, of course, is Mrs. Magnificent," Stuart said.

"Of course," said Evelyn and swallowed again. She watched, transfixed, as Stuart opened his bottle of mineral water and poured exactly half a glass.

By the time Susie returned with Freddie, Evelyn's eyes had adjusted enough so that she could glimpse their faces. Susie's appeared to be pert, Freddie's rough.

"Amy Girard, the columnist," Susie said.

"Amy . . . of course," said Freddie.

"Evie," said Evelyn.

"Right," said Freddie. "Of course. Stu, my man, it's a small world."

"Just incredible," said Stuart.

"I still don't believe it," said Susie.

"Do I gather correctly," said Evelyn, "that you three hadn't counted on seeing each other?"

"You do," said Stuart.

"Long time, no see?" Evelyn asked.

"No, that's the thing," said Susie. "We saw each other yesterday at the studio but that's what's so funny. I mean, we see each other every day but you get used to seeing someone in one place and then you see them in another, you know what I mean?"

"I guess that would be funny," said Evelyn.

"Well, maybe not exactly funny," said Susie, "but just sort of weird, you know what I mean?"

"Mmmnnn," said Evelyn, emptying her glass. "Weird."

"The point is, here we are and it's time for another round," said Freddie, snapping his fingers aloft.

"Exactly the point, Freddie," said Evelyn.

"Stu . . ." Freddie's voice dropped as he bent confidentially toward Stuart. "I just bumped into Manny Lazarus and he tells me . . ."

His words became inaudible and Evelyn felt Susie turn toward her.

"I thought the whole point was we weren't going to talk about you-know-what." A pout began forming around the edges of Susie's mouth.

Evelyn leaned toward her. "Why don't you just go right ahead and say it . . . bold as you please?"

"What?"

"You-know-what."

"Oh, that." Susie giggled. "I guess I think if I don't say it maybe it will go away, you know what I mean?"

"Oh, go ahead," Evelyn urged.

"Bus-i-ness. There! I've said it! It's just that I get so sick of it, Amy."

"Evie."

"I mean, if Freddie were just my boy friend, or just my manager, but since he's both it's like it's there all the time, you know what I mean?"

"I think I'm beginning to," said Evelyn.

"The other night we were at a dinner for my mother and father . . . they're visiting here to see me . . . and do you know that he managed to find someone there . . . they were almost all old friends of the family and stuff . . . to talk about *it?*"

"You-know-what?"

"Yes . . . all night long. At least tonight I have you which I didn't think I would have when we first came in and ran into Manny."

"You've got me all right," said Evelyn, lifting the glass which had just arrived.

"Cheers," said Susie, taking a sip.

"What are you drinking?" Evelyn asked.

"Boxcar," said Susie. "It's my favorite thing."

Evelyn opened her mouth to speak, then quickly closed it and nodded. Susie took her swizzle stick and ran it across Freddie's cheek. He brushed it away without looking.

"He hates it when I do that," Susie confided to Evelyn.

"Why do you do it?"

Susie looked startled. "I don't know," she said, genuinely puzzled, "but I do it all the time. I did it over at the other table when we first came in and I know I did it at the party the other night and I'm pretty sure I did it last weekend at dinner . . ."

"Maybe you should change drinks . . . something that doesn't come with a swizzle."

"I couldn't give up boxcars."

"Do you do it to other people?" Evelyn asked.

"Oh, no, only Freddie."

"Maybe you should give up Freddie," Evelyn suggested.

"Oh, Amy." Susie giggled. "I can see how you're a columnist."

"Evie . . . and I'm not a columnist."

"Do you have a syndication?"

"Not the last time I looked."

Susie giggled again and Evelyn was embarrassed. Her edge, obviously, was slipping away. She needed the third pill she'd put in her pocket. She lowered her head slightly and placed her hand on her chest. She pushed out her breath in short rasps, then reached for the pill and swallowed it under Susie's concerned gaze.

"Asthma," she said softly.

Susie gave a nod full of understanding. "Poor you," she murmured.

"Used to it," Evelyn panted. "Goes away."

Susie's eyes shone with reflected bravery. "Still . . . I don't think I could ever live with that, you know what I mean?"

"Probably won't ever have to," said Evelyn, somewhat moved herself. She reached over and squeezed Susie's hand. "Another boxcar? Sans swizzle?"

Susie nodded and giggled, breaking in two the stick she was holding.

By the time Evelyn finished her fourth drink, she knew she needed four or five bites of food to balance the equation. By the time dinner was over, she had had just that amount and the brandy sat nicely atop it. By the middle of her third brandy, she knew she was getting drunk.

Fabrizio's, it turned out, was crawling with singing waiters, operatic variety, and one nonwaiting singer, Fabrizio himself. He inaugurated the melodic portion of the evening while he was standing next to the Stupendous table. Because of his height (around five feet, Evelyn guessed), his shape (bulbous), and his proximity (his belly pressed against the table), the silverware tinkled when he sang in a timpanic accompaniment that Evelyn found quite lovely. She mentioned it to Fabrizio several times, insisting that he recognize his dual artistry: not only was he singing, he was also playing the silverware with his belly. But Fabrizio was adamant and insisted it was random, an accident.

Evelyn realized she was quite drunk while singing along with *Traviata*. The waiter she was singing along with suffered a sudden and complete voice loss while heading for a high note but Evelyn hit it, alone. This, in itself, was not necessarily an indicator of drunkenness. It was simply embarrassing. But the fact that she continued—to the end of the aria—alone—the last chorus rendered from a tabletop—was telling.

"The unvarnished truth," said Evelyn, sliding into her chair afterwards. "We artists, after all, must be truthful with each other."

"I doubt if you'll be besieged with offers," said Stuart, with unconcealed contempt.

"Well, I think she was real good," said Susie. "I mean, it wasn't even in your range or anything, you know what I mean?"

"Oh, Mrs. Magnificent, you really are," said Evelyn.

"That doesn't make sense," said Stuart, no longer hiding his rage either. Evelyn had embarrassed him.

"Perfect sense, Stupendous," said Evelyn. "Oh, Mrs. Magnificent, you really are . . . magnificent. The latter is implied . . . for those able to pick up on it. And I don't believe we've heard from Freddie."

"Stick to your column, Amy."

"Evie . . . and what is all this columnist shit, Stuart? I'm no more a columnist than you're an actor. Why do you need to tell people I am?"

"Freddie," said Stuart, ignoring her, "see about the check while I straighten out banquet arrangements with Fabrizio."

"Is there to be a banquet?" asked Evelyn. "I'm so sorry but I ate already. I must decline."

"That's fine with me," Stuart snarled.

"Why do you need to tell people that, Stuart?" Evelyn's voice followed him as he walked away. "Why?"

"The banquet isn't tonight, Amy," said Susie.

Evelyn bent toward her. "Do you know something, Sally? I didn't really think it was." She gave an enormous wink.

"Susie . . ."

"Anyway," said Evelyn, "I couldn't eat a thing. But I could certainly drink a nightcap and I think I just may join you in a boxcar."

"Join me in a boxcar . . . that's very funny. Freddie, did you hear . . ."

"I heard," said Freddie, signaling for drinks. "Last round, girls. Finish up what you got."

Evelyn upended her glass into her mouth. She felt the brandy go down, hit bottom, and bounce back up. With it came the small amount she'd eaten. Both landed on the napkin she had just taken from her lap and placed on the table. She was startled. Susie and Freddie were frozen.

"I am so sorry," Evelyn said after a few moments. "I am just as sorry as I can be that Stuart had to miss this. But you will tell him, won't you?"

"Well . . ." Susie began.

"And do tell him how I hit the napkin, dead-center. I think that's a nice touch, you know what I mean?"

Susie worked on a smile while Evelyn began wrapping her napkin around the vomit.

"Notice," said Evelyn, completing her package, "how

nicely it folds up. You can set it on your table, carry it in your purse, take it with you, or leave it behind. It is a bundle for all occasions."

"You want to cancel?" Freddie cut in as the waiter arrived with the drinks.

"Good God, no, Freddie." Evelyn picked up the package she'd made with her napkin and slipped it into her purse. "The timing is perfect, you know what I mean?"

Nine

As she began to fight her way out of sleep, Evelyn felt another presence in the room. After sweeping her arm across Regina's side of the bed and finding it empty, she raised herself up slightly. The pain of movement drove her head back to the pillow immediately. That was also painful and she whimpered as she hit.

"Missy is sick?" Evelyn recognized the voice of Rosita, the maid.

"Missy is dreadfully sick. Just dust around me, Rosita."

"I dust around," said Rosita.

Evelyn wrapped herself tightly with the sheet, as though it were insulation. But it wasn't and Rosita's dusting sounded like the beating wings of a flock of large birds.

Her perception is so acute that the most ordinary things take on another dimension in her hands. She views the sensory world through a magnifying glass, intensely.

She turned her head slowly to look at the clock. It was two-fifteen.

"Did you see Miss Ross?" Evelyn asked.

"First dust around," said Rosita.

"No, no," said Evelyn, recognizing one of Rosita's massive lingual lapses. "The other lady . . . did you see her?"

"No, no," said Rosita, smiling sweetly. Evelyn had no idea if she understood or not.

Evelyn desperately wanted a beer but she didn't want her desperation to show, even to Rosita. If she crawled on her hands and knees to the kitchen, the only way she could imagine getting there, it was bound to be evident. She pulled herself into a sitting position and waited until the pounding in her head and chest subsided. It felt like a very long time but the clock showed only two-seventeen. Then she swung her legs over the edge of the bed and, again, waited for the hammering to abate. When it had, she stood, pulling the sheet around her as she rose. Then she began to move slowly, and she hoped with dignity, toward the kitchen. She only got as far as the end of the bed before the sheet twisted around her feet and she stumbled. She caught herself just as Rosita started toward her.

"Is all right," said Evelyn with a thick accent, steadying herself.

Rosita backed off and Evelyn proceeded toward the kitchen, arriving at two-twenty. As she stood at the refrigerator, taking the first gulp of beer, Rosita came up behind her.

"I show stamps," she said, brushing against Evelyn as she reached for a bowl on top of the refrigerator.

"Stamps?" Evelyn wobbled slightly but kept a firm grip on the door handle.

"Oooh . . . many, many . . . oooh." Rosita crooned over the bowl as she carried it to the kitchen table.

Then Evelyn remembered. A few days earlier, Rosita had seen the bowl of trading stamps, accumulated during many trips to the supermarket, and become highly excited. Now her fingers danced through the bowl, pulling out strips of stamps and separating them into two piles. Evelyn slowly released her grip on the handle and headed for the table.

When all the stamps were on the table, Rosita looked up at Evelyn with an enormous grin. Evelyn tried to grin back and felt something twitch at the edges of her mouth. Rosita seemed satisfied with her response and reached into a shopping bag near her chair. She pulled out a sheaf of small booklets and held them aloft, triumphantly. Evelyn's mouth twitched again.

"Books," said Rosita, shaking them in her hand. "Books."

"Books," Evelyn repeated, and Rosita smiled with approval.

"Ones," said Rosita, pointing to one of the stamp piles. "Super-tens," she said, indicating the other. Then she stared across at Evelyn until Evelyn finally realized what she wanted and nodded.

"First super-tens." Rosita opened a book and very carefully counted the number of squares along one edge. "Five," she stated, glancing up.

"Five," said Evelyn, receiving another approving grin.

Then Rosita counted out a strip of five stamps and tore them off with a flourish.

"Five." She held them up so that Evelyn could see.

"Five," said Evelyn.

Rosita placed her fingertips at the ends of the stamp strip and stuck out her tongue as far as it would go. She waited until Evelyn nodded again. Then she ran the strip across her tongue, twice. Evelyn made a small retching motion. Rosita took it as a nod and carefully set the dampened strip onto the page. When it was in place, she balled one hand into a fist and brought it down on the stamps, pounding them in short, rapid bursts. Evelyn clung to the edge of the table.

When Rosita was through pounding, she lifted the book and turned it to face Evelyn.

"I see," said Evelyn. "Thank you, Rosita . . ."

"Now ones," Rosita cut in. "I show ones."

"Oh, Rosita, I don't think . . ." Evelyn began. "I mean, I couldn't let you spend any more time. I think I can see how it goes now that you've shown me."

Rosita couldn't have looked more stunned if Evelyn had upended her bottle of beer on the piles of stamps.

"I know you have other things to do." Evelyn reached out and touched Rosita's arm. "And I really do see . . . really . . . now that you've shown me."

Rosita began to take handfuls from each pile and stuff them back in the bowl.

"No, no. Leave them there. I'll do them later," said Evelyn. "Really."

That appeased Rosita somewhat. She straightened the two bunches of stamps into tidy piles, placed the booklets between them, and rose.

"Ones," she said sternly, pointing with her left hand. "Super-tens," she said, pointing with her right.

"Got it," said Evelyn. "Thank you, Rosita."

Rosita left the room and Evelyn sat staring at the stamps. She needed to get to the bathroom and then back to bed but sitting in the kitchen, contemplating the distances to be covered, they seemed too vast. She bent over and rested her head on the table, pulling the cold bottle tight against her forehead. When she closed her eyes, the darkness began spinning and she jerked herself upright. The vomit slid back down into her stomach. If she could keep it there, keep it from creeping upward and into her throat, she could deal with it. She finished the beer, tightened her sheet around her body, and started toward the refrigerator to get another. Before she got there, the phone rang.

"Please, Rosita . . . missy no home." Evelyn tried as hard as she could to will that thought into the other room.

"Missy . . . phone please."

Evelyn quickly grabbed a beer and lurched toward the bedroom.

"Yes?" She was short of breath and puffed the word into the phone.

"How are you? It's Ellie McKay."

"Oh, yes, Ellie . . . did you want Regina? She isn't here."

"No, I wanted you."

Evelyn was puzzled. Ellie and her husband, Bill, were old friends of an actress in the Ibsen play. Evelyn and Regina had met them only once, a week earlier, when they'd tagged along on a visit to the McKay's house in Malibu.

"Oh?"

"Did you sleep at all?"

Ellie was about fifty years old, a writer, a drunk who hadn't had a drink in ten years, a wise and supremely articulate woman, and Evelyn had liked her immensely. But none of those things explained why she was calling.

"I just woke up," said Evelyn.

"Can you think of eating?" Ellie asked. "Do you have anything there?"

"No, I can't, as a matter of fact but . . . I think I've missed something somewhere."

"You don't remember, do you?" Ellie's voice was soft but still Evelyn panicked. What was it? She tried to force her mind to clarity.

"You called last night." Ellie cut into the silence. "You were frightened."

"Oh, Christ," Evelyn whispered. "What time was it?"

"It doesn't matter," Ellie said.

"Oh, Jesus," said Evelyn. "I still don't remember."

"That doesn't matter either. Just tell me how you feel now."

"Really hideous," said Evelyn. "I'm shaking apart. I can't walk properly. My stomach keeps coming into my throat and there's a maid here who insists on showing me how to paste trading stamps into books."

"Do you have any food?"

"I'm drinking beer at the moment." Evelyn noticed then that the beer sat untouched on the bedside table.

"Try not to drink any more of it . . . unless you have to," said Ellie. "Do you have milk?"

"Yes . . . I'm pretty sure."

"Drink a glass of that, if possible, and get back in bed. I'll come as soon as I can."

"You'll come here?"

"I'll be there within an hour."

"I don't understand."

"You don't need to. Just try to get down a glass of milk and get back in bed."

"What did I say?"

"The same thing I said ten years ago: 'I'm terribly frightened. Is there any way to stop the fear?' "

"Oh, God, Ellie . . ." Evelyn felt her eyes begin to fill. "I actually said that?"

"That's what I heard."

"I can't go to one of those meetings, if that's what you're thinking. I can barely make it to the kitchen and back. And anyway, I don't know if I can not drink."

"Try not to think about anything right now except getting down a glass of milk and getting to bed."

"Why?" said Evelyn. "Why are you doing this?"

"It helps me."

"That's insane! That doesn't make sense."

"It will," said Ellie, "but don't think about it now. I'll be there very soon."

The hour passed slowly. Twice Evelyn reached for the beer on the bedside table but, each time, she just rested her fingers against the cool glass for a moment, then withdrew her hand. She didn't try to go to the kitchen for milk. She didn't go to the bathroom. She dismissed Rosita and lay unmoving in the bed, feeling the pounding in her head reverberate through the rest of her body.

When Ellie arrived, she rapped softly on the door and let herself in. Evelyn started to pull herself into an upright position but Ellie held up her hand.

"Don't move," she said.

Evelyn slid back down, her shaking accelerated by the movement.

"Oh, Jesus. I'm coming apart," she said.

Ellie stood by the bed and took hold of Evelyn's hand. "It feels that way, I know," she said.

"It *is* that way. Everything inside me is rattling and crashing. I just want it to end."

"It will," said Ellie, reaching into a bag she carried. "Try some of this." She pulled the top from an aluminum can and handed it to Evelyn.

It felt soft and cool going down and Evelyn drank until the can was almost empty.

"Sego?" She read the label aloud. "What is it?"

"Something that goes down and stays when nothing else will."

"I vomited on the dinner table last night," Evelyn said.

"You told me."

"I still don't remember calling."

"You probably won't. I still have lots of pieces missing."

"Regina says she once lost an entire year . . . blank . . . gone."

"I can't remember the first month of my sobriety."

"The only thing she knows is that it was 1962. I feel crazy."

"I know you do." Ellie reached out and touched Evelyn's cheek.

"I can't stand it. I only used to feel this way every *other* day. I couldn't drink with a hangover so I'd have a day off in-between. Now my days off are rare. It's not always this bad but it's never very good either. I black out more, puke more, shake more, function less . . . am I talking a lot? I suddenly heard myself."

"Go on. It's all right."

"I can't stand it. The inside of my head is like a fun-house mirror. Everything distorts . . . it's grotesque. Everything is frightening. I used to feel safe if I stayed in bed but even that's gone. With every hangover the dread and terror get worse."

"At the end of my drinking," Ellie said, "I couldn't open the front door to pick up the newspaper without a drink. I couldn't walk to the mailbox. There was a room in the house I couldn't go into because it terrified me. I never knew why and I still don't."

"You haven't had a drink for *ten years?*"

"It doesn't seem possible to me either. I couldn't live an hour without a drink."

"I don't think I can."

"You already have." Ellie nodded toward the untouched beer.

"That's a fluke," said Evelyn. "The only reason I didn't drink it is that I couldn't lift it."

"Don't demand good motives of yourself. The point is, you didn't drink it."

"So I managed an hour. It's very different from a day."

"A day is just a series of hours. Or break it down into minutes if you have to."

"Of course I think I have to now. But tomorrow, or even tonight . . . or an hour from now, for God's sake . . ."

"An hour from now doesn't matter," said Ellie. "Right now you're not drinking."

"I don't understand why you're doing this."

"It's keeping me sober. I should thank you."

"Oh, please . . ." Evelyn grimaced and turned her head away. "That kind of AA bullshit . . . I don't understand how you could believe it!"

"Sometimes I don't either." Ellie laughed. "But it's been proven to me over and over again."

"To keep it you must give it away." Evelyn's voice was disdainful.

"Exactly. Where did you pick that up?"

"I went to a few meetings years ago with my mother. My father's an alcoholic. And Regina was in AA years ago. She took me to a meeting in New York once. It didn't take."

"The first time someone thanked me for helping her to keep sober, I shut myself up for a week and drank around the clock."

"And?"

"And the next time I just said, 'You're welcome.' I was tired of the punishment."

"Maybe I'm not yet . . . tired enough, I mean."

"You are today. That's all that matters."

"I wish I could believe that."

"You can," said Ellie, "if you'll allow yourself. What have you got to lose?"

"Nothing . . . *nada*. It's all gone."

"No, it's not all gone." Ellie grasped Evelyn's hand again. "It feels that way now but it's not. Trust me."

"How do you know? You don't even know me."

"But I do," said Ellie. "I knew you the minute you walked into my house last week. It was like seeing myself twenty years ago. And I felt then that there was nothing left of me . . . nothing."

"Sometimes I think there is something left." Evelyn cried softly now. "But other times, like now, I can't find a shred . . . not anything. And I can't even remember what it is I've lost."

"I know," said Ellie. "I really do."

"I feel so mournful . . . like I'm grieving."

"You are. You feel an ending . . . and a loss. And it's all right. You have permission."

"No, I don't," Evelyn wailed.

"Of course you do. And you have a choice. As long as you don't drink, you have a choice."

"Between what and what?"

"Life and death, mourning or rejoicing, drinking or sobriety . . . whatever you like."

"I don't know . . . I really don't. God, I'm blubbering."

"It's all right." Ellie ran her hand across Evelyn's forehead, smoothing back the hair.

"I don't understand why I don't mind that I'm behaving this way with you . . . I don't understand anything."

"You will," said Ellie, continuing the motion of her hand. Evelyn closed her eyes. Ellie's fingers on her forehead muffled the pounding and, finally, erased it altogether. They smoothed out the sound until it disappeared. When Evelyn stopped crying, there was silence in the room. The last thing she felt before falling asleep was the quiet, inside and out.

Evelyn tried to appear casual as she walked into the meeting with Ellie, as though she were just dropping in for a look-see. But her fear seeped out and blurred the definition of the pose. Her whole body trembled, making her feel slightly out of focus.

"Ellie!" A man loomed with his hand outstretched.

"Sid." Ellie put her hand in his. "It's good to see you. This is Evelyn. She's new."

"You're in the right place," said Sid, pumping Evelyn's arm up and down. "Keep coming."

How, in Christ's name, do you know, Evelyn wanted to ask. Instead, she stood still for the pumping and eked out the approximation of a smile. Ellie guided her away from Sid and through the crush of bodies near the coffee machine.

"Evelyn, this is Marge." Ellie turned her toward a large woman pouring coffee. "She's been sober three months."

"Best three months of my life, sweetie," Marge said to Evelyn. "Boy, you look rough. Lemme get you a coffee."

"No." It sounded like a shout to Evelyn. "No, thank you. I don't think . . ."

"I got it," Marge cut in. "Me too. Couldn't touch the stuff for at least a month. Carbonation's probably what you need. I keep tellin' these cheapskates they should get sodas."

"I really don't want anything," said Evelyn. "But thank you."

"Sit on your hands, sweetie," said Marge. "It helps. And try to listen. It ain't easy but it's simple." Marge squeezed Evelyn's arm and started to walk away.

"And sweetie," she stopped and turned back toward Evelyn, "it gets better. That's a promise."

"This is her fifth time around," said Ellie, "but the most she ever made before was three weeks. Let's find a seat."

As they wove among the people all their words streamed together: Good to see you hang in it works don't drink a day at a time keep coming. By the time they found chairs, Evelyn's tremor had become a quake and she sat on her hands, as Marge had suggested. That simple act helped to still her entire body.

A pounding gavel finally silenced the room and Evelyn looked toward the young man on the podium.

"My name is Jack and I'm an alcoholic," he said.

"Hi, Jack," the room shouted in unison.

Evelyn jumped and her hands flew out from beneath her.

"Do they always do that?" she hissed at Ellie.

"It's a custom in California. I found it startling at first, too."

"Jesus," Evelyn muttered.

As Jack read from something he called "the big book," Evelyn's backbone rattled against her chair. She was certain everyone in the room must hear it and, when the sound became deafening to her, she raised her head and looked around. Everyone was facing the podium, listening to Jack—everyone but Marge, who was staring directly at Evelyn and flapping her hands. Evelyn stared back for a moment, then remembered and slid her hands back onto the seat of her chair. Marge grinned and gave her a big wink.

"Our first speaker," Jack was saying, "is Hallie from West Covina."

The room broke into applause and Evelyn jumped again but kept her hands firmly beneath her. A tiny woman, somewhere in her fifties, marched down the aisle and mounted the podium. After nearly disappearing behind it, she bobbed up and stated, "I'm Hallie Peterson, a surrendered winette."

"Hi, Hallie." The shout was mixed with laughter that continued for a full ten seconds. Evelyn heard herself join it although the sound seemed very far away.

"And I can just barely see you," said Hallie as the room grew quiet. There was another explosion of laughter.

"Well, they say you oughta use this," she said after a few seconds, picking up "the big book" and holding it aloft. Then she bent down, disappearing for a moment, and arose a few inches higher.

"Glad to see it's good for something." She threw the line away and dissolved the room a third time.

"I say I'm surrendered," said Hallie, "because I am through . . . finished . . . done. I don't have another drunk in me. And I say I'm a winette 'cause that's all I drank the last five years and I hate the word wino. I drank wine because I thought it made me more of a lady and I couldn't keep the other stuff down anymore. But, let me tell you, there's nothing very ladylike about lyin' in bed drinkin' a gallon in an afternoon . . . took me five years to figure that out though. I'm a little slow. Or I was then anyway. I notice I'm a little bit quicker now.

"Why, I used to sit across the room from Ben, bless his heart, and look at him sprawled in a chair, swillin' down the hard stuff, and I'd think, You pig, do you realize how you look sittin' there hoggin' down that rotgut? And I didn't only think it, I said it! And then I'd retire to my room and kill the jug . . . but only a glass at a time, you see. That's what made me different.

"The morning I realized maybe I wasn't as genteel as I

thought was when I woke up covered in my own vomit and reached for the bottle and didn't bother with the glass. That brought me up short more than the vomit, more than a garbage can of empties every few days, more than my teeth which were turning purple. When I didn't bother with the glass I thought, Hallie, maybe you're not quite the lady you think you are. Now I still didn't think I was a drunk . . . I just began to get the suspicion maybe I wasn't a lady. It took me another year to figure out that maybe I was a drunk. Like I say, I wasn't as quick then.

"I started drinkin' when I was fourteen years old and from then until the day I quit, it never occurred to me not to drink. I never went on the wagon, I never tried to cut down, I never thought booze caused any of my problems. Even when I couldn't stomach the hard stuff anymore, I blamed it on a childhood illness that left me with what I liked to call a 'weakened intestinal condition.' Now I never had any such illness but you couldn't have convinced me then. I even named the damn thing but I can't remember now what I called it."

Evelyn listened carefully while Hallie chronicled the years of bouncing from one man to another, one place to another, in and out of hospitals, in and out of jobs.

"But, thank God, these last ten years I had Benny." Hallie smiled down at a man in the front row. "I don't know any other man that would've stuck with me. 'Course I've gotta remember he could barely move out of his chair, let alone leave the house."

Hallie gave a full, deep laugh and the man in the front row joined her.

"Still, no matter why he stayed, he did. And that night when I begged him to get me some help, he managed to look in the phone book and get a number and call it up . . . which is more than he'd done in the last ten years put together. He was no prize, believe me! But he was another warm body in the house and he was there when I needed him. And I guess that night was the first time I ever did need him because as long as I had booze and it was workin' I didn't need another human soul. But when it stopped workin' . . . and it stopped that night . . . stopped dead . . . I was as alone as anybody's ever been. Booze was my constant companion for almost forty years and it was faithful to me, and true, and then one night it deserted me and I was as alone as anybody's ever been."

Evelyn felt the desolation in herself. It was as though Hallie had labeled something Evelyn hadn't defined and with the definition came recognition. She took comfort in a sense of shared experience until resentment forced the comfort aside. This woman had touched her in a way that was intolerable.

"There's something truly lovely about her," said Ellie, applauding as Hallie finished speaking.

Evelyn gave a noncommittal murmur.

"I want you to meet someone." Ellie stood up along with the rest of the room.

"Is it over?" Evelyn asked.

Ellie laughed. "Only halftime, I'm afraid, but we can leave if you'd like."

"No," said Evelyn, "I'm all right. I can't walk through all those people though."

"I understand," said Ellie.

"No, you don't." Evelyn's voice was sharp.

"But I do," said Ellie, "and so would anyone else here. That's the point."

"Well, I don't see how," Evelyn muttered. "It doesn't make any sense."

"Trust me," said Ellie, raising her hand and gesturing across the room.

A tall, elegant, fair-haired woman started toward them, winding through the crowd as gracefully as a stream tracing its way through a bed of boulders.

"Daria, I want you to meet Evelyn," said Ellie, when the woman arrived.

"How are you?" Evelyn was startled by the concern in Daria's voice.

"Just awful," said Evelyn, surprised again by her own response.

"Oh, I know," said Daria. "I could never have been up on my feet after a night like you had. It used to take me two or three days before I could even think of getting out of bed."

"I've told her about you," said Ellie, noticing Evelyn's puzzled expression.

"I wouldn't have considered getting up if it weren't for Ellie," said Evelyn.

"I would be lying there still if it weren't for Ellie. And as far as the phone call goes . . . you don't remember it, do you?"

Evelyn shook her head.

"Don't feel bad about that. My phone bill was always in the hundreds and I could rarely account for more than half the calls. And it's never easy for me to come to meetings."

"Why do you?" Evelyn asked.

"I don't really know," said Daria. "Sometimes because I'm told to . . . sometimes because I think I should . . . sometimes because I want to. But even when I want to it's not easy. Drunk or sober, I have trouble getting places. Getting out of the house is just not my strong suit."

"Are you glad once you get here?" Evelyn asked.

"Not always . . . but most of the time. I usually hear something I need to hear . . . that is, when I'm capable of listening."

"What determines that?" asked Evelyn.

"I wish I knew," Daria sighed. "I'm such a terrible snob

and so totally self-willed . . . it's true, isn't it, Ellie?"

"Absolutely," said Ellie.

"I guess I'm capable of listening when I'm capable of getting out of my own way. Does that make any sense?"

"Yes, I guess so," said Evelyn, "but I don't think I'm there yet."

"But neither am I," said Daria, "and I can't imagine that I ever will be all of the time. Nothing's ever absolutely complete and I've learned it doesn't have to be . . . at least I think I've learned that some of the time. Use what you can; discard the rest."

"I'll use you," said Evelyn, "what you've said."

"Please do . . . and here's my phone." She scribbled on a piece of paper. "Call any time."

"All right," said Evelyn, as the gavel began to pound. "Thank you."

Daria glided off and Evelyn followed Ellie back to their seats.

"I couldn't call her," she whispered.

"You may be surprised by some of the things you're able to do," Ellie said.

"Why would she want me to?"

"The same reason I wanted you to come with me tonight."

"To help her? To keep her sober? To keep it by giving it away? I can't believe that you believe that bullshit!"

"Be still and listen," said Ellie.

"I haven't had a drink or any mind-altering chemical or smoked any of those funny-looking cigarettes for three years, four months, and seventeen days." The man on the podium held up the appropriate number of fingers as he listed each unit of his sobriety. "And the only reason I haven't is through the grace of God and people like yourselves in rooms like these."

Evelyn groaned, louder than she'd intended, and felt

heads turn in her direction. She stared straight ahead and tried to freeze a look of boredom on her face.

"Now, I tried every way I knew how to put the plug in the jug. I tried preachers and doctors and promising my wife and I even once tried one of those headshrinks. I tried staying out of gin mills and changing my job and going back and forth across this whole country but not one of those things helped. Not until the day I got down on my knees and prayed for help and turned myself over to you people and the care of my higher power was I ever able to say no to a drink."

"I knew it," Evelyn muttered to Ellie.

"Use what you can, discard the rest," Ellie muttered back.

"And now my life is a beautiful thing," the man said. "I can do things now I never even thought of doing when I was drinking. I can make a plan to drive to Artesia to see my daughter and my grandchildren and know I'll be able to do it when the time comes."

"Big fucking deal," Evelyn said under her breath.

"I can set aside a little money for something special and know it'll be there when I want it," the man said. "I can walk into a room like this any time, night or day, and know I'll find my friends here . . . real friends . . . not like the friends I had when I was drinking but people who really care about me."

"Christ," said Evelyn. "I'd rather be drinking."

"And I know that as long as I'm sober, a day at a time, I never have to be lonely again."

"That is impossible," Evelyn hissed. "Just impossible."

"When the wife passed on last year, I was full of my old fears. I was scared, I don't mind admitting. But I got myself to a meeting that night and, do you know, by the end of that meeting, all the fear was gone? If I'd been drinking when she died it would have been an excuse to go on a bender to beat all benders. But as it was, I never thought of taking a drink. Instead, I came to you people and through you and the grace of God, I didn't find it necessary to take a drink."

"I don't think I can stand this." Evelyn spoke directly into Ellie's ear.

"Then let's get out." Ellie rose and took Evelyn's arm.

"But we can't just walk out," Evelyn sputtered, resisting Ellie's pull as she felt people turning toward them.

"Come on," said Ellie, gently raising her.

Evelyn felt more conspicuous than she had the night before singing from the tabletop and puking onto it afterwards. The walk along the aisle to the door was interminable. She felt her face become hot and blotchy. Her steps sounded loud and leaden. She thought she might have to scream. And then the air hit her and it was over.

"I thought I was supposed to sit still and listen," she said.

"There's a point of diminishing returns," said Ellie. "At least, I've found that to be so. The first priority is to do what makes you comfortable."

"A drink," said Evelyn. "A drink would make me comfortable."

"Can you finish the drunk in your head?" Ellie asked.

"What do you mean?"

"Think of the first drink, and the second, and the one after that. Think the drinks through to the end.

"I don't ever want to feel that again," said Evelyn.

"You don't have to," said Ellie. "You have a choice."

"That may be," said Evelyn. "Maybe that's so, technically. But what difference does it make if I'm incapable of choosing?"

"Let me help," said Ellie, putting her arm around Evelyn's shoulder and starting toward the car. "Remember, you answer only for now, not for an hour from now, not for tomorrow. Do you want a drink now?"

"I do but . . ."

"Finish the drunk in your head."

"No," said Evelyn, after a pause. "Not now."

Ten

When Evelyn awoke the next morning, she could tell she
hadn't moved all night. The minute she'd walked in the door,
she had taken two Sodium Amytal and two yellow Valium to
assure her being asleep when Regina came in. Slowly turning
over now, she saw they hadn't been necessary for that purpose. The other side of the bed was untouched.

Evelyn's entire body was stiff, her face felt swollen, and her
head hummed—all the earmarks of the second day of a hangover. She walked toward the bathroom tentatively, steadying
herself against pieces of furniture on the way. Rounding the
corner of the bathroom doorway, she gasped and fell back
against the wall. The pounding of her heart made it difficult
to breathe and she stood, propped against the wall, rasping.

"Regina," she growled, moving toward the figure on the
bathroom floor. "Regina!" She bent down and shook her.

"Act five, scene five," Regina mumbled, unmoving.

"Regina, sit up." Evelyn struggled to rearrange the dead
weight.

"Five minutes . . . five minutes." Her words slurred together.

Evelyn took her by the shoulders and tugged, finally raising her torso and leaning it against the toilet. Then she shook
hard. Regina's eyes flew open.

"Time . . . time." She stared straight at Evelyn, unblinking.

"About ten. You nearly scared me to death!"

"So sorry, darling . . . ten . . . supposed to be at the theater."

"What happened to you?" Evelyn asked.

"Oh, God, a long story . . . very long. I'd kill for a beer."

Evelyn rose and headed for the kitchen.

"And my purse? Do you see it?" Regina's voice followed her.

When Evelyn felt the bottle in her hand, she froze. Time stopped and her mind became empty.

"It might be by the door." Regina's voice wrenched her around and back toward the bathroom. She dropped the purse on the floor and handed Regina the beer.

"Thank you, darling . . . thank you." She took several deep swallows. Then she reached for her purse and tipped it upside down. The contents cascaded over her body and onto the floor. She pawed about in them until she hit on a small bottle of pills.

"I would never be able to get off this floor without these." She opened the bottle and took two. "Is F.B. out there?"

"I didn't see him."

"Oh, God, that's right. He decided to spend the night with the coat room lady at the Rehearsal Bar. Time?"

"A little after ten."

"Got to take a shower. I smell like a swamp." She pulled herself up by grasping the edge of the basin and stood, clutching it, weaving back and forth.

"The water will knock you over," said Evelyn.

"Have to try," she wheezed, "just have to."

Evelyn reached into the shower and turned it on.

"Steam will be good," said Regina. "Steam out the poison."

She turned from the basin and her feet shuffled about in the debris on the floor. "Oh, God. Could you just throw all this stuff back in? Just throw it in the purse? And stay here and talk to me?"

Evelyn knelt and began scooping things up as Regina got into the shower.

"For God's sake, be careful," Evelyn said. "You're still drunk."

"I guess I am," said Regina. "I guess I most certainly am.

Won't soap the bottoms of my feet. That would be dangerous."

Evelyn finished returning things to the purse, taking several pills from the small bottle and putting them in the pocket of her robe. Then she sat down on the toilet.

"I tried to call you last night," Regina hollered, louder than necessary.

"I can hear you," said Evelyn. "I was at an AA meeting." The water's sound filled the silence.

"I can't hear you now," said Evelyn, after several seconds passed.

"I think that's wonderful, darling. I really do. How was it?"

"Horrible," said Evelyn. "I'm going again tonight."

"I didn't know things were that bad for you."

"How would you? We never see each other."

"I know. And I hate it. But there's nothing I can do."

"You could come home once in a while before the middle of the night," Evelyn said.

"Did you go alone?" Regina's voice broke the silence.

"No, with Ellie McKay. I'm going again tonight."

The water stopped and Regina pulled aside the curtain. Evelyn could see the pills were beginning to work. Regina's eyes were focused and she stood upright.

"How did you happen to go?" Regina stepped out of the shower and began toweling her body.

"Couldn't stand it anymore," said Evelyn.

"Oh, God, darling, I've been such a wretch . . . so selfish. Come with me." Regina walked rapidly toward the bedroom closet. Evelyn followed and sat on the bed.

"If you can just stand it until the opening." Regina grabbed garments off the hangers and hurled them onto the bed. "It will be different then . . . I promise. Have you seen my blue with green dots?"

"Cleaners," said Evelyn.

"Shit! I have to wear blue today. Have to." She pulled on a navy shirt and rummaged through the clothes on the bed for a pair of pants.

"I'm getting fat . . . hugely fat," she said, sucking in her stomach while she pulled up the pants' zipper. "Do I look too disgusting?" She stood still for a moment.

"No . . . you look fine," said Evelyn.

"Oh, darling." Regina came and took Evelyn's face in her hands. "Forgive me . . . and try to understand." She kissed Evelyn's mouth quickly and turned to go.

"I know I'm a monster," she said from the doorway, "but I love you."

As the door closed, Evelyn began to count. On eight, it opened again.

"Purse," Regina panted, looking around wildly. Evelyn pointed toward the bathroom.

"I love you," Regina said, back in the doorway. "I really do."

When the door closed this time, Evelyn let herself fall back against the pillows. The heat in her eyes signaled tears and she squeezed them shut to hold back the flow.

Then she got up from the bed and walked to the bathroom. She leaned in close to the mirror and examined each part of her face closely. Each looked horrible. She reached into her pocket for the pills and swallowed them dry, staring at the beer on the sink.

Riding with Ellie to the meeting, Evelyn tried to think about the pills: why she hadn't mentioned them to Ellie; why she had no intention of mentioning them. One day at a time, one addiction at a time, she decided. She'd come apart completely if she relinquished them, too.

"Tell me about your day," Ellie said.

"I didn't drink," said Evelyn. "That's about all I can say for it."

"Don't minimize that. And try to take credit for your victories."

"What victories?"

"You didn't drink today."

"Not so far."

"That's a major accomplishment."

"Oh, Christ," Evelyn moaned, "you people all make it sound so simple."

"It is," said Ellie. "It's not easy but it's terribly simple."

"I know, I know. A woman told me that last night."

Ellie laughed. "You'll find plenty of repetition and it will enrage you, I'm sure. It did me. But sometimes we can hear things and sometimes we can't. Repetition increases the chances.

"I think I'll scream if I have to hear any more of that God crap," said Evelyn.

"Ah, the God crap. I think that's seized on more often than any other single thing as an excuse to drink. Ignore it."

"Ignore it? You must be joking. It's everywhere. It's in every one of those steps . . ."

"Not the first one," said Ellie. "And that's the only one that need concern you now."

"Well, how the hell am I supposed to remember one step from another?"

"You're not. The first step is, 'We admitted we were powerless over alcohol, that our lives had become unmanageable.' "

"Well, everything else just reeks of it." Evelyn could hear the petulance in her voice.

"God is just a word," Ellie said.

"I hate it," said Evelyn.

"Try to remember that semantics is a great refuge for resistance."

"I'm not resistant. I just hate the word."

"Of course you're resistant," said Ellie. "Most people are

to one degree or another. And it's all right. It really is. Just try to be willing to listen. That's the most you need to ask of yourself."

"This is Evelyn," Ellie said to a man at the door. "She's new."

"How's it going?" the man asked, shaking Evelyn's hand.

"Not well," Evelyn murmured.

"You're in the right place," he said.

"What did he mean by that?" Evelyn whispered as they passed into the room.

"If you're at an AA meeting, you probably belong here," Ellie said. "Not many people come and discover they're social drinkers."

"But there are other ways than AA," said Evelyn. "Nobody here ever seems to mention that."

"Most of us tried all the other ways before we got here," Ellie said.

"Where's the podium?" Evelyn saw that the chairs were arranged in an unbroken circle with a table in the circle's center.

"This is a discussion meeting," said Daria.

"*I* can't say anything!" Evelyn heard her voice rise.

"You don't have to."

"So who's the new baby?" Evelyn whirled toward the sound of the squeaky voice and saw a figure to match it. The young woman was just over five feet tall, her head covered in tight blond curls, her features extremely pointed. She looked, and sounded, like a rodent.

"Sylvia, this is Evelyn."

Sylvia pumped Evelyn's arm up and down. "I'd say about one day old."

"Right," said Evelyn, hating her.

"Don't get too hungry, don't get too tired, and come out for coffee after the meeting."

"Thank you but . . ."

"Don't think about it," Sylvia insisted. "Just do it. The more people you meet, the better it is."

"That is an impossible concept for me," said Evelyn.

"Don't analyze, utilize. Do what you're told and don't try to think your way out of this. Thinking's what got you here."

"Speak for yourself," said Evelyn.

"We all think we're unique when we come in here," said Sylvia. "You'll get over it. The Copper Kettle on Wilshire. Ellie knows the way."

"Jesus Christ," said Evelyn, as Sylvia moved away. "Who's that?"

"Try to remember we're just human beings," said Ellie. "You don't have to like all of us."

"Don't worry," said Evelyn. "She could drive me to drink."

"Kevin." Ellie reached out to a young man walking by. "This is Evelyn."

"Welcome," he said, putting out his hand, "and hang in. The beginning's pretty hairy but it's a beautiful trip."

Evelyn smiled and nodded.

"He couldn't put two words together when he came in," Ellie said as Kevin drifted away.

"How long ago was that?" Evelyn asked.

"Several months, I think. Let's sit down."

When the meeting began, Evelyn watched the faces carefully but could barely hear the words. After about fifteen minutes, she fished a pill out of her pocket and held it enclosed in her fist. She waited until the room laughed along with the woman who was talking. Then Evelyn faked a cough and raised her hand to her mouth, slipping the pill under her tongue. Moving her jaw imperceptibly, she summoned saliva and swallowed.

Here is a mind that is firmly disciplined and keenly imaginative at once.

"I prob'ly drunk more whiskey today than ya pissed in your whole life," a man's voice growled from the back of the room.

Evelyn turned and saw him sitting on the floor, his legs drawn up against his chest.

"An' I'll drink just as much when I get outta this fuckin' place." He shook a trembling finger toward the circle.

"That's your privilege," said the leader, a man named Artie.

"You're damn right it is," the man hollered. "An' nobody here's gonna tell me any different."

"That's right," said Artie. "Nobody can make you stop drinking and nobody can make you start."

"Jus' try it." The man started to rise but fell back to the floor, his legs sprawling. "Lessee any one a ya try."

"Nobody's going to try to make you do anything, pal, except quiet down so the rest of us can have our meeting."

"Everybody can speak here," said the man. "I know the rules."

"If you've been drinking, we ask you to be quiet and listen," said Artie.

"Been drinkin'! Been drinkin'!" The man laughed maniacally. "I been drinkin' longer'n you been alive. Why should I lissen to you?"

"I'm not asking you to," said Artie. "And since you'd rather not, maybe you'd better leave. There are other people here who are trying to stay sober."

"Well, good luck to 'em." The man turned around to the wall and began clawing up it with his hands. "That's what I say."

"And good luck to you," said Artie. "You know where to find us if you need us."

"Cold day in hell," the man muttered, standing now and speaking directly at the wall. "Very cold day."

He let his hands drop away from the wall to his sides, his

body weaving in a circular motion. Two men slid out of the circle and headed for him. He heard them coming and whirled around, nearly losing his balance.

"I don' need your help." He bared his teeth and flapped his arms to keep them away. "I don' need nothin' you're sellin'."

The two men stopped where they were and watched the drunk start toward the door. After each step, he stopped and swayed in place like a man on a tightrope. His muttering was background music. Halfway across the room, he did a partial pirouette which left him facing the circle.

"Blessings on all," he said, raising his hands in benediction. "Blessings on all."

Several people in the group murmured back at him as he resumed the long walk to the door: "Same to you . . . good luck . . . come back and see us sometime . . . take care."

He reached the door and had one foot through it when he suddenly whirled around again. "An' ya know what I think? Ya know what I think? I think all this crap about a disease is a lotta crap." He was shaking his finger at them again. "I think all this crap about a disease is something all a ya made up to make ya feel better. That's what I think!"

The final flourish with his hand destroyed his balance and he tumbled backwards through the doorway. The two men who had risen rushed forward.

"I said I don' need your help . . . I mean I don' need your help." He was flat on his back and his voice was muffled. Each man took an arm and pulled. He didn't struggle until he was upright and then he shook them off with a great show of ferocity.

"And to all a good night." He bowed from the waist and stayed bent in half for several seconds. Then he straightened up, made a smart turn in the doorway, and walked into the night, as slowly and precariously as he'd crossed the room.

"What will happen to him?" Evelyn whispered to Ellie.

"He'll be back . . . if he stays alive. He usually shows up here every two or three weeks."

"Is he ever sober?"

"No. But there's always a chance as long as he keeps coming. Maybe one night he'll be able to hear something. Maybe not."

"Can't somebody do something?"

"Pray that he stays alive until he does hear something . . . that's all. And that's the horror, isn't it?"

Evelyn looked at Ellie and nodded and felt it: the horror of the man walking down the street, night after night, on a tightrope; the horror of trying to hit that elusive point of balance; the horror of trying to maintain it once it was achieved; and the horror of the repetition of those efforts, day after day, endlessly.

"I can't believe there isn't something . . ."

"There isn't," said Ellie. "Unless you want it to be over, unless you want it to end more than you want anything else, there's nothing."

"I identified with you immediately," said Sylvia, leaning across the table, "the minute you came in the door."

"I wish I could say the same." Evelyn wanted to stop her dead. She had disliked Sylvia on sight and found her assumption of a link between them unforgivable.

"I was hostile in exactly the same way when I first came in," said Sylvia.

She was unstoppable and Evelyn was angry that she hadn't listened to her instincts and gone directly home.

"If you're uncomfortable, we'll leave," Ellie had said.

So here she was, uncomfortable, in an orange plastic booth at the Copper Kettle, between Ellie and Kevin, across from Sylvia and a woman named Barbara. Barbara was very carefully put together. The curls in her medium-length streaked blond hair were exact. The modulation of her voice was tightly controlled. Her smile was perfectly even, giving off just the right amount of warmth.

"You remember, Barb," said Sylvia. "Wasn't it exactly the same kind of hostility?"

"I'm not certain any two hostilities are ever identical," Barbara intoned.

"Don't nit-pick," Sylvia whined. "You know what I mean. I just wanted everybody to leave me alone, except for a chosen few."

"That's exactly the way I feel," Evelyn said pointedly.

"I smelled it when you were standing in the doorway," said Sylvia, triumphant. "That's what I'm talking about."

Since she wouldn't wither, Evelyn decided to ignore her.

"How long have you been sober?" she asked Kevin.

"Almost six months," he said. "It's still hard to believe."

"You're a miracle, Kevin," said Barbara. "It's so beautiful to see you." Her tone oiled her words and made them slither. Evelyn shivered.

"We're all miracles," Sylvia stated, "every one of us."

"I really object to that word," said Evelyn. "It implies that it's all so mysterious."

"But it is," Sylvia insisted. "It is."

"What's so mysterious?" Evelyn asked. "You all drank until you hit some kind of bottom. Then you quit . . . and helped each other to quit. What's so mysterious about that?"

"Just exactly what I would have said," said Sylvia, smiling tolerantly.

"Well," Evelyn sputtered, "what is? What's so goddamn mysterious?"

"There's no need for you to be concerned now with mysteries and miracles," said Barbara, giving *her* tolerant smile. "Just be good to yourself."

"And remember it's the first drink that gets you drunk," Sylvia said.

"You may have another drunk left in you," said Barbara, "but do you have another recovery?"

"First things first," Sylvia trilled.

"Easy does it," Barbara chanted.

Evelyn thought she might scream.

"We'd better be on our way," Ellie said, touching Evelyn's arm. "Evelyn's had enough of us for one day."

"I kept my hostility for at least a year," said Sylvia. "So don't let it worry you."

"It doesn't," said Evelyn coldly. "Believe me."

"We drop things when they no longer work for us." The words oozed out of Barbara.

"Stay cool," said Kevin.

Evelyn shook his hand, grimaced at Sylvia and Barbara, and followed Ellie out. She bargained with herself all the way to the hotel: If I still want a drink when I get there, I'll swim in the pool. If I still want a drink after that, I'll take a couple of Valium, lie down, and watch television. If I don't fall asleep in half an hour and I still want to drink, I will.

"Please pick up the phone if you feel shaky," Ellie said as she dropped Evelyn off. "And don't dwell on the Bobbsey Twins. AA is principles, not personalities."

"I'll try to remember that."

"Call any time. The phone is beside my bed."

As Evelyn walked into her room, she spoke aloud.

"I think I'm going to drink. I'm afraid I'll drink tonight. Why couldn't I say it?"

The liquor was in the kitchen. She could feel it sitting there, a room away.

Her sensory apparatus is unusually keen.

She went into the bathroom, stripped off her clothes, and climbed into her bathing suit.

Balancing on the edge of the pool, she watched the steam rise up around her body. It was warm but the air above it cool and she trembled. When she dove, she expected relief to flood over her with the water. It didn't come. She swam back and forth twice, the length of the pool, waiting to feel soothed. It didn't happen.

Back in the room, Evelyn dried herself with the roughest towel and put on a robe. From the drawer in her bedside table she took two blue Valium and swallowed them dry. She had always thought that one of the nicest things about Valium was their size. They never got stuck going down.

She turned on the television, turned down the bed, and slid her legs under the sheets, pointing the remote-control box at the screen like a gun. She flipped past news, a talk show, something with canned laughter, and finally hit on a movie.

"This young man will drill men, not teeth," said an army commander, draping his arm across a private's shoulder.

"Oh, mother of God," said Evelyn, dropping the box and swinging her legs out of bed. She stalked into the kitchen and took a tray of ice from the refrigerator. She filled a glass with ice, took a bottle of Scotch from the cupboard, and returned to the bedroom, placing the glass and the bottle on top of the television. She flipped the dial until the talk show appeared and crawled back into bed. If the ice hasn't melted in fifteen minutes, I'll make a drink, she decided, checking the bedside clock.

"A lot of people probably think it's been easy for me," a young woman was saying in a breathy voice.

"Not me, sweetheart," said Evelyn.

"I mean, just because my father is big in the business doesn't mean I don't have the same problems as anyone else."

"Of course not," said Evelyn.

"In fact, I have one additional problem which is living down the idea that I somehow have it made because of him."

"Who would think such a thing?" Evelyn asked.

She stared at the glass and saw that a thin line of water had already formed in the bottom. She looked at the clock. Only two and a half minutes had passed.

"So you could say," the host was saying, "that there are both advantages and disadvantages to being your father's daughter."

"Exactly," said the young woman. "And, after all, if it weren't for Daddy I wouldn't be here at all." She giggled and the host and audience joined her.

"A point well worth making," said Evelyn.

As they continued talking, Evelyn's eyes drifted from screen to glass to clock.

"Well, I understand from those who've seen a screening that you're a natural, a real pro," said the host.

The audience clapped and the young woman smiled with great modesty.

"I suppose there are certain things about me that just fitted the part naturally," she said, when the applause quieted. "But I still have a lot to learn."

Eight minutes had passed and there was an inch of water in the glass.

"We'll take a break now," said the host. "Don't go 'way."

Evelyn leaned back her head and closed her eyes. She should be feeling the Valium by now, at least in her hands and feet, but she felt nothing. Her entire body was tight.

"Our next guest is a fella we're always glad to see," said the host. "The San Fernando Valley's answer to Henny Youngman . . . Bernie Wald."

"Jesus Christ," Evelyn muttered, getting out of bed and heading for the bathroom.

"Funny thing happened to me on the way here tonight," said Bernie Wald. "A drunk came up to me outside the studio . . ."

Evelyn slammed the bathroom door, cutting Bernie off. When she came out, twelve minutes had passed and there were two smallish cubes left in the glass. She got back into bed and flipped away from Bernie Wald.

She stopped at an image that appeared to be a panoramic view of the inside of a supermarket. There was no sound at all except for the ringing of cash registers and the whine of baskets being wheeled up and down the aisles. It was as though the network accidentally had gotten plugged into the remote control camera in the market itself. Great idea for a program, Evelyn thought. Call it *Shoplifter* and let the viewers see if they can spot one.

Just as she turned to check the clock—fourteen minutes elapsed—a man appeared on the screen and began talking in a low voice.

"Good evening, ladies and gentlemen," he said. "We're stationed tonight near the checkout counter of the Food Fair market in downtown Hollywood. No one presently shopping in the store knows we're here but three of these shoppers will have a chance tonight to be our lucky winners when we play . . . Big Basket."

He shouted the last two words and, behind him, shoppers screeched to a halt and whirled toward the sound.

"Checkers," he hollered, "freeze your lines!"

The camera quickly panned to the checkout lines. The checkers ran out from behind their machines. A man appeared with a rope strung between two poles. The checkers set up one pole behind the line at the register near the bottom of the screen. Then they unwound the rest of the rope, stretching it behind each successive line until all the lines were cordoned off from the rest of the store.

"I was here! I was here!" a woman screamed, trying to snake her basket around the rope barrier.

"The lines are frozen," said the M.C., approaching the

distraught woman. "So near and yet so far, eh?"

"I was here," the woman shrieked.

"But for being such a good sport, we have these for you."
He reached out and grabbed several items from the front of
the checkout counter—a *TV Guide,* some razor blades, two
candy bars—and dropped them in her basket. "And next
time, you leave your house a little bit earlier, hear?"

She opened her mouth as though to scream again, then
shut it and slunk away. She began muttering as soon as her
back was turned but the words weren't clear.

"We hate to disappoint anyone but we've gotta play by the
rules," said the M.C., "and those rules are . . ."

He moved dramatically toward a spot near the center of
the checkout lines as an organ played frantically ascending
arpeggios.

Evelyn looked at the clock. Eighteen minutes had passed
and she could see a small piece of ice floating in the glass. I'll
wait until the first commercial, she decided.

"No contestant may remove anything from, or add anything to, his or her basket. The contestants will be handed a
pencil and a piece of paper before approaching the register.
They will write down their estimate of the value of the groceries in their basket and hand that paper to me. When the
checker has rung up the total, she will hand the tape to me.
If the amount on their paper comes within one dollar and
fifty cents of the amount on the tape, they're a lucky winner
and get all their groceries free. So ready . . . set . . . go. Let's
play Big Basket!"

A commercial came on and Evelyn started to get out of
bed. Before her feet hit the floor, she stopped and pulled her
legs back under the sheet. I'll wait until after the first contestant or ten minutes, she decided, whichever comes first.

"While you were away," said the M.C., after the commer-
cials, "we picked our three lucky contestants. Number One

is a lovely lady from Reseda and maybe she'll tell us what she's doing over in these parts so late at night. It's a long drive to market!"

He thrust the microphone toward a middle-aged woman who was clinging to the basket handle to steady herself.

"Yes, it is," she said, "but I'm not . . . I mean, I didn't drive here to market. My sister lives just down the street."

"And you're here to visit and she sent you out to market!"

"Yes . . . well, actually, she couldn't . . . yes, sort of."

"I think maybe we've confused you a little but what a surprise you might have for Sis! I bet they don't do things this way in Reseda, do they?" He gave her a big wink and turned away.

"No . . ." she murmured. "The markets aren't even open at night."

"Contestant Number Two," the M.C. boomed, "is a young man and by the look of things in his basket he's a very health-minded sort of fellow. What are some of the things in your basket?"

"Lotta dried fruit, whole grains, juices." The young man slouched over his basket and poked among the items with his hand. "Sea salt, carrots, greens . . ."

"He's into health foods in a big way," the M.C. interrupted, "and they can run ya a pretty penny. Keep that in mind when you tally, young fella."

"Right," said the young man.

"And Contestant Number Three, this gentleman over here . . ."

"Hi, Bill. I've seen the show." The man was enormous, his basket overflowing.

"Then you know how to play and if *you* win, you win big!" The M.C. rolled his eyes and pointed toward the basket, both unnecessary gestures.

"I'd be watchin' it now if I weren't here." The man began

to laugh and Evelyn could see the laugh rippling over his gigantic body. He had trouble stopping but when the M.C. handed him paper and pencil it subdued him immediately.

"You have thirty seconds to make your estimate," the M.C. intoned, passing slips of paper to the other two. "Just thirty seconds . . . but don't rush it. Take all the time you have to guess how much is in your Big Basket!"

Again, he shouted the last two words. Then a loud ticking noise began, marking the seconds. The woman stood frozen, staring down into her basket, her pencil poised over the paper in her hand. The young man continued poking about in his groceries, moving his mouth as though he were counting. The behemoth circled his basket with narrowed eyes, twice bending down with great effort to glimpse what was at the bottom of the mound.

"Contestants," the M.C. yelled when the ticking stopped, "may I have the papers, please."

He collected the pieces of paper and held them aloft. "One, two, maybe all three of these could be lucky winners when we come back to play . . . Big Basket!"

A commercial came on and Evelyn got up, grabbed the glass from the top of the television, and hurried to the kitchen. She dumped out the water and refilled it with ice. She put it back next to the bottle when she returned to the bedroom. She resolved to drink if there was ice left by the end of the program.

When *Big Basket* returned, Contestant Number One was piling her groceries on the checkout counter. One of the checker's hands flew over them, touching each item and slapping it down the sloped counter. The other hand danced over the keys of her register. It was dizzying to watch.

When the last can crashed against all the others lying at the far end of the counter and the register emitted its last mad cadenza of staccato notes, the M.C. stepped forward.

"The tape, please," he said to the checker.

She tore it off with a flourish and handed it to him. He stepped back a few paces until the distance between him and Contestant Number One was about three feet. He held up his hands, the tape in one, Contestant Number One's paper in the other.

"Contestant Number One wrote on her paper . . . forty-three dollars and ninety-six cents! And the tape reads . . ." He paused and looked around, grinning. "And the tape reads . . . twenty-seven dollars and thirty-nine cents!"

The shoppers in the background groaned in unison and Contestant Number One slumped visibly.

"Either prices in Reseda are mighty high or we've got a pessimist on our hands!" exclaimed the M.C. "But tell you what I'm gonna do."

The M.C. stepped over to the groceries of Contestant Number One and lifted from the pile a package of meat, a six-pack of soda, and some breakfast cereal. He placed these in her basket.

"These are on the house," he said. " 'Course you don't have to tell Sis that if you don't want. Good luck and thank you for playing."

As the crowd applauded, the woman lifted her purse onto the counter and the checker totaled the deductions. It embarrassed Evelyn to watch the woman reach for her money.

Contestant Number Two's groceries were already being tallied by another checker. This time the discrepancy between paper and tape was only about three dollars. The young man's consolation prize was four boxes of Familia.

Contestant Number Three had so many groceries that the M.C. took a commercial break while they were being tallied. If he wins, I'll drink, Evelyn decided, whether there's ice left or not.

When the program returned Contestant Number Three

stood presiding, with a grin, over a mountain of groceries that nearly obscured the checker.

"Our last chance tonight for a lucky winner," said the M.C., reaching over the pile for the tape. "Contestant Number Three said . . . seventy-three dollars and forty-eight cents. And the tape reads . . . seventy-*four* dollars and forty-nine cents! We've got a winner!"

The huge man began to jump up and down and an organ exploded in runs up and down the scale. The crowd broke into applause and cheers and the M.C. set down the microphone and joined in the clapping.

"I won," the man crowed. "I won!"

Evelyn reached for the remote box and clicked off the set. The man had won and there were still distinct cubes of ice visible in the glass. Either way, she thought, that was the deal. But she didn't move.

When she did, it was to reach into the bedside table drawer. She fished another Valium out of the bottle, got up, and took it with the water made from the melting ice. She got back in bed and looked at the clock. It was twelve-twenty-five.

She stretched out flat and closed her eyes. If I'm still awake at quarter of one, she decided. Her last thought was that she couldn't feel the Valium beginning to work. She was asleep by twelve-thirty-five.

Eleven

Evelyn sat straight up in bed. She was sure she'd heard something but only the clock sounded in the silence. She fumbled for it and saw it was ten minutes after four.

"Motherfucker!" The cry came from the kitchen.

When Evelyn got to the kitchen doorway, she saw Regina standing before the refrigerator, her feet encircled by food. One of the refrigerator's metal shelves lay on the floor also.

"Every time I try and get ice out of this motherfucker, something else comes with it," Regina muttered.

"You must have pulled the wrong thing," said Evelyn.

"Don't tell me what I did. It's this goddamn machine! Everything's tied together. You pull one thing and everything moves."

"Do you want me to help you?" asked Evelyn, starting forward.

"I know how to do it, for Chrissake. It's this goddamn machine!"

Evelyn reached past Regina into the ice compartment and extracted a tray. While Evelyn carried it to the sink, Regina kicked free of the food and reeled over to the kitchen table.

"What did you want?" Evelyn asked.

"Brandyandsoda." The words came out as one.

Evelyn set the ice, a glass, brandy, and a bottle of soda in front of Regina and went over to the pile of spilled food. She began picking things up and replacing them in the refrigerator.

"If you're trying to make me feel guilty, it won't work," said Regina, fixing her drink. "I am beyond guilt . . . so don't even try."

"I'm not," said Evelyn, continuing to pick up the food.

"You always are. Why not now? Have you given that up too?"

"That's unnecessary, Regina."

"Unnecessary, perhaps . . . but very true, my dear. You have tried to make me feel guilty from the moment we met . . . guilty for spending time with anyone else, guilty for working, guilty for talking to people, and now guilty for drinking, guilty for spilling food on the floor, guilty, guilty, guilty!" Her voice rose as she wrenched out of her chair and wove into the living room, holding the brandy bottle by the neck.

"Then clean up your own goddamn food!" Evelyn shouted after her.

"I will," Regina yelled back, "when I'm good and ready . . . and that's not now."

"You are dead drunk," said Evelyn, entering the living room.

"That is very possible," said Regina, slumping into the corner of the sofa. "And so fucking what?"

"You're dead drunk practically every night," said Evelyn.

"Possible again." Regina nodded her head vigorously.

"You're obliterating yourself," Evelyn said.

"That is *my* privilege," Regina shrieked.

"How right you are," said Evelyn, heading for the bedroom.

"That is my privilege," said Regina, getting up and following her, "and coming home whenever I want to is my privilege, and seeing anybody I want to see is my privilege, and never going to bed until six o'clock in the morning is my privilege . . ."

"You're absolutely right, Regina. I'm not arguing."

Evelyn got into bed and lay flat on her back. Regina stood on the opposite side, bending over so that her hands rested on the edge.

"And it is *not* your privilege to tell me anything or to judge me or to lecture me . . ."

"I'm not saying anything, if you'll notice," said Evelyn.

"And don't patronize me . . . how dare you patronize me!"

Evelyn turned her back to Regina and curled up in a ball under the covers.

"And don't turn away from me either!" Regina reached across the bed, grabbed Evelyn's shoulder, and slammed her onto her back again. "I can kick you out of here anytime I want, baby."

"You won't have to," Evelyn said quietly.

"What's that supposed to mean? What the fuck is that?"

"I've been thinking about leaving. I'll go tomorrow."

"Where would you go?" Regina spit out each word.

"There are a couple of places . . ." Evelyn began.

"Well, take one. Take one of 'em because, baby, I can't stand the way you make me feel."

Regina lurched away from the bed and banged into the bedroom wall. When she recovered her balance, Evelyn heard her shuffle into the living room. Then there was silence, broken only by the occasional clink of ice against glass.

Evelyn lay very still with her eyes closed. Tears squeezed out from beneath her eyelids and ran into her ears, forming puddles. "I've got tears in my ears from lying on my back on my bed while I cried over you"—the song was absolutely right, she thought.

She tried willing the Valium in her system to take over but it remained dormant. Eventually, she shook her head to disperse the tear pools in her ears but, other than that, she didn't move. She listened to the clock marking time and the ice marking swallows and she tried to make herself empty of feeling.

Light was beginning to show beyond the window shade when she heard the ice approaching. The bed undulated as Regina crawled onto it. When Evelyn opened her eyes,

Regina was beside her on all fours, a glass clutched in the hand closest to Evelyn.

"It's very late, darling," Regina whispered, engulfing Evelyn in brandy fumes.

"It's very early," Evelyn murmured.

"I'm so sorry, darling . . . so sorry. I hope I didn't wake you."

She took her weight off the hand with the glass and began to reach out with it toward Evelyn's cheek. Then she toppled sideways across Evelyn, splashing the drink on Evelyn's neck, thumping her head down onto Evelyn's chest. Immediately, she began to omit heavy snoring sounds.

Evelyn lay pinned beneath her, feeling the dampness spread. Several minutes passed before she pulled her arms into a position that would give her leverage with her elbows. Then, using all of her strength, she pushed her body upward, throwing Regina's off to the side. It rolled into a ball and Evelyn covered it with the sheet. She got towels from the bathroom and covered the wet spots on her side but when she lay down on the towels, the smell penetrated them. It was like being curled up in a cask of brandy.

She took the light bedspread from the end of the bed and trailed it behind her into the living room. There she wrapped it around her and lay on the sofa, watching the onslaught of day.

When the alarm rang, Evelyn heard Regina slap at the clock and it crashed onto the floor. The wail continued for about a minute after it landed and, even after the sound died, an echo reverberated in the room. Evelyn couldn't remember setting it. She couldn't remember any reason for wanting to get up.

After several minutes passed, she rose and went into the kitchen. Food had leaked out of some of the containers strewn on the floor and rivulets of different colors streamed away from the pile. She tiptoed around them and got a bottle of milk from the refrigerator. She poured a full glass and drank it, standing at the sink. Then she returned to the sofa and curled up under the bedspread, feeling the milk seep through her body and soften its shaking.

The only noise from the bedroom was Regina's snoring, punctuated by snorts. It sounded, Evelyn imagined, like pigs at a trough.

Miss Girard's sensitive ear makes us listen afresh. She redefines the commonplace with a rare exactitude that makes us feel we are, indeed, in virginal territory.

Evelyn started when the telephone rang, the movement reactivating her trembling.

"Evelyn? It's Ellie."

"Good morning."

"How was your night?"

"Minute-by-minute torture," said Evelyn, "using every trick I could think of. What helped most was a really atrocious TV program called *Big Basket.* Very diverting."

"You just have to do it the hard way, don't you?" said Ellie.

"I'm sure there are tougher things in this world than half an hour of *Big Basket,*" said Evelyn, "although I can't think of one offhand."

"I mean picking up the phone, you dope. Why didn't you call?"

"I couldn't," said Evelyn.

"Wouldn't," Ellie corrected her.

"Okay," said Evelyn, "wouldn't. Anyway, I didn't drink. I also didn't sleep more than a couple of hours."

"Nobody ever died from lack of sleep," Ellie said.

"I find that hard to believe this morning," said Evelyn. "I feel so close. Regina came in around four. We had a scene and I never went back to sleep."

"Could you drive out here today?" Ellie asked.

"Yes . . . I suppose. I have to get out of here." Evelyn began
to cry. "I know I have to get out and I can't bear to leave."

"It's not irrevocable," said Ellie. "You can leave today and
go back tomorrow . . . or tonight. You can turn around and
go back the minute you get here."

"I can't stand to leave her."

"The most important thing today is your sobriety. Without
it, you won't have her . . . you won't have anything. Try, if
you can, not to make conditions impossibly difficult for yourself."

"I don't know how," Evelyn wailed.

"Let me help," said Ellie. "That's what I'm here for."

"Just tell me what to do," said Evelyn.

"Put a few things in a bag . . . toothbrush, bathing suit, a
change of clothes, a book . . ."

"I can't read," Evelyn cut in.

"Shut up and listen, as they say. Put a few things in a bag,
get in the car, and drive here . . . slowly. Don't think about
it, don't weigh the pros and cons, just do it. It's not final; it's
not forever. It's just an action that's right for you today."

"How do I find you?" Evelyn asked. "I can't remember."

Ellie gave her directions and they hung up. Evelyn felt
very resolute—until she reached the bedroom doorway.
Regina was breathing more softly now. Her mouth was
closed and she looked utterly serene. Evelyn went to the bed
and stood looking down at her.

"I love you," she whispered, bending over to kiss Regina's
hair. She wanted to get in bed, wrap her body around Regina's, and sleep. Instead, she turned away, took some clothes
from the closet, and went into the bathroom. She showered
quickly—first very hot, then very cold—dressed, and packed
a small suitcase. She debated whether or not to wake Regina.
She was probably due at the theater and wouldn't awaken by
herself. But if she confronted Regina directly, Evelyn knew

she would never leave. She decided to write a note and, on the way out, ask the desk to call the room.

"I can't believe I'm writing this," she wrote, "but I know I have to to survive—today. I'm going to Ellie's because I'm told it will be easier for me if I'm out of a 'drinking environment.' It feels, however, like the hardest thing I've ever done. I'm sorry I've imposed my dilemma on you. I'm sorry I've caused you to feel guilty. At least my going should alleviate that.

"I hope we can see each other before too much time passes. I will miss you. I love you."

She scrawled a large letter "E" at the bottom of the page and placed it near Regina's purse on the living room table. Then she looked in the purse and took a few pills from a bottle she found in it.

Evelyn stopped three times on the way to Ellie's. Once, before she got to the Pacific Coast Highway, she pulled up in front of a liquor store. She thought about beer: how the cold wetness would feel on her dry tongue; how her stomach would stop gnawing after a couple of large swallows; how the trembling in her arms and legs would diminish; how she would want a second after the first. She drove on.

She stopped again when there was a sudden break in traffic coming down the Coast Highway from the north. She turned left across the highway into a parking lot on the ocean side. She wanted to turn around and go back to the hotel, tear up the note she had left, and get into bed beside Regina. Her mind jumped back and forth between the warmth of that fantasy and the despair she would feel when Regina awakened and left. She tried to concentrate on the latter and, finally, got back on the highway, heading toward Ellie's.

The third time she stopped was when a motorcycle roared past, so startling her with its sound and speed that she veered off to the side. It took several minutes for her body to stop vibrating violently. Then she continued.

Bill answered the door.

"Come in, come in," he said.

Evelyn stood rooted before the door and began crying. Bill reached out his arm, wrapped it around her, and guided her in.

"These are the roughest days," he said. "It'll never be this bad again."

"I'm sorry," Evelyn snuffled. "I'm not usually a crier."

"Nothing usual applies when you're coming off the booze," said Bill. "Please don't apologize."

Evelyn looked up and saw Ellie approaching through a film of tears. She shoved something cold into Evelyn's hand.

"Drink," she said.

It was strawberry Sego and Evelyn drank almost the entire can standing in the front hall.

"Come and sit." Ellie took Evelyn's hand and led her into the living room. The ocean was pounding beyond its windows.

"God, that looks wonderful," said Evelyn, rubbing the haze from her eyes. "How incredible it must be to wake up to it every morning."

"Sometimes I think it's the only thing that keeps me sane," said Ellie, sitting down across from Evelyn.

"Gotta get back to David's scene with Liz," said Bill, sounding rather disgruntled.

"We took over a soap about a month ago," said Ellie, "and our lives have become unrecognizable."

"He has to explain that he can't see her anymore because he's the father of Margo's illegitimate baby," said Bill. "And it's one of those days when I don't give a shit about any of them . . . one of those days when I can't remember why I'm doing this." His voice trailed off as he walked heavily up the stairs.

"I know you have work to do," Evelyn said to Ellie.

"How did I get stuck with this scene?" Bill's plaintive voice floated down into the living room.

"Because I did his scene with Margo yesterday, you creep," said Ellie, laughing. "We both hate David. He's such a prick."

"Can't you change him?" Evelyn asked.

"We inherited him, just the way he is, and the audience wouldn't stand for it. They love him."

"Doesn't that make you hate the audience?"

"No," said Ellie. "I can't afford to. If you do a soap with contempt, it shows."

"I have a feeling that's going to be my problem with AA," said Evelyn. "Contempt."

"It's just a device," said Ellie, "and maybe you'll be able to discard it."

"What kind of device?" asked Evelyn.

"To keep people away from you, to hear what you want to hear, to protect your right to drink."

"But I don't want to drink," Evelyn protested. "Doesn't last night prove that?"

"Still, you had to do it the hard way, to make it as difficult as possible, to test yourself. You had to do it your own way, and you had to do it alone."

"But that's the way I am," said Evelyn. "That's the way I do everything."

"One of the things that happens when we stop drinking is that we get rid of old ideas about ourselves."

"Well, there's no way I could get rid of that."

"Maybe you'll surprise yourself," said Ellie. "Look what you're doing today."

"What? What exactly is it that I'm doing? I've been asking myself."

"You're taking a step toward breaking an old pattern," said Ellie. "You've put yourself first, your sobriety first."

"But I don't even know if I believe that. I'm only here because you told me to come."

"Then you're listening . . . and that's something."

"I'm pretending to listen . . . and that's nothing."

"It's not nothing." Ellie leaned forward. "Get used to the idea that you're going to be faking some of the time. That won't be easy with your fierce honesty but get used to it. You'll do a lot of things you don't want to do and it helps sometimes if you can pretend to like them."

"Well, I can't," said Evelyn. "I don't see how."

"I know you can," said Ellie. "I have great confidence in you."

"How can you say that?" Evelyn wailed. "I can't talk to those people; I can't pick up a phone; I can't make a decision; I can't read or think or articulate anything; I can't eat; I can barely drive; I can't stop crying . . ."

"My God, you're hard on yourself," Ellie said. "Do you think you could suspend judgment for a little while?"

"I certainly can't do that! And I can't stop blubbering and I can't stand it!"

Ellie got up, took a box of Kleenex from the raised fireplace hearth, and placed it in Evelyn's lap. Evelyn pulled a couple of tissues from the box and clapped them against her running nose.

"It's so disgusting, among other things." The words gurgled in her throat.

"You just never let up, do you?" said Ellie.

"Never," said Evelyn.

"Do you have such a need to be punished?"

"Apparently," said Evelyn.

"Do you know why?" Ellie asked.

"Because I'm alive? Because I'm a drunk? Because I'm a lesbian? I don't know. Because I'm a fraud and nobody knows it but me?"

The telephone rang twice and stopped.

"Evelyn," Bill called from upstairs, "it's for you."

"You can take it in there." Ellie pointed toward a phone in the dining alcove and then started up the stairs.

"Hello," said Evelyn.

"Darling, I just woke up." Regina's voice was still fuzzed with sleep. "I got your note. Are you all right?"

"I'm fine," said Evelyn, sniffing loudly.

"Are you crying?"

"All the time lately, it seems."

"Oh, darling, I'm so sorry. What happened last night?"

"Nothing," said Evelyn, "the usual . . . it doesn't matter."

"I say terrible things when I'm drunk, you know that. Things I don't mean. Did I say terrible things?"

"Regina, it doesn't matter."

"Oh, God, darling, please forgive me. I'm a monster lately. I know that. And I know how awful it must be for you. Things will be better as soon as this fucking play opens. I promise."

"You don't have to promise me anything," said Evelyn. "I wish you wouldn't. I always believe you."

"I understand if you can't be here," said Regina. "God knows, it's a drinking environment."

"No question there, I guess," said Evelyn. "How do you feel?"

"Like death. What happened to the refrigerator?"

"You pulled out a shelf."

"And woke you up crashing around?"

"Right."

"God, I'm sorry. I'm so sorry. Did I sprinkle brandy on the bed perchance?"

"Splashed."

"Oh, Jesus. It's very pungent this morning."

"It was even more so last night," said Evelyn.

"Oh, Christ. How awful for you. I'm a big help, aren't I?"

"It's not your problem."

"I understand why you have to be away," said Regina. "I'll miss you terribly. I miss you now. Can I call you?"

"Of course."

"How long will you be there?"

"I have no idea," said Evelyn. "I can't think five minutes ahead."

"I think what you're doing is wonderful," said Regina.

"Well, I'm not doing it very well."

"I don't believe that. How long since you've had a drink?"

"About forty-eight hours."

"My God," said Regina, "that's impossible. You are doing the impossible!"

"Minute by minute," said Evelyn. "I've never felt time move so slowly. Oh, God, Regina, I don't want to be here . . . I want to be there, with you."

"I want you here," said Regina. "I can't believe how selfish I am. I want you here because every night when I come reeling in, dead drunk and crazed, I see you and it makes me feel a little bit sane. At least I know where I am."

"It's *my* sanity I'm trying to work on," said Evelyn.

"I know," said Regina, "and you must. You must think of yourself and take care of yourself and I understand. Really I do. And now I must plunge into today's insanity."

"Try to take care of *yourself,*" said Evelyn.

"I will, darling. You too. Can I call tonight if it's not too late?"

"Yes . . . but I'm sure it will be."

"Yes, I suppose. But if it isn't?"

"Yes," said Evelyn.

"I love you, darling. Please try to believe that. I love you."

"Good-bye." Evelyn hung up quickly as she felt the crying begin again. "Shit!" She got up and went toward the Kleenex. "I can't stand it!"

Ellie came down the stairs as Evelyn grabbed a handful of tissues and mopped off her face.

"And what I really can't stand is saying I can't stand it. God, the repetition! And, of course, I can stand it. I'm standing it right now, standing here and standing it. Oh, Christ, I don't know what to do."

"Follow me," said Ellie.

Evelyn trailed after her into the kitchen, snuffling. "One of the worst things about crying is the sounds," she said. "If there weren't any sounds, it wouldn't be so undignified. It wouldn't be so humiliating."

"I was told at the very beginning to face the fact that I wouldn't get well with style," said Ellie. "Are you humiliated?"

"No, actually, I'm not," said Evelyn, continuing to cry. "I don't give a damn. It feels rather good, as a matter of fact. I may never stop."

"We're all such extremists." Ellie laughed. "Half an hour ago you were determined to control it. Now you may never stop."

"I'm sick of control," said Evelyn. "I am sick to death of control."

She opened her mouth and released a long, lamenting sob. It began in a low register, climbed to a high, thin pitch, and fell back into a groan. She did it twice. By the end of the second cry, Ellie had placed some cheese in front of her.

"Start with this," she said. "Pretend you're hungry."

"Another thing about crying," said Evelyn, sobbing, "is that it makes it very difficult to eat."

"You like things the hard way," said Ellie. "Eat."

"It's not even real now," said Evelyn. "It's involuntary."

"Eat," said Ellie.

Evelyn put a piece of cheese in her mouth and began moving her jaws.

"Is this right?" she asked. "I can barely remember."

"Looks right," said Ellie.

Evelyn finished crying as she was chewing the last piece of cheese. Ellie put a bowl of soup in front of her. When Evelyn reached out to touch the china, it was cool.

"How did you know I couldn't possibly eat anything hot?" she asked.

"I remember," said Ellie.

"You're amazing," said Evelyn, lifting a spoonful toward her mouth.

"Oh, God, forget the spoon," said Ellie, noticing Evelyn's wobbling hand. "Just drink it."

Gratefully, Evelyn put down the spoon and drank from the bowl. When the soup was gone, Ellie gave her a sandwich and, when she finished that, a dish of ice cream. Evelyn felt her eyelids growing heavy as she ate and by the time she finished the ice cream, she was fighting to keep them open. Ellie took her by the hand, led her to a den near the front door, and pointed to a couch. Evelyn didn't even remember lying down.

She stayed at Ellie's for nearly a week, sleeping away great pieces of days and at least twelve hours each night. When she wasn't sleeping, she went to meetings or talked with Ellie. She ate high-protein meals three times a day. She took walks on the beach, never in the midday sun or longer than fifteen minutes. She talked to Regina twice—once when Regina was drunk, once when she was sober. She stopped taking any pills but never spoke about them. She did not go into the ocean because, suddenly, she found it frightening. She met a woman named Bea who said, "Alcohol is a great teacher. Sometimes when you want a drink, you may have to take one. Maybe you need a refresher. Maybe you need to be reminded." And she tucked those words into a corner of her mind.

She met another woman who was going away for a week, leaving her house empty. She offered it to Evelyn and Evelyn accepted.

"I must give you back your house and your life," she said to Ellie.

"You haven't taken either of them away," Ellie replied. "But do whatever makes you comfortable."

"I need now to be alone for a while."

"For some part of each day that's fine. But don't isolate yourself."

"No," said Evelyn, "of course not. We'll talk."

And they did speak each day while Evelyn stayed alone in the strange house set on the edge of the Pacific Palisades. She spoke of her feeling of suspension, the difficulty sometimes of fighting a drink, her loneliness for Regina. The pain will pass, Ellie assured her. Be patient and it will pass.

Evelyn also went to meetings, sometimes two or three a day, but her mind meandered away from the rooms even as she sat in them. To quicken her concentration, she began again to take the occasional pill. This allowed her to focus on a meeting's content but it didn't decrease her distance from it. The only voice that pierced her detachment belonged to the woman named Bea.

"Do you understand what's at stake here?" Bea asked her at a meeting one night.

"What do you mean?" said Evelyn.

"This isn't a game," said Bea. "Drinking is a matter of life and death for you. You're in a situation where you're playing with your life."

"You mean Regina? Yes, I know the situation's bad now. That's why I've gotten out for a time. But it won't always be like this."

"You don't know that," Bea said. "Accept the things you cannot change. Regina is one of them. She's drinking—you're not. She may be a luxury you can't afford."

"Perhaps I can't right now. But it may be different after the play opens."

"There are very few certain things in this world," Bea said, "but I can give you one absolute guarantee: If you don't drink, things will get better; if you do, they'll get worse. That's one promise I can make you."

And Evelyn believed Bea as she spoke. But afterwards, when she was by herself, the words slid away and she couldn't retrieve them even when she tried. Powered by sheer obstinacy, however, she did resist seeing Regina. When the woman arrived to reclaim her house, Evelyn moved to a motel on the beach instead of returning to the hotel.

"I'm glad you've found a sanctuary," Regina said when they spoke on the phone. "I only wish it could be with me."

"Maybe soon . . ." said Evelyn.

"I don't *want* to be separated from her," Evelyn told Ellie. "And I know she doesn't want it either. She loves me . . . I know that some of the time."

"You need to be your own person," said Ellie. "It's not enough for you to be a hanger-on."

"Can't I belong to myself without moving away from her?"

Ellie did not answer the question and Evelyn couldn't.

"*They* say my sobriety must come first," Evelyn told Regina the day of the opening, unable to assume responsibility for her refusal to attend, afraid Regina would be angry.

"I understand," Regina said, "I really do. I'll come out to the beach after the party."

When she had not arrived by the following afternoon, Evelyn's anger was colossal despite a large dose of pills. By early evening, with Regina still among the missing, the pills still failing to give insulation, she drew out the phrase "alcohol is a great teacher" and let it move about in her mind. By ten o'clock she had bought a bottle of Scotch and poured her first drink. When Regina arrived at three in the morning, Evelyn was quite drunk.

"There was a horrible little man staring out of the office so I put F.B. in a bag." Regina, not entirely sober herself, was panting as she hauled several valises through the door.

"Good idea," said Evelyn. "He's not allowed."

"But I can't remember which one." Regina pulled at the zippers until F.B.'s head popped out. Evelyn fell into a chair, silently watching, as Regina extricated the dog and brushed bits of tobacco and Kleenex from his fur.

"You're drinking," she said, noting the glass in Evelyn's hand.

"Quite obviously," said Evelyn, "and thanks to you."

"I'm sorry I'm late." Regina retreated to the bathroom and shouted over the water running into F.B.'s bowl.

"You're screaming," said Evelyn.

"Oh, God, darling, it's been a nightmare," she hollered. "Drunken party, drunken driving, all night at the police station . . ." She stopped suddenly and appeared in the bathroom doorway. She and Evelyn stared at each other.

"I thought I'd never get here." Regina's voice was quiet now.

"It crossed my mind," said Evelyn, trying to hang onto the rage, wanting to punish Regina for what she'd made her feel.

"I thought it might just make things worse if I called. I didn't want to do that."

"You couldn't have." Evelyn wished her ferocity weren't attenuated by liquor.

"No, I don't suppose so." Regina was hesitant. "I missed you terribly."

"I bet." It had no bite at all.

"I did." Regina started toward Evelyn. "I never want to be without you again."

The last whisper of wrath vanished as Regina stretched out her hands and grasped Evelyn's. Evelyn rose and longing streamed through her as their bodies came together.

"Did we always have this great passion?" Regina asked as they made love.

"We did," said Evelyn, "and then we didn't and now we do again."

"How could I have forgotten?"

"All that matters is that you've remembered."

It was difficult a few hours later for Evelyn to fight her way out of sleep even with the sharp sounds hammering at her. It took several long moments for her to identify the noises. One was F.B.'s piercing bark. The other was the motel owner's scream.

"No pets," he shrieked, "no pets."

When F.B.'s howls threatened to drown him out, he began pounding his fists on the door as well.

"Shut up, F.B.," Evelyn hissed. "Regina, wake up."

"No pets, no pets." His fury was growing.

"Be right with you," Evelyn sang out, hoping to calm him.

But he continued pounding and screaming, F.B. continued barking, and Regina didn't awaken. Evelyn wrenched herself away from the bed, her head pounding as she ran across the room, picked up the dog, and threw him under the covers next to Regina.

"For God's sake, Regina." She jostled her roughly. "Wake up and keep him quiet."

"Quiet, F.B.," Regina murmured. His cries were somewhat muffled now by the sheet over his head.

Evelyn ran to the bathroom, each step sending waves of pain reverberating through her body, and grabbed her robe. As she threw open the door, the owner's mouth was poised for a new shriek.

"I know, I know," said Evelyn, stepping outside and closing the door behind her.

"No pets," he screamed, unable to stop himself.

"I'm so sorry." She clapped a hand over her brow as the

sunlight bore into her eyes. "I didn't know."

"There is a pet in that room," he cried, waving his fist toward the door.

"Yes, there is," said Evelyn. "A dog, actually."

"A barking dog who is not allowed."

"Could you please lower your voice?" Evelyn felt faint.

"You must get out," he bellowed. "You and your barking dog."

"The dog is just visiting . . ."

"He is not allowed to visit." The man's red face deepened a shade.

"I realize that now," said Evelyn.

"Out! You out and the dog out!" He stalked away, still waving his balled-up fist.

Evelyn clung to the balcony railing, willing her body not to retch. When the owner reached the courtyard below, he turned and looked up at Evelyn.

"Out!" he screeched.

The noise drove her back against the door and she fumbled for the knob. It didn't move.

"Oh, Christ," she whimpered. "Regina . . . Regina . . ."

The only sound she heard from within was F.B.'s renewed barking.

"No pets," she cried, banging on the door, "no pets."

She is, quite simply, without peer among today's young writers.

"This is a dog in here, not a pet." Regina was indignant as she flung open the door. "Oh, darling, come in."

"Thank you. I will."

"What happened?"

"We're being evicted."

They began packing, prodded by regular and hysterical phone calls from the owner, and managed to leave within an hour.

"Beer," Evelyn whispered as they pulled away, barely able to squeeze the word through her parched lips.

"Yes," said Regina with equal effort, turning in almost immediately at a small weathered building with a Budweiser placard in the window.

"I can't face going back to town," Regina said after gulping down a beer and struggling halfway through a taco.

"I think we belong at the beach," Evelyn agreed.

"I wouldn't want to stay at some filthy place that didn't want animals. They must be vile people."

"They are."

"Maybe we should rent something. Let's see what they have over there." She gestured with an arm streaked with hot sauce at a real estate office across the highway.

In the office, Regina talked while Evelyn tried to fish about discreetly in her purse for some pills. There were two agents present. One was talking to Regina; the other, Evelyn was certain, was watching her. She didn't really care, she decided. This was the worst hangover she could remember. Her fingers struck a vial.

"I'll check on F.B.," she said, excusing herself.

Outside, she threw several pills in her mouth and washed them down with a beer she'd left in the car.

"It wasn't supposed to be empty until the end of the month," the agent was saying as Evelyn reentered. "But the people left unexpectedly yesterday. I don't see why it wouldn't be available."

Regina turned toward Evelyn. "Five miles north of the Colony, at the end of a private road, six rooms, all glass across the front facing the ocean, doesn't it sound perfect?"

"It sounds lovely. What's the rent?"

"They've been getting six hundred fifty dollars," the agent said.

"It doesn't matter," Regina said. "We'll take it."

"They might require a year's lease," said the agent.

"Would you excuse us a moment?" Evelyn moved to a corner of the office and gestured to Regina to follow.

"Darling," Regina whispered before Evelyn could speak, "I have a feeling about this, an instinct. Why would it just be miraculously empty if we weren't supposed to have it?"

"Why would it be six hundred and fifty dollars if we *were* supposed to have it?" Evelyn hissed. "I'm almost out of money."

"But I have plenty at the moment. Or at least I can get it. That'll all work out."

"And a year's lease?"

"I just feel this is meant to be our house."

"Maybe we should take some time and think it over."

"Wouldn't it be nicer than a motel?"

"Well, of course it would be nicer than a motel . . ." Evelyn began to sputter.

"We'll take it," Regina said, turning back to the agent. "When can we move in?"

AUTUMN

Twelve

"Regina!" Evelyn hadn't meant to scream but heard that she had. "Put it down."

Regina stood before a glass wall of the beach house with a movie projector poised over her head, about to throw it.

"Put that down!"

Regina let it fly toward the pane where it bounced once and thudded onto the floor. Evelyn ran to the glass, astounded to find it intact, and then examined the crumpled machine. Their dinner guests simply stared in silence.

Only one of them had been formally invited and it was an invitation neither Evelyn nor Regina remembered.

"Hope I have the right night," the woman had said, her girth filling the doorway at six o'clock that evening.

"Are you sure you have the right house?" The instant Evelyn spoke she realized there was something familiar about the leviathan.

"You did say six?"

"Yes . . . probably. Please come in."

"Nice pad," said the woman as she glided in on the balls of her feet, removing from her shoulders a shawl the size of a double-bed sheet. She handed it to Evelyn, who stood paralyzed near the door, noting the newspapers strewn on the floor, the bundles of laundry piled on the table, the shopping bags filled with groceries.

"Let me get you a drink," said Evelyn, moving now. "We seem to be running a little late, as you can see. Maybe you'd like to take your drink out on the deck and watch the sunset while we get pulled together in here."

"That's cool," said the giantess. "Bourbon and water."

Evelyn made her a drink, steered her outside, and flew to the back of the house where Regina was struggling with a clogged toilet.

"There's a huge strange woman out there," Evelyn said, "and I'm afraid she's come for the evening."

"Did we invite her?" Regina asked.

"We must have," said Evelyn, "but I can't even place her."

Regina emerged and crept to the window. They could see the outline of the woman spilling over a chaise.

"Oh, my God, that silhouette," said Regina. "It has to be Deanna. You remember . . . from the Albatross."

"Keep going," said Evelyn.

"She plays the piano."

"Oh, my God."

"You must have invited her."

"I didn't," said Evelyn. "You probably did. You're the one who remembers her."

"I couldn't have. How could I?"

"Well, the point is, she's here and she's obviously planning to stay."

"That does seem to be the point, doesn't it?"

They stood staring out the window toward their unexpected guest.

"I'll straighten up if you'll deal with her," Evelyn said finally.

"Perfect," said Regina. "And please call Dalton about the john."

As Evelyn was putting away the last of the groceries and preparing to join Regina and Deanna for the final light of the day, there was a knock at the door.

"I'm coming in but only for one quick drink because I have to see one of my movies and it goes on at eight." It was Imogene Rose, who lived three houses away and could not resist dropping in when she saw Evelyn and Regina had company. "I wouldn't impose if you didn't have such interesting friends. I get to see so few people these days and, anyway, I know you don't mind."

"These days" were the months since Imogene's husband had died a sodden death. Imogene spoke freely of this, apparently unaware that she was heading for a similar end. And Evelyn and Regina did mind because once Imogene was in, there was no way, short of turning off the lights and going to bed, to get her out. Still, she almost always managed to get past whoever opened the door.

"The usual?" Evelyn asked her.

"You are so good to me," said Imogene, smiling her misty, heartbreaking smile. "Yes, the usual."

While Evelyn made her a dry Manhattan, Imogene drifted over to the window to gaze at their guest.

"Tell me about her," she urged. "You always have such interesting friends."

"Her name is Deanna."

"Oh, come on. Who is she? What does she do?"

"Actually, she's sort of a mystery guest." Evelyn handed Imogene her drink.

"Oh, that's even more interesting," Imogene said. "I'll go introduce myself."

As Evelyn was making herself a drink, Dalton, the handyman, arrived. The night before Regina had stuffed a burning shirt into the toilet. Then, with the shirt still floating in the bowl, she had flushed and now it was lodged somewhere in the pipe. Evelyn didn't know quite how to explain this so she said nothing.

"Have any idea what mighta got caught in there?" Dalton asked after his preliminary investigation.

"Can't you tell?" Evelyn tried to keep hope from suffusing her voice.

"Hafta get my snake in there." He took a towel from a rack on the wall and mopped his face with it. Dalton was a flabby man, the color of Wonder Bread, and any exertion caused him to sweat heavily. "I got it in the truck. Hafta get it in there."

Evelyn guessed, correctly, that he was waiting for a beer and when she offered him one, he went on with his work. Regina was convinced that to get and remain on the good side of a handyman was crucial to life. She achieved this by the proffering of abundant food and drink. Dalton, Evelyn knew, would be staying to dinner.

When Regina came in the house for refills, they decided to cook Mexican food. That meant they would need margaritas and the tequila was low. Regina placed a call to their liquor store, asking for immediate delivery. The delivery man became the sixth for dinner.

Conversation at the table was sprightly. Imogene told in detail of her career as Ilona Valdez, punctuating her account with little outbursts of feigned resentment at Evelyn and Regina.

"If you didn't have such interesting friends, I'd be seeing one of my films right now." She tried to pout prettily but her muscles were too slack.

Dalton continued to speculate on what had clogged the toilet. The delivery man, consuming a good portion of what he'd delivered, remarked incessantly on the happy accident of their being his last call of the night. Deanna's contributions were never more than two words long—"right on," "far out," "heavy trip"—but she made them often.

"I don't think I can stand another minute," Regina said when she and Evelyn met at the bathroom door about midnight. "I can feel tears of boredom squirting out of my eyes."

"Let's kick them out."

"We can't kick out the dumpling."

"Which one?"

"The white one. We need him. And we can't kick out the delivery man . . . Adolph."

"Aldo."

"Aldo. Our bill there is enormous. We need him."

"We don't need Deanna," said Evelyn.

"We invited her," Regina pointed out. "And we know it's impossible to get rid of Imogene. I think I'll show some movies. At least that'll keep them quiet."

Regina had recently bought a camera and shooting film was her current obsession. The movies she selected to show this particular audience were a study of the kelp beds that lay in the Pacific several hundred feet offshore, F.B. devouring a roast he'd apparently lifted from a neighbor's table, a young man and a much older woman rolling about at the surf's edge in front of the house, a gigantic spider web that hung in the corner of one of the bedrooms, and Evelyn, somewhat less than sober, standing in front of the phonograph conducting an opera.

It was in the midst of this last one that the film caught in the projector and began to burn, causing Regina to hurl it at the window.

"Well," said Regina, breaking the silence, "I think what we'll have to do is just make another little film right now to replace the one that burned."

"I can dig it," said Deanna.

"It's such an interesting idea," said Imogene.

"I wouldn't have missed this," Aldo crowed.

Dalton grunted.

Evelyn had retreated to the bar where she poured herself another large brandy.

"Me too, darling," Regina called out. "Now I want you to come over here." She pulled Imogene from the recesses of her chair and tossed her onto Aldo's lap. She arranged the

two dumplings next to each other on the sofa. She placed an
early Supremes record on the phonograph and turned the
volume to its upper limit.

"All right, darling." She motioned to Evelyn. "In the center, dancing."

Still clutching her snifter, Evelyn moved to the middle of
the room, her head thrown back, her eyes closed, and began
to dance.

*What she does is deceptively simple. She trusts absolutely
in the power of line and movement.*

"Now I want to see you reacting to her," Regina shouted
over the music as she prowled around the room, pointing her
camera at them like a gun. "React! This is a beautiful thing.
You wish you could be doing it. Yes, Adolph. That's good.
C'mon, Deanna. You want to be up there."

"I'm hip." Deanna jiggled her bulk a little more feverishly.

"As the tempo speeded up in the next song, Evelyn's motion became larger, her body more elastic.

"Okay, Dalton," Regina commanded, "I want you to dance
toward her. Get up, Dalton."

When it became clear that he couldn't, or wouldn't, Regina
took her finger off the trigger and examined him more
closely. He was out cold.

Evelyn, adrift in the center of the room, continued to
dance.

"Okay, Imogene." The camera was running again. "You
can't stand it anymore. You have to get up and dance. Go
ahead. That's right."

Imogene slithered out of Aldo's lap and snaked her way
across the floor toward Evelyn, circling her with a strange
little hopping step.

"That's good," Regina cried. "Just terrific."

Next she summoned Aldo and finally Deanna.

"Now don't stop," Regina screamed when they were all up

and swirling. "Just keep going. Don't stop."

She disappeared briefly, returning with three brightly colored chiffon scarves which she placed in their hands as they twirled by her.

"Move the scarves." She began filming again. "Touch each other with your scarves. That's right. Good. Now faster . . . faster."

Evelyn could feel the frenzy building as the material whipped by her. Regina urged them on.

"Now kneel, darling," Regina called to her. "Kneel down. That's right. Be still. The rest of you keep moving. She's the center of the flower, you're the petals."

Regina climbed onto the arm of the sofa and shot downward. "Now the petals begin to close. Adolph, kneel down. Drape your scarf over her. That's right. That's beautiful, Adolph. Imogene! Don't stop until I tell you. Okay, now. Now, Imogene. Begin to kneel. Drape the scarf. Softly, that's right. That's lovely. Good. Okay, Deanna. You can start to kneel . . ."

There was a terrible ripping sound and Evelyn felt herself flattened against the floor as Deanna landed on her. She would have screamed but her breath was driven away on impact.

"Oh my," Imogene murmured, "oh my."

"Jesus Christ," muttered Aldo.

Deanna didn't move.

"Get her off." Evelyn managed to squirt the words between her clenched teeth.

She felt Aldo tugging at Deanna. Each pull sent waves of pain coursing through Evelyn's body. Finally, he dislodged her.

When Evelyn rolled over onto her back, the first thing she saw was the mound of Deanna beside her. Raising herself onto her elbow, she saw that the ripping noise had been

Deanna's garment which was split up the front, leaving her
body billowing out. The next thing she saw as she lifted her
eyes was Regina, still balancing on the sofa arm, filming.

When Evelyn and Regina regained consciousness early the
next afternoon, what confronted them was not remarkable.
They had seen it, or its approximation, many times before.
The evening's debris filled the front of the house and spilled
over into one of the bathrooms: puddles of tequila on the
floor with glass shards floating in them; cigarette filters hanging on table edges, their wormlike ashes on the rug below;
dishes caked with enchilada sauce set in precarious towers on
the bar; half-empty bottles of Carta Blanca beside the
volumes in the living room bookcases, set down there and
forgotten; part of a tortilla and a Beatles record jacket in the
bathroom basin. Poking out from several places in the rub-
bish were pieces of Deanna's garment. Wound throughout it
were the chiffon scarves. And in each room there was at least
part of an F.B. bowel movement, his way of assuring that
they received his message: either you remember to let me
out or I go in the house.

"I think we have to cut down on our socializing," Regina
said after Evelyn had crawled to the refrigerator and brought
two beers back to bed.

"The pace is killing, I agree." The cold liquid appeased
Evelyn's throat.

"Why should I pay for those swine to come here and soak
up gallons of booze, hour after hour?" Regina asked.

"You shouldn't." Evelyn hoped her swift agreement would
block any further talk of money. The subject made her very
uncomfortable lately.

Regina had managed to charm the landladies down to a
$500 rent during a lavish luncheon she and Evelyn prepared
for them shortly after moving in. Regina had also assumed

the entire burden of the rent, an act that necessitated her selling some stock her detested aunt had purchased in an obscure munitions concern. She pointed out to Evelyn that she needed to divest herself of the stock for moral reasons and that had she been living alone she would have been paying the same rent anyway. Evelyn overlooked the weakness of her arguments and agreed to provide her own food and spending money.

To accomplish this, she sold the furniture she'd left behind in New York and lied and forged her way into receiving unemployment insurance. Her reporting time at the unemployment office was eight A.M. Monday mornings. Hangovers had so far prevented her from keeping two of her four scheduled appointments. And since these lapses had occurred, the subject of money had begun to make her very uncomfortable.

"Those loathsome creatures think they can come here anytime and drink all they want and stay as long as they please. I'm sick of it."

Any reference to hospitality abused made Evelyn's guilt quotient soar.

"Maybe I'd better get a job." She insisted on raising the specter of proper employment although she and Regina continually agreed that it would only impede Evelyn's efforts to write.

"Don't be silly. It has nothing to do with you." Regina dismissed this notion even though Evelyn had not yet begun her efforts. She understood that Evelyn needed time to adjust, time to become acclimated to their new life. "It has to do with those pustular pigs barging in here. I hate them all!"

"Let's not let them in anymore," said Evelyn.

"That is a brilliant idea, darling," Regina said.

"I think we need to get on a schedule."

"Perfect."

"For me," said Evelyn, "that's going to mean a little less drinking."

Time and time again, her gift for understatement carries the day.

When they moved into the beach house, Evelyn had stopped attending AA. The time just was not right, she decided. This was a time to devote to living without restrictions, to relishing her reunion with Regina, to building their relationship, to exploring herself, to exercising her talent. An AA effort could be enormously demanding. Her limited energies dictated that she set priorities. And Regina agreed, although she could see, as could Evelyn, that AA might be a fine idea sometime in the future. Perhaps after the first of the year. Maybe they'd even go together.

Evelyn, of course, had no intention of returning to an unrestrained intake of alcohol and pills. Having felt the effects of addiction, she had no wish to feel them again. This morning, however, she could see she might have to tighten up somewhat her regulatory measures.

"It's the brandy after dinner that's killing me," Regina said, emptying her beer. "I can't even think of sleeping until dawn."

"It would help a lot if we didn't have big groups of people," said Evelyn.

"No big groups, no brandy after ten o'clock."

"Two drinks only before dinner," Evelyn said.

"No more than a bottle of wine with a meal."

"Asleep by midnight, up by eight."

"And we'll do it a day at a time, darling. After all, isn't that the way they say to live?"

SPRING

Thirteen

The end of winter in California was indistinct. There wasn't a day when the air suddenly softened and the ground felt spongy. There were no promises of renewal carried on lion-like March winds. There were no March winds. It just got slightly warmer each day and spring arrived by the calendar.

But in homage to an old memory, sometime in the middle of March, Evelyn planted seeds in the sandy soil in front of the house. It was an arduous task. In their months in the house the only landscaping effort she and Regina had made was to hack down with an ax a nicotine plant threatening to close up one of the doorways. Their minimal gardening and a rainy winter had caused the growth around the house to thicken into a jungle. When the landladies visited, Regina made a point of extolling the beauties of wildness.

"I hate a manicured look," she said. "Things should be allowed to grow free, especially at the beach. It's much lovelier. Don't you think so?"

The landladies murmured something noncommittal and, although Evelyn and Regina suspected their sensibilities were offended, they didn't actually object and they didn't offer to send their Japanese gardener.

To make room for her seeds, Evelyn tore away the jungle's outer edge with garden shears and her bare hands. Along the slender border she planted rosemary, thyme, basil, sweet savory, and a mixture of flowers. She monitored them closely. Each morning when she awakened, she went outdoors to see what, if anything, had happened to them in the night. Each evening, just before the sun plummeted into the ocean, she noted how they had been affected by the day. The temptation to look on them as symbols was irresistible. She became convinced they were reflecting her life.

She cleared out a corner of the extra bedroom in the house and set up a table. She bought several notebooks and pens with different-colored ink. She spent a part of each day thinking about what she would write. And the morning when she found the first green shoot piercing the ground, she went to the table and sat down.

Perhaps the last several months might look wasted to some. Much of the time appeared to have passed unnoticed. Her fidelity to the rules of moderation and discipline had seemed ragged. She had not been able to begin writing. Often she was nagged by echoes of the previous summer: if you don't drink, it will get better; if you do, it will get worse . . . unless you want it to end, more than you want anything, there's nothing . . . there is nothing.

But Evelyn knew she could make useful what seemed useless, make fertile what appeared to be barren. Time past was grist and she was ready. After all, last night she'd drunk only wine, a few glasses with dinner, and she hadn't had a pill for nearly a week.

Two hours later she heard Regina stirring in the next room. She pulled the notebook cover closed over the empty page and went in and flopped onto the bed.

"Gently, gently," Regina muttered. "Jesus! Whole Polish army . . . barefoot in my mouth . . . no, with boots, disgustingly filthy boots."

"Want a beer?" asked Evelyn.

She has an uncommon gift of perception.

"Kill," said Regina. "Kill for one."

When Evelyn returned with the beer, Regina was framed in the open bathroom doorway, sitting on the toilet, her head supported by her hands.

"You are an angel of mercy." She raised her head and took the beer. "How long have you been up?"

"Hours," said Evelyn, lying down again on the bed.

"Why?" asked Regina. "How?"

"I didn't drink much last night, if you'll recall."

"I recall very little. What have you been doing?"

"Working," said Evelyn.

Her powers of invention are without limit.

"I think I sent some telegrams," said Regina.

"Who to?"

"That's the part I can't remember." Regina got up and returned to bed. "I had things I wanted to say but I didn't want to talk to anyone. I thought telegrams would be just the ticket."

"I wonder which is cheaper," said Evelyn, "telegrams or phone calls?"

"I'm afraid they may have been very long," said Regina. "The telegrams."

"Anonymous?" asked Evelyn.

"God, I hope so," said Regina. "And I was also going to arrange all the vitamin bottles in alphabetical order. Can't remember if I did or not."

"I had trouble finding the niacinamide and it's usually right in front," said Evelyn.

Her observations are penetrating.

"Must've then. Do you want to finish this?" Regina offered Evelyn the beer. "Got to go back to sleep for a while."

Evelyn took the bottle and carried it outdoors. She stood at the edge of the deck, facing the ocean, and drank the rest of the beer.

The next morning she was sitting at her table ready to work by nine o'clock. At noon, she wrote the date on the blank page and shut the notebook. She lay in the sun for a couple of hours, watered her border, read *Time* magazine cover to cover, and went to market. That evening, she and Regina each had a single martini before dinner, two glasses of wine apiece with the meal, and a small snifter of brandy afterwards.

Evelyn was at her table again the next morning at nine. At eleven o'clock, after carefully marking down the date on an empty page, she closed up her notebook and went out to walk on the beach.

The days passed, indistinguishable from one another, and Evelyn moved through them like a phantom, waiting for her mind to take hold. On the morning that she found traces of brown along the edges of the three plants that had pushed through the ground, she decided to take one Dexedrine to help her focus.

She knew it was ridiculous to be taking her cue from the plants. She also knew that she needed direction and thought perhaps the plants were better than nothing at all. The pill took a very long time to work and sharpened her only slightly. This, she decided, was because she'd taken it on a full stomach. She would avoid that in the future.

That evening, to help her unwind, she had three martinis before dinner and half a bottle of wine with her meal. To enable her to sleep, she had Valium after dinner instead of brandy.

The next morning she took two Dexedrine as soon as she got up and made a large pot of coffee. She had resolved not to fall into the old trap of using her notebooks for psychic catalogs. She was determined to write *some thing,* to create an entity, a work.

In the middle of the day, she put brandy in her coffee, took another pill, and continued to sit at the table. Her material was certain: suspension of life in the midst of life—patching oneself with chemical glue—insulation—disintegration. She must now decide on her form.

During the next several days, although she fueled herself with pills and fortified them with brandy and caffeine, she could not begin. At the end of a week, she decided perhaps she was trying too hard. She would try approaching her table completely without design. She would will her mind to emptiness. Then, seated, with a blank page before her, she would lift the embargo and write down whatever entered.

She took special care with the coffee that morning and, while it was brewing, she lined up her Dexedrine on the kitchen counter. There were five pills and she placed them end to end. She took from the cupboard a glass and her favorite cup. She filled the glass with water and set it next to the row of pills, concentrating fully on these small physical tasks, keeping her mind vacant.

Light spilled onto the counter, glancing off the tiny orange spheres in the capsules. Evelyn stared at them until the coffee was ready. Then she took them, one at a time.

When they were gone, she carried her cup of coffee to the table in the next room. She sat down, opened her notebook, selected a pen, and placed it on the empty page. She sipped the hot coffee, patiently waiting for the right moment. When it arrived, she raised the curtain in her mind.

"When it stopped workin' . . . stopped dead . . ." The words were clear. They came from that first meeting, months ago.

"It stopped dead . . . and I was as alone as anybody's ever been." The voice belonged to Hallie from West Covina.

"When it stopped workin' . . . I was as alone as anybody's ever been."

"Miss Girard concurs," Evelyn wrote. Then she closed up the notebook and went out to lie in the sun.